It Had
to Be Them

D1269914

ALSO BY TAMRA BAUMANN

It Had to Be Him
It Had to Be Love
It Had to Be Fate

It Had to Be Them

TAMRA BAUMANN

Montlake
Romance

Text copyright © 2016 Tamra Baumann
All rights reserved.

Published by Montlake Romance, Seattle

www.apub.com

Amazon, the Amazon logo, and Montlake Romance are trademarks of Amazon.com, Inc., or its affiliates.

ISBN-13: 9781503939622
ISBN-10: 1503939626

Cover design by Eileen Carey

Printed in the United States of America

This book is dedicated to Matt and Traci, who I love even more than chocolate. You make me so proud to be your mom.

CHAPTER ONE

A hypochondriac could be a doctor's worst nightmare, but Ben Anderson had reason to be particularly fond of the one sitting on the padded exam table in front of him. She was the mother of the only woman he'd ever loved.

He'd run every test he could think of on Kline Grant's mother but could find nothing wrong with her. She'd developed a new dire illness every Monday for the last six weeks, and today was no exception. He was tempted to borrow her phone and delete her WebMD app.

"I have just the thing you need." He grabbed a small bottle of vitamins from his white lab coat and handed it to her. "Take one every morning for a month, and you'll be good as new."

Mrs. Grant flipped her glasses to the top of her gray-haired head and frowned at the label he'd had his nurse, Joyce, dummy up for him. "What is this?"

"It's a new miracle drug and perfectly safe." He laid a hand on her shoulder. "You trust me, right?"

She lifted her chin and smiled at him. "You know I do, Ben. Did I mention Kline is finally coming home?"

Her words were a punch to his gut. It'd been over ten years since Kline had been back. "No, you hadn't mentioned that." He looked away from her curious eyes and busied himself with notes in her chart while his system settled.

"I told her I wasn't well enough to travel all over the darn world to visit wherever she's teaching now like I have in the past."

Tahiti, last he'd heard. Kline had wanted out of Anderson Butte so badly, and had lived in four other cities and three countries since their breakup. Not that he kept track of her or anything. "You're well enough to travel if you want. Sand, blue water, and warm weather might do you good." Of course, that made him think of Kline in a bikini, dammit.

Mrs. Grant waved her hand. "Oh, she's done with that job. It was only temporary. I told her we desperately need a science teacher here while her cousin takes maternity leave soon. But you know Kline. Itchy feet. No way she'd ever come back to live in this one-stoplight town . . . blah, blah."

Good. Because losing Kline had hurt. So much that he had sworn he'd never get close enough to another woman to let that happen again. He'd let her go, thinking she would come back after a year or so because she missed him. After five had passed, he realized he had made the biggest mistake of his life by not telling her the truth. She probably hated him for it. Hopefully she'd be in and out and they wouldn't run into each other.

"She's coming tomorrow and plans to visit through the end of the month. Then she's thinking of substituting in Denver for the rest of the school year."

That meant she'd be in Anderson Butte for three long weeks. Hard not to run into someone in their small town for that long.

He helped Mrs. Grant off the table. "Have a nice visit with Kline. And be sure to take those pills now, okay?"

"Will do." She slid a purse big enough to hold a fifteen-pound turkey over her shoulder. "I'm going to try to set Kline up with Wayne

Jacobs while she's here. He always asks about her. That way she'll have a date on her birthday."

Kline's birthday was next Saturday, November 15. Exactly a month after his. But his neighbor, Wayne Jacobs, was the last person Kline would be attracted to. Wayne had been the big jock in high school, entitled and rude, and hadn't changed a bit. Not Ben's problem, though. He couldn't care less who Kline dated.

Mrs. Grant shook her head and walked toward the door. "Kline is going to be the death of me, always just dating for fun. She says no commitments and especially not marriage for her. But I'd like a grandchild before I kick the bucket. I imagine your dad feels the same about you, Ben. Both you and Kline are so good-looking, it's odd neither of you ever married, don't you think?"

"Nope. And you're only sixty and not going anywhere anytime soon. Bye now."

"Thanks for the pills." After she waved goodbye, the exam room door softly closed behind her.

Ben tossed her file onto the table and rubbed his tired eyes. The last time Betty Grant had been in, she'd whipped out a handful of pictures. Kline still looked fantastic, a tall, slender brunette with the deepest caramel-colored eyes he'd ever seen. Eyes that used to gaze at him like he was the last chocolate éclair on earth as he made love to her. Eyes that had cried when he told her that he was going back to Anderson Butte after med school.

She might have stuck it out with him if he'd told her the truth. That his father, and obligations to the town, had forced him into coming back home after he finished college. He'd wanted to do the right thing by her, so he'd let her go. He'd broken up with her so she could live her dreams and have her adventures. But for her to never come back for even a single holiday? It had to be because she wanted to avoid *him*.

She'd accused him of not loving her as much as she loved him, of always putting his family's needs before hers by staying in town rather than leaving with her as he'd promised, and then she had thrown her engagement ring at his head.

He couldn't help that his mom had died and they had a father who wasn't a parent to his younger brother and sisters. Someone had to raise them, and it *had* taken a lot of his time and effort. She wasn't wrong about that. She'd been extremely patient with him—until he'd broken the bad news.

He'd lost the love of his life and the best friend he'd ever had in a single moment.

Shaking off the memories, he stood to go see his next patient. Luckily, he was swamped trying to take care of the patients he had, and with his plans for a brand-new clinic that would serve even more people from the surrounding area. That was, if he could convince his father to let him use the piece of land he had his eye on.

Yeah. He had plenty of excuses to avoid Kline.

But Wayne Jacobs? What had Kline's mom been thinking? The guy wasn't good enough for Kline. He couldn't think of a man in town who would be.

Kline Grant laid a hand on her roiling stomach as she negotiated the curvy, icy mountain road she had vowed she'd never drive again. When she passed by the sign that said "Welcome to Anderson Butte, Colorado," childhood memories swarmed all at once inside her head.

She passed the hotel Ben's sister Casey ran, and then the General Store, run by Santa Claus, aka Fred. Next she passed the diner located across the street from the Town Square with its pretty white bandstand in the middle. Remnants of a recent snowfall sparkled on the roof in the waning sunlight. Not much had changed.

Glancing through her passenger-side window, she caught her first glimpse of the beautiful lake between the buildings. The bright

November setting sun reflected long, thin lines across the smooth surface. She rolled her window down and drew in a familiar breath of cold air, pine trees, and lake water. Maybe she'd missed *that* a little, but she hadn't missed the nosiness of small-town life, the lifelong battle between the Andersons and her family, the Grants, and the memories of her difficult childhood.

After hearing her mother describe her odd symptoms and how she was too sick to travel, not to mention the signs of confusion, Kline had no choice but to break her vow and come home. She loved her mom—the one constant in her ever-changing life—so very much.

So she'd have to talk to Ben again. It'd probably be awkward. Their breakup hadn't been pretty. She still regretted throwing her ring at his head. She should probably apologize for that. On second thought, he should apologize to *her* for stringing her along all those years. He made promises he'd never intended to keep. Just like her last boyfriend had. She was through with men.

Her stomach seized again at the thought of seeing Ben.

She'd just keep things professional with him, ask what the deal was, and then get out. Then she'd stop by the diner and pick up supper so her mom wouldn't feel the need to cook.

She pulled into the clinic's driveway and wound around the back to park, hoping she wouldn't be too late to catch Ben. After she turned off the ignition, a marching band of nerves reverberated up and down her spine. She hated to be so intrusive, to go around her confused mother for the truth, but her mom's strange symptoms just didn't make sense. Well, according to WebMD, anyway.

She grabbed her purse and headed for the clinic. By the time she tugged on the glass door her stomach had gone from being upset to seriously hurting.

She started for the familiar waiting room, but had to stop when a wave of dizzying nausea hit. She leaned a hand against the wall to steady herself.

The sound of heavy footsteps made Kline look up and into Ben's striking blue eyes. Still as handsome as ever. He hadn't changed a bit. How unfair was it that men aged so much better than women?

"Kline? Are you okay?" A frown creased his brow as he reached out to help her.

She nodded, but then lost the battle with her stomach and leaned over and puked on his designer shoes.

Still bent in half, staring at the mess, she moaned. Seriously? Had that really just happened? Worse, were those expensive Ferragamos?

Could the earth open up and swallow her whole, please?

She hadn't seen the man in years and what did she do? Ruin his shoes. And humiliate herself on top of it.

"I'm so sorry, Ben." Cringing, she slowly lifted her head and met his strangely calm expression. "I'll replace your shoes." When her stomach rolled over again, her hand flew to her mouth. "Oh, God."

She turned and ran toward the ladies' room, dodging Ben's nurse, Joyce, who carried an armload of towels. To clean up the mess, no doubt. She'd help Joyce as soon as she could.

This was not at all how she'd pictured her homecoming. She'd lain in bed the last few nights, dreading her first encounter with Ben and playing out all the possible scenarios. She'd covered the one if he pretended not to recognize her at first, and even the one if he was cold and indifferent to her. She hadn't anticipated the barfing-on-him reunion.

After she was sure there couldn't be anything left in her gut, she hobbled weak-kneed out of one of the two metal stalls in the ladies' room. Ben leaned against the counter waiting for her, now wearing a pair of tennis shoes. He reached inside his white lab coat and pulled out a lollipop.

"Thanks." It'd have to do until she could unearth some mints from the depths of her purse. The sweet cherry flavor quickly eliminated the rancid taste in her mouth.

"Pregnant?" he asked.

That was about the last thing she'd be, seeing how she hadn't slept with a man in months, but she wouldn't tell him that. "No. More like a bad convenience store egg salad sandwich."

"Ah." He crossed his arms then angled his head as if studying her. "Your mom told me you weren't coming until tomorrow."

Humiliation took a quick backseat as concern for her mother weighed on her again. She mumbled around her sucker, "I must've told Mom five times I was coming today. Not tomorrow. I'm worried about her. That's why I'm here." She crunched the candy off the stick, tossed the white cardboard into the trash, and then turned on the water to wash her hands and face. With her eyes still closed, because when she opened them she got dizzy, she reached for a paper towel.

Ben slipped a wad of paper towels into her hand. "Well, you certainly made an entrance. Welcome home . . . finally."

"Thanks. I'm sure everyone in town will hear about this from Joyce. And won't ever let me live it down." After she'd patted her face dry, she drew a deep breath and then faced him. "I really am sorry about your shoes." They probably cost more than she made in a month. Ben had always liked expensive footwear. That much hadn't changed about him.

He shrugged. "They're just shoes. Don't worry about it." He slowly reached his hand out as if approaching a skittish horse and laid the back of it on her forehead. "No fever. And your color is coming back."

Yeah, her cheeks were probably a deep shade of mortification red.

"What do you mean, just shoes?" She held onto the counter to steady her wobbly legs. "You used to covet shoes harder than any of my girlfriends—"

He held up his hand to cut her off. "Save me the speech about how many starving children you could feed for the price of one pair. Maybe I've changed?"

"I wasn't going to say that." Only because she was a bit off-kilter at the moment and it hadn't occurred to her yet.

He cocked a brow.

"Oh, all right. I would've eventually, but that's not the point. I'm worried about my mom. What's going on with her?"

The bathroom door swung open and Joyce's wrinkled face appeared. "Nice to see you again, Kline. Hope you feel better soon. *Wheel of Fortune* starts in ten minutes so I gotta run. See you tomorrow, Doc."

Ben raised a hand. "Have a nice evening."

Kline called out, "Nice to see you too, Joyce. Sorry about that!"

After the door swung shut, Ben's eyes locked with hers again. "I can't talk to you about a patient. Even if it is your mother. You need to ask her." He scooped up her purse from the counter. "I'll drive you home."

"I can drive myself. It's a whole two minutes away." She stuck her hand out for her purse and nearly toppled over. She *was* still a little dizzy.

He wrapped his hand around her arm to steady her, then motored her out the swinging door. "You need to be in bed. Lots of ice chips tonight. Dry toast and crackers in the morning if you feel hungry."

"Will do." She leaned against the stucco wall outside while he hit the lights and locked the door. The cool air felt nice on her clammy skin. "Seriously. You must be busy, Ben. I can drive myself." And then she'd bury her head under the covers for a week and hope to forget the most embarrassing moment of her life.

"Still so stubborn." He slid his arm around her waist and tugged her toward the only car in the parking lot. Hers. "How are you going to charge an electric car in Anderson Butte? Your mom said you're staying for three weeks."

Crap. She hadn't thought about that. "Maybe I'll ask Uncle Zeke. He could probably rig me up something." Leaning against the hood of her car, she dug around in her purse for her keys. And found her tin of mints. Bonus! And then the keys.

When Ben just stood there with his big palm sticking out, she gave in and handed over her fob. She wasn't feeling so hot again anyway.

She popped three mints into her mouth. "I wasn't being stubborn about you driving. I was trying to let you off the hook. Things are awkward enough between us as it is without being trapped—" She was going to be sick again. With no time to go back inside, she ran to a nearby trash can and stuck her head inside. It was just lucky that Mondays were still trash day in Anderson Butte, so the can was empty.

A set of cool fingers slipped through her long hair and pulled it away from her face as she finished up her business. Ben had always been kind and considerate. But still, he'd misled her and couldn't be trusted.

She whispered, "Thank you."

"Welcome." He gave the makeshift ponytail in his hands a slight tug. "Let's get you home before another round hits."

Good idea. Or next she'd be the talk of the town as they drove down the road with her head stuck out the window like a dog. Her car was brand-new. She didn't want to mess it up.

Ben beeped the locks and opened the passenger-side door for her. After she'd collapsed into the seat, her eyes followed his tall, lean body as he rounded the hood. His thick, dark hair, wavy in all the right places, fell just above one of his stunning blue eyes, and his arms flexed nicely when he removed his lab coat and neatly folded it inside out before opening the driver-side door and tossing it in the back. He'd filled out, become more solid muscle than before, and he still had the same blindingly white pretty smile. The new crinkles around his eyes when he grinned actually looked good on him, as opposed to hers.

So unfair.

She closed her eyes and laid her head against the seat so he wouldn't catch her staring and get the wrong idea. She wasn't interested in him. She was just noticing, that's all. She had no intention of opening the can of worms their relationship had turned out to be.

Once he was settled beside her he said, "Okay. I give up. How does this go-kart start?"

"For your information, this is an environmentally friendly, high-tech vehicle. Press your foot on the brake." She leaned forward and hit the ignition button. "There. It's ready to go."

Ben blinked at the dash in the silent car. "How do you know?"

She chuckled. It had taken her a day or so to get used to that too. "The light right there says so."

"Huh. Let's see how many hamsters are under the hood."

He put the car in reverse and sped backward, nearly giving her whiplash and making her stomach do weird things again.

Then he put the car in drive. "It can actually move."

"Uh-huh." Talking was making her nauseated again so she closed her eyes and hoped he'd hurry.

As soon as they pulled up in front of her mother's log cabin, Kline opened the car door and made for the rear to get her bags.

As she reached inside the trunk, Ben gently brushed her hand away. "I've got them."

"Thank you." She hadn't relished the idea of dragging her heavy suitcases up the front steps in her weakened state. Instead, she slowly moved ahead of Ben and grabbed the knob on her mother's front door. She wasn't surprised to find it turned freely. No one locked doors in Anderson Butte. She called out, "Mom?"

Her mother appeared from the kitchen, wiping her hands on a towel. A huge grin lit her face. "Kline. You're a day early! And just in time for dinner. I made your favorite. Spaghetti and meatballs."

The aroma of garlic and her mom's famous red sauce made Kline's stomach threaten to act up again, but she pushed that aside and hugged her mom—hard. A year and a half ago, Kline had been unjustly locked away in a foreign prison cell and hadn't been sure she'd ever see her mother again. It had made Kline realize how much she loved and missed her mom. And how short life was.

The horrific experience had made her appreciate the little things in life too, and it had proved to her that it was time to settle down and grow some roots.

Anywhere but Anderson Butte, that was.

Kline finally released her mom and then took a step back to examine her. Her mom looked like her usual tall, thin, spry self. "Why would you make my favorite dinner tonight when you thought I'd be here tomorrow?"

Her mom blinked rapidly. "I don't know."

Kline exchanged a "see what I mean" glance with Ben. He nodded slightly and closed the door behind him to keep out the cold. Then he hauled her luggage to her old bedroom for her.

Mom let out a little squee. "I'm so glad you're finally back, Kline. We're just going to have the best visit ever!"

"I'm so glad to see you too. But tell me what's been going on with you. How are you feeling?"

Ben returned, texting someone on his phone.

Mom asked, "You'll stay for dinner, won't you, Ben?"

"I'd better not." He exchanged another glance with Kline. "Kline's sick and needs to rest. And I need to do some *serious* online shoe shopping tonight."

Kline crossed her arms. "Very funny. But forward me the bill, please." Thank God he'd refused to stay. She couldn't bear another uncomfortable minute with him.

Mom's forehead crumpled. "I'm sorry you're sick, sweetheart. We'll get you tucked into bed right away, then." Her eyes took in Kline's outfit. "That's what you wore to come home after all this time?"

"Yeah?" Kline glanced down at her blue TOMS sneakers, jeans, and black V-neck sweater. Why would her mom care what she wore to ride in the car?

Her mom turned Ben's way. "She cleans up much better than this usually."

"I'm sure she does." Ben grinned as he continued to tap away on his cell.

If her mom only knew. He'd seen a lot worse earlier. She wanted to die every time she thought of it.

He reached for the door handle and said, "Take care, Betty. Come see me tomorrow if you're not better, Kline. I'll be sure to bring my galoshes with me." He paused to fix a crooked picture on the wall, and then when his phone rang, answered it as he made his hasty escape.

Kline laid both hands over her face and shook her head. Was this indicative of how her visit would be? How would she ever last the three whole weeks she'd promised her mother she'd stay?

CHAPTER TWO

*K*line pried her eyes open and then rolled over to check the time. She'd been up sick most of the night, but had finally fallen asleep about four a.m. She picked up her phone and blinked in surprise. How could it be almost three thirty p.m.? She hadn't slept that long ever.

She threw her covers back and slowly stood, waiting for the wave of dizziness to hit, but it didn't. She actually felt a little hungry. Maybe after a shower she'd try some toast. And then get some answers about her mother's health.

She scooped up her robe and headed to the bathroom. A quick glance in the mirror made her cringe. Her eyes had dark circles under them and she looked like crap, but she felt a whole lot better.

After her shower, she wrapped her hair on top of her head with a towel and slipped into her silk robe. As she made her way to the kitchen, memories of the horrors of the day before hit. On the bright side, maybe Ben was so disgusted by her that he'd avoid her just as she planned to avoid him. And since Ben wasn't willing to help her figure out what was wrong with her mom, maybe Joyce would. Everyone in town knew that Ben's nurse had a weakness for chocolate mousse pie from the diner. Who didn't? It was Kline's favorite thing too. Maybe a little good old-fashioned bribery was in order. After all, she was just trying to help her mom.

A loud knock sounded on the front door, so she changed direction to answer it. She swung the door open and a broad smile tugged at her lips. It was Ben's grandmother. Ruth Anderson was full of piss and vinegar and one of Kline's favorite people growing up. She'd never known her own grandmothers so Ben's held a special place in her heart. "Hi, Mrs. Anderson. How are you?"

She thumped past Kline and into the house, leaning heavily on her cane. "The same as usual—old and cranky." She stuck out a tall plastic container. "Heard you weren't feeling well, so I brought you some of my famous chicken soup."

"Thank you. It was just something I ate. I'm much better now." Kline accepted the still-warm plastic cylinder and then gave Ruth a hug. "Come in and let's catch up. I've missed you."

"We've all missed you too. Heard you saw Ben yesterday. Ruined a pair of his fancy shoes. That's no way to win back my grandson's heart."

Kline shook her head. "I'm not trying to win any man's heart. I'm giving them up for good."

"Hi, Ruth," her mom called out as she stirred something on the stove. "And Kline, you can't give up men quite yet. I promised Wayne Jacobs you'd go out with him."

"What? Now you're making dates for me?"

Ruth plopped herself down in the kitchen nook. "Someone has to. You're way too pretty to be alone. And it's harder to have children when you get past a certain age, you know."

Kline wanted to roll her eyes. Instead, she popped the soup into the microwave. "The last man I'd date would be one who lives here." She turned toward her mother. "I only came home because I'm worried about you, Mom."

Ruth asked, "Is that dizziness any better, Betty?"

"No. As a matter of fact now that you mention it, I'm starting to feel a little faint too."

Kline zipped to her mother's side and slipped her arms around her shoulders. "Then sit down, please. You'll get hurt if you fall."

Ruth dug out a cell phone from her apron. "I'm going to text Ben."

It seemed seeing Ben might be inevitable during her stay. For her mom's sake, she'd try to forget how she'd humiliated herself in front of him and try to have a cordial relationship with him.

After her mom was settled in a chair, Kline grabbed a cloth and wet it. She laid it on the back of her mother's neck. "How's that?"

"A little better. Thank you, sweetheart." Mom forced a smile. "I'm so glad you're here."

Ruth slipped her phone back into her apron pocket. "Ben's on the way."

Mom's forehead scrunched. "If Ben's coming, maybe you should go put some makeup on, Kline. You wouldn't want him to see you looking like that, would you?"

"I'm not worried about Ben seeing me without makeup." Although he used to tell her he thought she looked great without it. "How long has this been going on, Mom?" Her mother had danced around every question Kline had asked about her health so far.

Her mother shrugged. "A while now. It's no big deal. It'll probably pass in a few minutes like it usually does."

The microwave beeped, so Kline grabbed the soup and bowls. "Maybe you need some of Ruth's magic healing soup too."

"No, thanks. I don't have much of an appetite either."

That couldn't be good.

Kline spooned up a bowl for herself and dug in. Nothing better than Ruth's homemade chicken soup. The added hit of New Mexico green chile was enough to clear out her sinuses too.

As Kline scraped the last of her soup from the bowl, a knock sounded. "Must be Ben." She laid her spoon down and stood to answer the door.

When she swung it open, Ben's eyes widened. And then his gaze slowly ran up and back down her entire body. She'd forgotten she was dressed in a skimpy robe. And what it used to do to her insides when he looked at her like that.

She grabbed her lapels with one hand and closed the gap at the top. "Hi. Come in. Mom's in the kitchen."

His gaze finally moved to her eyes instead of her cleavage. "You look like you feel better today."

A cool breeze floated past Ben and fluttered the hem of her robe, so she quickly closed the door behind him. "Much better, thanks. But I wish you'd talk to me about my mom, Ben."

"HIPAA rules don't allow for that." He fixed the same picture by the door that had gone crooked again and then turned and started for the kitchen. "Why don't you go get dressed while I examine your mom? Then after, ask me questions in front of her."

"Okay. Be back in a few."

Yeah, that just might work.

Ben headed toward the kitchen, thankful Kline had left to get dressed. It was bad enough he was still attracted to her on every level, but seeing her in that sexy robe, without makeup, and her hair up in a towel brought back memories of when they'd lived together and he saw her like that every morning. If he had the spare time during his residency, he'd often scoop her up and take her back to bed. Kline wearing that robe tempted him to do it again.

But he'd burned that bridge and she wasn't going to stick around, so why torture his heart? Better to keep his distance.

Pushing the memories from his mind, he greeted his grandmother and pulled out a chair next to Betty. "Hi. Do you want my grandmother to leave or stay?"

Betty waved a hand. "Of course she can stay."

He wrapped a blood pressure cuff around her arm. "Kline's worried about you. Why aren't you talking to her about your health?"

He leaned down to get his stethoscope and could have sworn he saw a wink pass between Betty and his grandmother. He listened to Betty's heart beat true and strong. She took a deep breath and everything was clear. And no fever. When he shone a light into her brown eyes, they twinkled back at him, as if in bemusement.

He said, "Everything checks out just fine. How long has the dizziness been bothering you?"

She shrugged and her gaze slid toward his grandmother again.

Grandma said, "She's been complaining about it to me for a couple of weeks now, right, Betty?"

Betty nodded.

Then why hadn't she mentioned that along with all the other symptoms she'd detailed one by one in his office the day before? What had gotten into her in the last six weeks? Why the change from someone who never went to the doctor to weekly visits?

Suddenly a thought occurred to him. "How long have you known Kline was coming?"

Betty examined her nails. "A little over a month. Why?"

Uh-huh. Now things were making sense. He turned to his grandmother. "Are you in on this scheme too?"

Grandma pretended to look shocked. She was the world's worst actress. "I have no idea what you're talking about, Benjamin."

Yep. That's why he'd been shown so many pictures of Kline recently and her name had been continually brought up during the appointments with her mother. They were trying to get them back together, dammit.

He packed up his things. "It's not going to work, ladies. Kline and I want different things out of life. It's why we broke up all those years ago. And Betty, this is a dangerous game you're playing. Making up false symptoms." He crossed his arms and glanced back and forth between the two matchmakers. "What do you two have to say for yourselves?"

Grandma said, "Kline looked pretty darn cute in that robe, don't you think?"

Betty finally let her smile bloom. "And you have to keep our secret, right? Doctor-patient whatever that is?"

"I do." He pinched the bridge of his nose. "So I'm not sticking around for the Q-and-A session with Kline. You need to come clean with her. She's worried about you."

He turned to his grandmother. "And you, of all people, should know better than to pull a stunt like this."

Grandma shrugged. "All I know is you're serial dating and unhappy. And it needs to stop."

"What needs to stop, Ruth?" Kline walked into the kitchen, her hair dried and cascading around her shoulders. She wore jeans and a tight pink sweater. He liked all her new curves. A lot.

He said, "Grams isn't happy if she's not complaining about something I'm doing wrong." He looked away before she saw the desire in his eyes, and his gaze landed on Betty's nonalphabetized spice rack. Things out of order bothered him, so he rearranged the small bottles while he pulled himself together. "There. That's better." His phone vibrated with a text so he pulled his cell out from his pocket. It was Joyce asking if he could squeeze in one more patient this afternoon. He texted her back with an affirmative and then said, "I have to get back to work. See you ladies later."

He made for the front door, but before he reached it, a slender hand wrapped around his bicep and tugged.

"Wait. I thought we had a plan back there." Kline's brow crumpled in genuine concern. He hated that now he was going to have to be part of lying to her too.

"She specifically said she doesn't want me to discuss her health with you." Betty had talked about patient confidentiality, so that wasn't a total lie. But she'd been talking about their crazy scheme, not her health.

Kline's shoulders dropped. "My mom and I used to tell each other everything. I don't understand why she'd do that."

The crushed expression on her face poked him straight in the heart. "Why don't you let me worry about your mom so you can just enjoy your visit?"

"No. I'm going to get to the bottom of this one way or the other." She crossed her arms and hitched her chin. "Even if I have to resort to being sneaky."

He remembered that look. It was the one where she strapped her stubborn determination on and didn't take it off until she got her way. "Good luck. Nice sweater, by the way. See you."

Kline didn't know quite how to respond to the sweater comment, so she ignored it and called out, "Be back in a bit, Mom!" and then followed Ben.

Picking up the pace, she caught up with him, but wished she'd grabbed a coat. It was sunny out, but the wind blowing off the lake was chilly.

Ben glanced her way, but kept walking. "I hope part of you being sneaky doesn't include badgering me to death. Because I won't cave on this."

"Nope." She circled her arms around herself to stop her shivering. Keeping up with Ben's aggressive pace should warm her up soon enough. "Got many appointments still today?"

He frowned. "Is this polite small talk? Or do you really care?" He grabbed his phone from his pocket and answered texts while they walked.

"Just trying to have a pleasant conversation on my way to the diner." And to figure out if he'd be too busy to catch her bribing his nurse for information about her mom.

A grin curved one side of his mouth as he typed. "I'm sure there's an ulterior motive in there I haven't figured out yet, but yes. I'm booked solid until five o'clock. Since old Doc Rhodes retired from down south, I'm the only doctor in a fifty-mile radius, so it keeps me busy." Ben tucked his phone away.

"Busy is good." They walked side by side, careful not to touch. Together but separate. "So, still loving being a doctor?"

He nodded. "I am. Do you still love teaching? And being a tree hugger?" He reached out and turned over her pendant that had flipped backward.

That he'd touch her when he was clearly trying so hard to keep his distance was odd. As was the quick tingle that danced up her spine when his fingers brushed her neck. "Your habit of straightening things is new. When did that start?"

"I don't know what you're talking about." He stopped walking and faced her. "Or is this your way of avoiding my question?"

No, but it seemed he was avoiding hers.

Standing still made the cold seep through her sweater again. "Yes, I still love teaching and especially *tree hugging*." She smiled. Ben always teased her about her environmental causes. "I've been involved in some meaningful projects in developing countries. Things that really made a difference in people's lives." She started walking again so she wouldn't freeze to death.

He appeared by her side. "Just what you set out to do."

"Yep." But they were supposed to do those things together. An uncomfortable silence fell over them as they crossed the grassy town square.

Ben cleared his throat. "Are you heading to the diner for a piece of Gloria's chocolate mousse pie?"

He knew her well after living together for so many years. Then he'd ruined things by dropping the bomb that had exploded all over her life.

"I am, actually. It's the only thing I miss about this place."

"Yeah." His jaw clenched. "You made that perfectly clear." They were in front of the diner so he opened the door for her. "Enjoy your pie."

Perfectly clear? Did he mean because she hadn't come home to visit for so many years? Or that she hadn't missed *him*?

Crap. She hadn't thought before she'd said that. She'd had no intention of hurting his feelings.

She opened her mouth to apologize, but he said, "Don't. It's over and done. And you'll be gone as soon as you can. Let's not go there. Deal?"

The pain in his eyes made her feel like a total heel.

"Okay." She laid a hand on his that held his medical bag and squeezed. Hopefully he'd take that as the apology she'd meant it to be. "Thanks for checking on my mom."

He slid his hand from her grasp. "No problem."

Ben waited as she entered the diner and then he let the door slap shut behind her.

She headed for a stool, sighing at the painful memories seeing Ben conjured up again.

Their plan since high school had been for her to finish up her teaching degree, get a job to support them until he was done with med school, and then they'd travel the world to help others. She'd teach and he'd heal those who needed care the most. Then one day, out of the blue, he came home and told her he didn't want those things anymore, that they were just the dreams of two naïve kids, and now that they were adults it didn't make sense. He still loved her, but she should just go on without him.

Trusting men had never been easy after that. They'd say they loved her, but she'd never said it back because she feared they'd do to her what Ben had done. Abandon her. Crush her heart.

Easier to just stay loose and single.

So where was all that pain and emotion coming from on his part?

CHAPTER THREE

𝒦line pushed all the bad memories of her and Ben back into the little box where they perpetually lived and then glanced around the diner. She waved to all the familiar people who'd smiled and held a hand up in greeting. Rachel, the last person she'd want to talk to, called out, "Kline. Great to see you. Come join me."

It was inevitable she'd run into one of her high school nemeses. Rachel and Lisa Anderson were Ben's cousins and had made Kline's life hell.

Being the daughter of the school lunch lady and the high school's janitor had already been two strikes against Kline, an ugly duckling who didn't find her inner swan until high school. Amazing what contacts, getting braces removed, and growing boobs had done for her social life.

But she'd had to put up with the humiliation when kids like Rachel and Lisa would dump stuff on the floor just to watch Kline turn red when her dad appeared. He'd smile and wave to her, then clean up the mess.

Refusing to be bullied anymore, she laid a hand on her stomach and drew a deep breath for patience as she approached the red booth in the fifties-themed diner. But she wouldn't sit. Just in case she needed to make a hasty retreat. "Hi, Rachel. How are you?"

Rachel laid her burger down and wiped her hands. "Brewing kid number three now. Hence this burger two hours before dinnertime. Cravings don't help the battle with my waistline, a problem you obviously don't have. You look incredible. How've you been?"

That was pleasant enough. "I'm great. And that glowing-when-pregnant thing must be true. You look fantastic." Seeing a classmate pregnant sent a little pinch to Kline's heart. Not having a baby of her own had recently made her biological clock start clanging in alarm.

Rachel waved a hand. "Thanks, but I feel like a cow. How long are you staying?"

"Just home for a short visit with my mom."

Rachel nodded and then took a humongous bite and closed her eyes. "God, I need to stop, but I can't." She picked up a chocolate milkshake and took a long pull from the straw. "Heard your first meeting with Ben didn't go so well."

Here it came—just when things were looking good, the usual taunting was about to begin. Joyce must have told everyone, as predicted. "Yeah. I've had better days."

Rachel chuckled. "I did the same thing to him a few weeks ago. This pregnancy has brought along with it my worst bouts of morning sickness yet. Ben's used to it. Don't worry about it."

Huh. She hadn't expected kindness from Rachel. "I suppose he is."

Kline still needed to get her bribery pie before Ben's office closed, so she said, "Nice to see you again, Rachel."

"You too." Rachel grinned. "Be forewarned. My mom has started a new betting pool. How long it'll be before you and Ben get back together. There's already over a grand in there. Everyone saw how Ben changed after you guys broke up, so the whole town is rooting for you two."

"Well, I hope you didn't waste your money because that's not happening." Kline chewed her bottom lip, debating if she should ask. "How did Ben change after we broke up? He seems the exact same to me." Except for his new habit of straightening and organizing spices, and a different kind of confidence about him that was really sexy.

Rachel shook her head as she finished off the last of her burger. "I don't want to spread gossip about my cousin and his dating habits, so maybe you should ask him."

Rachel *had* changed. For the better.

"Okay. I'm sure I'll see you around. Take care." What the heck could that have meant? Obviously, they'd both dated others. And Ben must be single now, or else they wouldn't have a pool going. Geez. One more mystery she'd be compelled to solve during her visit.

Kline walked up to the counter and was instantly embraced by two strong arms. It was hard to breathe with her face smashed into Gloria's cleavage. Wearing her typical bowling shirt, blue eye shadow, beehive hairdo, and a perpetual smile, Rachel's mom was always a breath of fresh air. "Hi, Gloria. So good to see you."

Gloria finally released Kline so she could breathe again, then said, "You too, sweetie. Heard you had a little incident with Ben. Are you pregnant, honey? Is that why you've finally come home?"

"No! Food poisoning is all." She held up her hand. "Scout's honor."

For God's sake. Someone must've posted the news to the town's private e-mail loop, which had been set up years ago so everyone could keep up with who the latest visiting celebrity was, not to gossip about people in town. Anderson Butte was the world's best-kept secret celebrity hideout. The mayor's lucrative 401(k) and profit-sharing plan encouraged the town's residents to keep their lips sealed about their famous visitors. But man, a girl couldn't even barf on a guy's shoes without the whole world knowing, and instantly assuming she was knocked up. One more reason she'd made the right choice to stay away.

"I'm feeling much better today, thanks. I was hoping to get a chocolate mousse pie to go?" Joyce might want the whole pie, not just a slice, in exchange for a quick peek at her mom's chart.

Ben rapped a knuckle on the exam room door before he stuck his head in. Joyce had said Eric might need stitches. His youngest sister, Meg, the family mischief-maker and newly adoptive mother of Eric, sat in the chair beside the exam table. "Hey, guys. How are you?"

Eric said, "Okay, except I cut myself pretty bad."

"We'll get that all fixed up." Ben glanced at Meg. "And my prying baby sister? How are you?"

Meg rolled her eyes. "I haven't said a word about Kline, Mr. Neat and Orderly."

"Yet." Ben laid Eric's chart down and washed his hands. "But no doubt you will. And there's nothing wrong with wanting a little order in my life."

"Okay, Doctor Delusional, if you say so." Meg beamed a mischievous grin. "But you have to admit, Kline coming back is the biggest news we've had around here in a long time."

"Kline is just home for a few weeks. So knock off whatever scheme you're brewing up, Meg." Ben shook his head. It was going to be a long three weeks while Kline was home. She'd touched him twice, and both times it had sent an unwanted blast of desire straight through him. The smart thing would be to keep his distance. But all he craved was an hour alone with her in his bed, to show her how much he'd missed her.

He needed to snap out of it and keep his head in the game.

Scooping up the supplies he'd need, Ben kicked his rolling stool across the small room. "So Eric, how'd you end up with that big gash?"

Eric stuck out his hand covered with bloody gauze. "I found a broken beer bottle one of the lodge's guests left out by the lake. I didn't want my dogs to step on it and cut their paws, so I picked it up and tossed it into the lake. Guess that wasn't so smart, huh?"

It was a deep cut, so Ben held out a lollipop for Eric and then got the novocaine ready. "Nope. But your heart was in the right place. Bet you'll never do that again?"

"Nuh-uh," Eric mumbled around his candy.

Meg said, "Back to Kline . . ."

"Dim that unholy gleam in your eyes, Meg. Nothing is going to happen between Kline and me. She just made it perfectly clear that the only thing she's missed since she's been gone is Gloria's pie."

"Ouch." Meg winced. "She said that? Straight up? Kline was never mean on purpose, Ben."

"Maybe she's changed." He shrugged a shoulder to make it appear he didn't care. But Kline's words had stung. More reason to shut down his feelings for her. After so much time had passed it should have been easier. But just being in the same room made him realize how much he'd missed her.

He prepped the area on Eric's hand, then handed over his cell as a diversion tactic. "Think you can beat my top score in Zombie Wars? I'll give you a hundred-point handicap for only having one thumb."

Eric's lips tilted into a grin as he killed zombies on the phone's screen. Ben hurried and neatly closed up the wound.

Meg asked, "So how's the fight going with Dad about your new clinic?"

Ben shook his head. "He doesn't understand how badly we need a bigger facility with maybe one or two more docs to keep up with demand. As it is, sharing after-hours calls and days off with a doc sixty miles away isn't cutting it. We both usually end up working on our off days anyway. And it makes more sense to turn this building into commercial space because it's closer to Town Square, and then let me have the land currently earmarked for the new distillery. There's plenty of room for the distillery just outside of town."

"Yeah, but then it'd be on Grant land, and you know Dad would never go for that."

"The land across from the hotel is the only large parcel left. The council is casting the final vote tomorrow night to change the zoning."

"So it's not even final, and yet Dad has already announced the groundbreaking ceremony will be next week? That's not looking good for you."

"I'm going to try to talk to him one more time before the vote. Try to rally some support."

"Good luck with that."

"Gonna need it!" He finished up the stiches then laid a bandage over his handiwork. "Time's up. Let's see how you did." He took the phone from Eric. "You obliterated my score. You're killing my zombie-hunting ego. Get out of my office before I have to hurt you."

"'Kay." Eric laughed and hopped off the table.

Meg said, "Thanks for stitching him up. And while you're fighting for your clinic, maybe Casey and I will work on Kline so you can have *everything* your heart wants. You coming to Brewsters tonight?"

"Yes. Now go away. I'm busy." He tossed a tongue depressor at her.

Meg caught it and laughed as she walked out the door. He should tell Casey and Meg not to bother, that it'd do no good. But his sisters were as stubborn as two rusted-out lug nuts. Their family gathering after work was going to quickly turn from a fun time to catch up into a "how to get Kline back" session. But trying to win her back would surely just end badly again.

Kline, pie box in hand, opened the clinic's front door. The theme from those Pink Panther movies ran through her head, tempting her to tiptoe in time to the *da-dum, da-dum*s echoing in her brain as she snuck to the front desk. She must be spending too much time around her middle school–aged students.

Laughing at herself, she looked both ways to be sure Ben wasn't around, then she darted for Joyce's station.

It was near closing time and the waiting room was empty, but where was Joyce? Maybe it was a good time for a quick snoop. If she found the file on her own, maybe she'd just keep the pie for herself. Total win-win.

One last glance over her shoulder showed the coast was still clear, so she laid the pie on the high reception counter and then circled behind. It was so quiet the only audible sound was the second hand moving rhythmically on the clock above her head, reminding her to hurry.

The file cabinets were labeled alphabetically so she headed for the Gs. There was a whole vertical file drawer dedicated to just that letter. Probably because more than a quarter of the town's residents were Grants.

She slowly slid the drawer out, making as little noise as possible, and quickly fingered through the tabs. Aunt Abigail was first, then her uncle Andrew. Cousin Barbara was next but then it skipped to her aunt Connie. Betty was missing. Or misfiled, darn it. She glanced over her shoulder again and noticed a large stack of files on the countertop next to Joyce's coffeemaker.

Her mom had mentioned she'd been to see Ben just yesterday. Maybe her chart hadn't been refiled yet.

She quickly closed the drawer and then crossed to the messy stack of files. She tilted her head to read the mishmash of name tags sticking out and she finally saw it. Betty Grant.

Bingo.

She reached out to slip the file from the stack, her hand shaking a bit with nerves. Just as her fingers were about to tug, Ben's voice sounded from behind her. "What are you doing?"

Crap!

Her eyes darted to the coffeepot beside the stack of files. Snatching up a cup, she poured out a mug and then spun around. "Just pouring you some coffee to go with the pie I brought you as a peace offering." She pointed to the box on the countertop. "That is if you still like coffee with your pie these days?"

"Peace offering?" He smirked and crossed his arms. He didn't believe a word of her BS.

Ben was going to make her say it. No doubt as punishment for her almost crime. "For the 'only missing the pie' comment. I didn't think before I said that, and I clearly hurt your feelings. I'm sorry for that." She *was* sorry for hurting his feelings.

He opened the box and looked inside before quickly snapping it shut. "So was the pie really the only thing you missed after you left?" He stared deeply and longingly into her eyes as he waited for her answer.

The same look he always had in his eyes right before he made love to her.

After seeing him the day before, part of her wondered. Would her body still crave his touch like it did before, even though her heart had written him off?

Without breaking their shared gaze, he rounded the counter and moved slowly toward her.

Her heart galloped and left her with a distinct lack of air in her lungs.

Ben wanted her to say it out loud. But she'd been so hurt she'd sworn to never admit how much she'd missed him to anyone. Rather, she'd learn from her mistake and never make it again.

She stalled by offering him the mug, but he just shook his head and then tidied the crooked stack of files, so she laid the cup on the countertop.

After the files were aligned, he still stood so close she could detect traces of his sexy aftershave. A scent as dangerously alluring as Ben.

He said, "So your lack of an answer means the pie really was all you missed?" His right eye twitched like it used to when he was really irritated.

She swallowed the lump forming in her throat, blinked back the tears that threatened to fall, and whispered, "No. I missed one other thing in particular too. So much, and for such a very long time, I didn't know if my heart would ever heal."

He nodded in understanding, slipped his arms around her, and pulled her against his hard chest. "I missed something that much, and for as long too, but now I understand how futile it was to ever think it would work. So I had to let it go."

A rogue tear slid down her cheek. "And I had to learn to forget. But looking back, it was never wrong . . . just not entirely right?"

"Yeah." He wiped her tear away with his thumb, then whispered, "But this part was always right between us, don't you think?" His mouth slowly moved closer to hers, giving her the chance to push him away, but damn if she didn't meet him halfway. He gently laid his soft lips on hers and kissed her.

Warning sirens in her head screamed that it was a mistake to kiss him. But she couldn't deny how much she'd missed it. The way his lips fit so perfectly with hers. How his touch was so soft and gentle on her mouth, but at the same time filled with so much passion he made her spine turn to a puddle of goo.

So she had her answer. Their chemistry hadn't dimmed in the least.

Really, she should make it stop. It'd be the smarter thing to do rather than closing the little gap between their chests and wrapping her arms around his neck like she'd just done. And to angle her head just a bit to the right, at the same time he leaned his to the left so it'd deepen their kiss even more.

His kiss left her in need of air but she didn't want to stop long enough to take a breath. Her hormones screamed for more while her oxygen-deprived brain tried to talk some sense into her. But then, thinking—and breathing—were overrated. Every nerve in her body was on fire. And she wanted Ben to put the flames out.

When he let out a low, sexy moan she was tempted to drag him into an exam room and put them both out of their misery. Then as if reading her mind, he wrapped his big hands around her waist and lifted her onto the countertop. With his lips never leaving hers, he used a muscular thigh to spread her legs apart and then moved between them.

She parted his long lab coat and tugged his shirt from his pants. She wanted her hands all over his tight abs and chest again. She'd always loved the way he was built, all lean muscles and sexy definition.

Joyce's voice called out, "Well, looks like I lost the pool at Gloria's. I thought it'd take at least another day for you two to figure things out."

Ben pulled away so fast she almost toppled forward and off the countertop.

He stuffed his hands into his lab coat pockets, then turned to face his nurse. "What pool?"

"The latest one at the diner. Everyone's betting on how long it'll be before you two are back together again."

Ben growled, "We're not back together. That wasn't what it looked like."

Joyce cocked her head to the side like a confused puppy. "I may be getting old, but I don't think much has changed about kissing."

Feeling like she'd just been caught making out in high school by the principal, Kline hopped down and moved beside Ben. "He's right. That wasn't your run-of-the-mill kiss. That was . . ." She glanced his way for help. She'd have liked to say it was the best kiss she'd had in a very long time, but that wouldn't help their cause. She whispered, "What *was* that?" and raised her brows in question.

His eye did that twitching thing again. "Nothing. It didn't mean anything." He brushed past his nurse. "I'm not on call tonight so I'm going to Brewsters for a damn beer. Lock up on your way out, Joyce. And not a word about this to anyone or you're fired!"

The slamming of the back door made both Kline and Joyce flinch.

Joyce asked, "What was that about? Ben's never raised his voice to me before."

"I'm . . . not entirely sure." She turned, picked up the pie box, and held it out. "Here. Ben will feel bad for yelling at you. So tomorrow when he apologizes, tell him it's okay because you enjoyed the pie he forgot in his haste to separate himself from me. *Again.*"

Joyce accepted the box and sighed. "Maybe you should go after him?"

"Nope." She shook her head. "He hates to lose his temper, so I'll just let him cool down and talk to him later. Instead, I'll go home and have a nice dinner with my mom. After all, it's her I'm here to see. Not Ben." She waved and started for the door.

As she gathered her things, Joyce mumbled under her breath, "Didn't look to me like you were thinking about anyone *but* Ben."

Joyce was right. He was stirring up all sorts of emotions she'd thought were long buried. Maybe she should go after Ben and get things straightened out between them. Once and for all, so they could both understand the rules while she was in town.

She pulled her phone out and texted her mom to let her know she'd be a little late.

As she headed toward Brewsters, a familiar voice called out, "Kline? Wait up."

She turned and smiled as Ben's brother caught up in two long strides. Ryan wrapped her up in a bear hug. "Missed you, Kline."

"Missed you too." Ryan had always held a special place in her heart. He was handsome, built like a pro athlete, and didn't see the need to talk much. Because he was the middle child between his two sisters, they tended to do the talking for him, but he used to talk to her. A lot. Mostly about his father, the mayor, who tended to have a heavy-handed, mean way about him that affected Ryan more than he had ever let on to the others. He was the little brother she'd never had.

She leaned back and said, "I hear you're the sheriff these days. And that you actually have a serious girlfriend? Is she quiet like you?"

"No. She's the new dentist in town. Casey and Meg can't figure out how a quiet guy like me snagged her. Or how I keep her."

"You must actually talk to her then, huh?"

He nodded. "Yeah. It's not a chore with her. She's great."

And Ryan was clearly in love with her. It made Kline's heart swell. "I look forward to meeting her."

"You're going to love her. Really good to see you again, Kline." He gave her a friendly shoulder bump as they walked. "Heard you and Ben got off to a rocky start, though."

Of course he'd heard that. Little did he know how much rockier things had just gotten with that kiss. Hopefully Joyce could keep a secret for a change. "I'm headed to talk to Ben right now. Set some things straight between us."

Ryan frowned. "So I've wasted my ten bucks in Gloria's pool then, huh? No hope for a reconciliation?"

The sharp pang to Kline's heart at the thought of reconciliation reminded her of the pain Ben had caused her. She had no desire to go through that again, no matter how the man had grown even more handsome and maybe a tad more confident and interesting since she'd left. "Nope. Sorry about your ten bucks."

CHAPTER FOUR

When Ben pulled open the door to Brewsters, country music annoyed his ears, while the aroma of greasy sliders and fries turned his stomach. Why the hell had he kissed her? It was like shoving the dagger into his heart even deeper. She'd killed him when she questioned why he'd done it. Why did she think he'd kissed her? And why the hell had she kissed him back like . . . that?

It had been damn lucky they'd been interrupted, because ten more minutes and Joyce would've gotten a real eyeful. No way they should ever sleep together again. It'd just make everything worse. Now if only he could convince his libido of that.

He ran a hand down his face and searched for calm before he took someone else's head off. Yelling at Joyce for no reason had been a jerk move. He'd be sure to apologize for that in the morning. Better yet, he'd call her at home later. For now, he needed to pull it together because his siblings were like vultures on a carcass if they sensed he was upset. His sisters would want to talk about feelings. His were so raw he couldn't bear anyone poking around there.

He found Meg seated at a table. Thankfully it was two-for-one happy hour so there were two pitchers of beer in front of her. He planned to put a dent in one of them. He pulled out a chair and sat down while Meg finished up a phone call. He grabbed a beer mug and filled it, then downed half the glass in one gulp.

God, he was an idiot! What had possessed him to kiss her?

When Meg's call was finished, she laid her phone on the table and hitched her brows.

Showtime.

He plastered on a fake grin. "What?"

"What's really going on with you and Kline? Casey saw you walking with her earlier."

His sister Casey had a big mouth. He took a long drink, debating how much he wanted to tell. His sisters were pretty damned nosy, but gave good advice when it came to women. "I honestly don't know."

Meg took a long drink from her mug and then banged the glass onto the table. "Why don't you tell her why you signed that contract with Dad and the town in the first place?"

He'd been tricked into signing that contract and had felt like an idiot for it. Maybe his ego back then was as much to blame for not telling Kline as was his desire to let her live her dreams. "It doesn't really change why we're still fundamentally never going to be together. And after all this time, do you think it'd even matter?"

"I'm sure it couldn't hurt." Meg's face lit with a smile. "Casey said Kline looked really good. Does she seem happy?"

He shrugged. "She's not happy to be home. She's here to see her mom, but plans to leave again as soon as she can. She hasn't changed her mind about not wanting to live here."

Meg's grin turned mischievous as she picked up her phone again. "The pool at the diner keeps growing. The whole town wants to see you two get back together. And we need a new science teacher. Maybe we all just need to show Kline what she's missing here. I can send out an e-mail on the loop to rally everyone. She'll be so welcome home she won't know what hit her!" Meg's thumbs quickly tapped out her post. "Do you think Kline's mother will keep that a secret from her?"

"She'd like Kline to come home too. So yeah. I'm sure of it." He wished he could tell her that Grandma and Betty were way ahead of her, but he had to keep that to himself. "But I'm not sure that's a good idea, Meg."

Meg ignored him as usual. She hit one last button on her phone and then put it away before she glanced up and said, "Oh. Hey there."

He turned to see who she was looking at. Kline stood behind him next to Ryan with her hand lifted.

She said, "Hi, Meg. Sorry to interrupt. I just need to talk to Ben for a minute." She glanced at him. "Please? It's *important*."

About the kiss, most likely. Why the hell had he kissed her?

———

Kline's heart warmed when she saw Meg, Ben's youngest sister, who'd hopped up to hug her and told her how much she'd missed her. Kline had worried his siblings would take Ben's side over hers, but neither Ryan nor Meg seemed to have done so. She'd missed them too.

"So good to see you, Meg." Kline leaned back to study her. Meg was still short and adorable. A mini version of her sister, the beautiful Casey, who was tall and willowy. Both Ben's sisters had dark hair like Ben's and big smiles. "Congratulations—I hear you just got married. And you run a lodge now across the lake?"

"Yep." Meg held her hand up, showing off an impressive rock. "Josh is the best."

"I look forward to meeting him." Kline glanced at Ben, who was ignoring everyone and rearranging the condiments on the table. She needed to clear the air between them.

After Ryan pulled out a chair next to Ben, she said, "I'll let you have Ben back in just a minute." They needed a little privacy, so she grabbed his hand and pulled. "Let's dance while we talk."

Ben reluctantly followed behind her to the dance floor just as the music turned from a two-step to a slow tune. He was a good dancer and usually enjoyed it. But the expression on his face was of a man about to have a root canal. Or in his case, deal with an unorganized closet. His new habit was a little confusing. And maybe a touch concerning.

He tugged on her hand to make her stop walking. "Look. I'm sorry I—"

"No. Don't." She shook her head. "I kissed you back, so we're even there."

"Then what are we doing, Kline?" He pulled her close and into the fray of people dancing.

Enjoying his strong arms wrapped around her more than she should, she said, "Dancing?"

He let out a frustrated grunt and pulled her closer. His warm breath feathered across her cheek, sending a delicious shiver up her spine when he whispered, "You know what I meant. What are we going to do about . . ."

"Us?" More out of habit than conscious effort, she snuggled her chest against his hard one and circled her hands around his neck. "That's what I wanted to talk to you about. What happened in the past is over and done for good reasons, but obviously we're still attracted to each other physically. It's basic science, really, and probably can't be helped."

"Big understatement there." He slowly slid his hand lower toward her butt, stopping just before he'd earn them an R rating from the spectators.

Straining to stay focused on their conversation and not what she knew those hands could do to her in bed, she said, "You hurt me, Ben. And it took me a long time to get over that. Seeing you again has stirred up lots of feelings. Not all of them good."

"For me too. But mine are mostly good." He nuzzled his stubbly cheek against hers.

He wasn't making things any easier by being so nice to her. And by being so damn sexy. "I'll never live here, and you'll never leave your family, so anything long term will never happen."

His face nodded against hers in response.

"We could go one of two ways here. We could give in to basic human desire and sleep with each other again, thereby enjoying the physical release while it lasts, or we can use the higher, more developed parts of our brains, decide we're just going to be friends, and then keep our hands and mouths to ourselves."

He leaned back and stared into her eyes. "Cut the science crap, Kline. What do *you* want?"

You, naked in my bed was the first thing that popped into her traitorous mind. "I hope we can be friends again, but I'm afraid the only way that's going to happen is if we leave our physical desire for each other out of it and keep things platonic."

He studied her for a long moment before he finally nodded. "You're probably right."

"Okay then. Friends with *no* benefits it is." She laid her head on his shoulder and closed her eyes, determined to enjoy the rest of the dance, while familiar sadness washed over her. It'd be nice to be friends again, though. He used to be her *best* friend. She'd never found another like him. She snuggled closer and breathed in his familiar scent.

His phone vibrated in his pocket against her leg. He ignored it, but a moment later it started up again. She said, "Aren't you going to get that?"

"I'm not on call tonight. And I'd rather enjoy a dance with you."

"Thank you." When they were in high school Ben didn't carry a cell, and yet his family still seemed to find a way to interrupt whatever they were doing. Now that he was a doctor, it must be twice as bad. But she appreciated that the new Ben seemed to have found some better work-family-life balance for his own good.

Wayne Jacobs suddenly appeared and cleared his throat. "I'm cutting in, pal."

Ben shook his head. "Go away. We're having a conversation here."

"I didn't see any talking going on. Besides, Betty sent me to find Kline."

She lifted her head. "Is my mom okay?"

Wayne tried to cut in, but Ben blocked him with his shoulder. Wayne matched them step for step as they danced. "Betty said she was going to go to bed early and didn't want you to eat alone. She wanted me to take you to the diner and keep you company. She asked if you could bring home a chocolate mousse pie."

Whoops. Gloria would get suspicious about two pies in a day. But she'd rather just go home. It'd been a long, emotional day. "I appreciate the offer Wayne, but—"

"Your mom said it'd mean a lot to her if you'd have dinner with me. She said you need a decent meal after you've been sick and all."

Kline glanced at Ben, who rolled his eyes. It made her laugh.

She *was* starving. "Well, okay then." She stopped dancing and leaned back but Ben still had her wrapped up and wouldn't let her go.

Ben whispered, "Why don't I take you to dinner? We could go to the hotel for a quiet meal. It'd give us a chance to catch up."

The hungry look in his eyes made her stomach clench. Having dinner at the hotel could very well lead to them going upstairs to one of the rooms for dessert. Better not go there. "Maybe another time, Ben. Wayne went out of his way to find me."

"Fine. Have fun." Ben slowly released her.

"Thanks." She turned to Wayne. "Okay, let's go."

She led the way, winding between people standing in clusters talking. At the front door, Ben appeared beside her. He held out his jacket. "I noticed you didn't have a coat. Take this."

God, that was so sweet. "But then you'll be cold. I'll be fine."

Ben glanced at Wayne, who wore a leather jacket. "You walked, right?"

He nodded. "Yeah. It'll be a cold walk home, Kline. You should take it."

Obviously Wayne wasn't going to offer up his.

Ben slipped his coat over her shoulders. "I'm going to drink enough beer tonight that I won't care about the cold." He turned and walked back toward his table.

"Wait. Ben?"

He lifted a hand over his head and just kept on walking.

So maybe he wasn't happy with their friends-with-no-benefits agreement, but it was for the best.

Wayne slipped his hand around her arm and tugged. "Let's go eat. I'm starving!"

When they stepped outside, a blast of cold air sent a shiver up her spine, so she slipped her arms fully into Ben's jacket. It smelled like him, a combination of sexy aftershave and soap. Yum.

Luckily it was a short walk to the diner. Wayne held the door open for her. "After you, babe."

Babe? She'd better make sure Wayne understood right away that nothing was going to happen between them. Sure, he was tall, muscle-bound, blond, and cute in his own way, but not her type. He'd always been all about sports and chasing women. In that order.

She dated casually, but she didn't sleep with guys just for the sake of having sex. Ever. Although, with Ben she was sorely tempted to make an exception. But he was different. She'd once loved him.

Gloria walked up to their table with two glasses of water and a frown. "Didn't expect to see you two here for dinner. Where's Ben, Kline?"

Gloria was the hub of all relationship gossip in town so Kline needed to clear things up, pronto. "Ben is with his family. Mom wasn't

feeling well so she asked Wayne to keep me company. It's not a date."
She glanced at Wayne to gauge his reaction.

His forehead crumpled, but he didn't say anything.

Relief softened Gloria's expression. "Sorry Betty's not feeling well.
So, what can I get you two?"

Before Kline could answer, Wayne said, "The usual."

"Chicken-fried steak with a double serving of mashed potatoes.
You got it." Gloria turned to Kline. "Meatloaf is the special tonight."

"Meatloaf sounds perfect. And I ended up giving away that pie I
picked up earlier to Ben, so I'll need another." She wouldn't complicate
the story by telling her that Joyce ultimately ended up with the pie.

"Shared it with Ben, huh?" Gloria smirked, probably thinking how
that would increase the action in her betting pool. "I'll have your food
right out. And Kline, your dinner and the pie are on the house. Call it
a welcome home gift."

Gloria left before Kline could thank her. So she turned her attention to her non-date. "Last I heard, you were teaching in Denver. Why
would you ever decide to come back here?"

He shrugged. "We needed a PE coach, and the pay is five times
better here when you factor in the town's profit-sharing plan for keeping our yaps shut about the celebrities who visit. The board promised
me that whatever the school's money won't cover for supplies, the town
council will. I just have to ask. My equipment is top notch. And all of
our teams have winning records."

Kline took a sip of water as she processed that. Five times more pay
was a lot. "But that's the athletic department. They always get all the
glory and budget. What about the arts and sciences?"

"It's all the same. You just gotta ask." He paused for a drink then set
his glass down with a thud. "I was just a glorified babysitter in Denver,
but here, the kids know you might run into their parents at the store so
they think twice about cutting up too much. This job is so much easier
and lots more fun."

She'd always had to spend all her free time begging for beakers and Bunsen burners, rather than planning exciting experiments for her students. That'd be a real change from any of her other experiences. "That sounds pretty nice."

"I'm not looking forward to taking over one of your cousin's class periods while she's out, though. I don't remember a damn thing about science."

"Maybe Barb has good lesson plans all ready to go?"

Wayne nodded, then his gaze wandered around the diner like he was bored. Maybe because she'd made it clear they weren't on a date, therefore he wasn't getting lucky after.

Looked like it was going to be up to her to keep the conversation going. "Tell me the whole story behind the whiskey. Something about people finding barrels that were hidden during Prohibition?"

Gloria slipped their meals in front of them and said, "Yeah. Ryan's girlfriend, Tara, and Eric, Meg's newly adopted son, found the secret recipe and the whiskey stored in an old mine right before it caved in. So a crew was hired to get the barrels out for the kids who'd gone looking for them and ended up hurt. And Tara's father, a bigwig businessman from Denver, is going to start making the whiskey again and Eric will be the owner once he turns eighteen. Now you're up to date."

Kline laughed. "Thank you."

After Gloria left, Wayne added, "I'm looking forward to the big party next week for the distillery groundbreaking." Then he attacked his plate like a starving caveman. The guy had no manners whatsoever. She couldn't watch.

She hurried and ate so she could get their not-even-close-to-a-date over with. Thankfully he inhaled his food.

When he was done, Kline pushed her half-empty plate forward. "That was great but I'm full. Ready to go?"

Wayne leaned closer and smiled. "Why don't we go back to Brewsters? Play some pool, shoot some darts? Have a few drinks before we head home?"

That would be *way* too close to a date. "Thanks, but it's been a long day. I'd just like to go."

"Okay. Going home works too." Wayne put his meal on his tab and then they bundled back up and started for home.

As they passed by Wayne's house, which her mom had mentioned was right next to Ben's, Wayne stopped walking and breached the boundaries of her personal space. "Since you're not going to be in town long, I might as well just cut to the chase. The ladies all tell me I'm good in the sack. Why don't you come inside and I'll show you just *how* good?"

Charming.

She took a half step back. "Geez, that's awful tempting when you put it like that, but I think I'd better get home and check on my mom. And put this pie in the fridge. As a matter of fact, you don't have to walk me the rest of the way. Thanks for having dinner with me."

He blinked in confusion. "Oh. Okay." Then he leaned down for a kiss. She turned her face at the last moment so his lips landed on her cheek. "Night, Kline."

"Good night." She hightailed it away, hoping her mom would refrain from making her any more dates while she was home. As she passed by Ben's house, she checked to see if there were any lights on. Looked like he was still out. When a big hand slipped around her elbow and stopped her forward progress, she yelped.

She turned to tell Wayne she still wasn't interested and was surprised to see Ben standing there, grinning at her. "Oh, it's just you."

"I'll walk you the rest of the way home." He still had her elbow so she had no choice but to follow along as he guided her up the street.

"You don't have to, Ben. It's cold and I can manage the *mean streets* of Anderson Butte on my own."

"I'm not letting you walk home alone. Wayne was a jerk to do that."

"Well, evidently he's so good in the sack he never gets turned down. I probably threw him off his game."

Ben chuckled. "I heard that. I've been behind you guys ever since you passed Brewsters. What an ass."

"Oh, believe me, I've met worse."

He was quiet for a moment, then whispered, "I'm glad you didn't take him up on his offer."

She tucked her arm through his and snuggled closer, telling herself it was to keep him warm, but she'd missed the deep connection she'd always felt when they touched. "You set the bar pretty high right out of the gate for me. It takes a lot for me to decide to sleep with men."

He shot her a sideways glance. "It took two long years before you were ready to sleep with me. And then I had to endure the whole senior prom before we could sneak off."

"Thank you for being so patient with me." They walked up her mom's front steps and stopped under the glowing porch light she must've left on for Kline.

Ben leaned close and whispered, "I waited because I was in love." He stared so deeply into her eyes it stirred up faint whispers of that sweet first love again in her heart.

"I was too. You made my first time perfect. That's something a woman never forgets." She laid her hand on his ice-cold cheek. "Thank you for that."

He took her hand from his face and then laid a soft kiss in her palm. "I've never stopped loving you, Kline. I couldn't figure out how." He gave her hand a squeeze and then turned and walked down the steps. "But you obviously don't feel the same, so I'll keep my distance."

She stood on the porch, tears burning her eyes, as he disappeared into the night. He still loved her? Then why did he let her walk out of his life without a fight?

Bitter memories from that night he'd told her he was breaking up with her clenched her stomach. That he'd changed his mind about all the plans they'd made together for their future. Med school made him realize there were plenty of people to help in their hometown. But that she should go on and do what she'd felt she needed to do since she was ten years old, when she'd vowed she'd never live in Anderson Butte.

He'd said he realized he wouldn't make her happy because he wouldn't be happy without being near his family who still needed him. But what about her? She'd needed him too. More than he knew.

How hadn't she seen that big a change occurring in him? It was as if a light switch flipped one day and Ben suddenly wasn't the person she thought he was. Worse, he hadn't asked her to come home with him. He'd just decided they were through. Probably because he was tired of having to convince his father that she was good enough for him. The mayor had never liked her and had made no bones about telling her so.

But then, Ben had always done things like that. Made decisions for her as if he were protecting her, rather than discussing things with her.

Looking back, part of that might have been her fault for letting him. She was loyal, determined, and always kept her promises, but communicating her feelings had always been hard for her. It had become even worse with all the bullying she'd endured in school, always afraid of the consequences if she spoke up, so maybe their relationship had been doomed to fail. Ben just saw it before she had.

She sighed and opened the door to her mom's house.

Her feelings for him were definitely confusing, but she'd hardened her heart so firmly against love after they'd broken up, she wasn't sure she'd be *able* to fully give it to a man ever again. Especially one already married—to Anderson Butte.

CHAPTER FIVE

While Kline wiped down the kitchen counters after breakfast, her mom came in with a pair of high-powered binoculars and held them out. "Your dad always intended for you to have these. I found them in the hall closet the other day when I was looking for something else."

Kline smiled as she ran her fingers over the spots that were worn from so much use. "Dad loved these. You should keep them, Mom."

A quick flash of her father's sweet smile brought a sharp pang to her already tender heart. It conjured up memories of her college days when she'd come home for visits. The thing she'd looked forward to most was bird watching with her dad. He had loved the outdoors and nature as much as she did.

After he died, knowing her mom was alone had made Kline feel guilty for being so happy living with Ben, free from the shackles of small-town life as they attended school in Denver. It'd been heaven. But Betty Grant was rooted in Anderson Butte as deeply as Ben and had never taken Kline up on her offers to live with her elsewhere.

"You'd get more use out of them than I would, honey." She took the rag from Kline and finished wiping the countertop. "As a matter of fact, I can't believe you haven't been out tromping through the woods yet. You've never lasted two hours before you were off exploring, much less two days."

"That's where I'm headed now. There won't be many birds this time of year—most have flown south—but I might see some owls, eagles, or a sage grouse. Want to come with me? Might be good for you to get some fresh air."

"No." Mom pursed her lips. "I think I'll go lie down and read a book while you're gone. I just don't have a lot of energy these days. I've even given up yoga."

Her mother loved yoga. It had been a passion of hers for years. She must have owned twenty workout DVDs. "Mom, seriously. If Ben can't figure out what's wrong with you, then let me take you to Denver. We'll find you a specialist." She looked closer, searching for physical signs of illness that might be a clue to her mother's constant fatigue. But her color was good, and her eyes clear.

Mom shook her head. "You've been staying with your teacher friend since you've been back in the country. I couldn't impose."

"I'd planned to find a place of my own as soon as I leave here anyway. We can stay in a hotel for a few days until I figure it out. Please? I'm so worried about you." She laid a hand on her mom's shoulder and stared into her eyes. "Losing Dad was bad enough. I don't want to even think about living without you too." After her prison stay had made her realize how precious life was, she'd vowed to spend as much time with her mother as she could.

"Such a good girl." Her mom patted Kline's cheek. "Maybe this is just part of growing old. How would I know? I've never done it before. Go. Have fun. I'll be fine after I rest a bit." She started to leave, then said, "Oh, if you think of it while you're out, will you please stop by the store? Fred has some new books he's holding for me."

"Sure. Be back in a while." She'd just have to keep nagging until her mom gave in, that's all. Because Kline couldn't leave town until she knew her mom was going to be okay on her own. Luckily, that temporary teaching position was open in case it took a while to figure out what was going on with her mom. She could just put off teaching in Denver until next fall if that's what it would take. Her mom trumped any vows she'd made to stay away from Anderson Butte. And Ben.

She grabbed her backpack that held her bird guide and a bottle of water, then slipped the binoculars inside. She snatched up her fleece that hung next to Ben's jacket on the hooks beside the front door.

Ben was probably missing his coat, but she didn't relish seeing him again so soon after their painful encounter the evening before. Maybe she'd just drop the jacket off on his front porch after she got back from her trek. He'd made it clear he'd rather not see her anyway.

She headed down her mom's drive with thoughts of Ben and worry for her mom warring within her mind. When she caught glimpses of the lake between homes, her dad's solution for worry popped into her head, and she smiled. She could still hear his voice saying, "To feel truly grounded and peaceful from the inside out, a body needs to be connected to the earth, Kline. Burrow your feet into the sand by the lake, or wrap your arms around a tree and then close your eyes and visualize a positive outcome. You'll feel better in no time."

Pushing her thoughts aside, she looked up and found herself right in front of the store. So she tugged on the door, which set off a loud chime above her head, and stepped inside. Fred's familiar laugh alerted her to his location in the corner by the cell phone kiosk. He stood watching TV, his white beard having grown even longer and his belly having filled out a bit too. Probably made him look even more authentic in his Santa suit these days.

When he saw her, his face lit up. "Well, look who finally came back. Great to see you! How are you, Kline?"

She weaved through the short aisles and joined him in the electronics section. It amused her how Fred actually labeled all the sections of his business as if he owned a Walmart instead of the small general store. "I'm great. Good to see you too, Fred. My mom sent me to pick up some books for her."

"Got them right here." He reached behind the counter and came up with a handful of historical romance novels. "Betty does like to read. She goes through three or four of these a week."

"Really? I had no idea."

He nodded. "Someone like you would appreciate that it'd save quite a few trees if she had an e-reader or a tablet."

"That's true. Do you have any of those?"

"Abso-betcha-lootly! Got the latest, greatest one right here."

Kline studied the box. She'd wanted the same model to replace her old one and had just mentioned it to her mom the other day when she'd been fishing for birthday gift ideas. "This might be a little too high-tech for my mom. But I'll take it. Maybe I could talk her into joining the electronic age with mine that's easier to use, and I'll buy this one for myself."

"Sounds like a plan. Oh, and this just came in for your mom too." Fred handed over a yoga DVD.

"When did she order this?" It was odd that her mom would buy a new workout DVD if she didn't have the energy to do her beloved yoga anymore.

"'Bout a week ago, I guess."

Maybe her mother really was losing it. That made no sense. She needed to get her mom to a doctor in Denver as soon as possible.

Kline followed behind Fred to the front checkout counter and then realized she didn't have her purse. "My wallet's at home. Will you save this for me? I'll come back and get it this afternoon."

Fred bagged up the books and the tablet. "I wasn't going to charge you anyway. It'll be my welcome home gift to you." He popped her favorite candy bar into the bag too. "We're all glad you're finally back."

"Thanks, Fred, but I'm only here for a few weeks. I insist on paying for this." She pocketed the candy in her coat and then slipped the bag into her backpack. "I'll stop by later."

"Nope. Don't want your money. I'm hoping after being home for a while, surrounded by folks who truly care about you, and your mom, you'll see what you've been missing and stay."

"Sorry to disappoint, but I've made plans to substitute teach in Denver." Maybe later rather than sooner with her mom ordering yoga DVDs she couldn't use, but Fred didn't need to know that.

"We've got a *permanent* science teacher job open and it's yours if you want it. I'm on the school board these days and we're in desperate hiring mode now. There's no one else interested in the job."

That stopped Kline's retreat. "I thought Barb was only going on maternity leave for a few months."

He shook his head. "She gave her notice yesterday. She's decided to stay home with the baby."

Interesting. Barb had always insisted she'd be a working mom. That she'd go nuts if she had to stay home all day. "Well, I appreciate the offer. Maybe I'll think about it. And I'll bring you the money later." Kline quickly slipped out the door before Fred could argue with her about paying.

What was up with everyone giving her welcome home gifts? They'd never done that when she'd come home on college breaks. Had they started a bribery campaign to keep the younger people from moving away?

Kline grabbed the candy bar from her pocket and unwrapped it while she headed to her favorite birding spot. She bit into the gooey, nutty, caramel-and-chocolate treat, and blessed Fred for remembering what her favorite candy bar had been as a kid. Couldn't get that kind of treatment in the city. On the other hand, no one could buy condoms or hemorrhoid cream without Fred knowing either.

As Kline passed by the hotel, Ben's sister Casey power walked up the paved drive. "Hi, Kline."

Kline gave Casey a hug. "So good to see you. Heard you've snagged a bad-boy rock star. That's just about every woman's fantasy."

Casey chuckled. "Zane is just a regular guy. You'll see when you meet him. I was just looking for you. I wanted to give you a keycard to use the hotel gym."

She *would* like to use their fancy gym. From what she'd heard, it rivaled the best she'd ever been in. "Thank you, Casey. That's the second fantastic gift I've gotten today. What's up with everyone?"

Casey smiled. "We're glad to have you back."

That was nice, but she probably hadn't talked to her brother since last night. "I'm going to disappoint everyone by accepting all these gifts when they figure out I'm not staying permanently. And I'm not getting back together with Ben."

"They're simply gifts. Given freely and from the heart. No strings attached." Casey laid a hand on Kline's arm and gave a little squeeze. "Everything will work out with Ben the way it's meant to."

Or *not* meant to, in their case. Coming home and seeing Ben had conjured up all the hurt from when they'd parted ways. Some wounds to the heart cut too deep to mend. She was happy that Ben's sister seemed to understand. Maybe Casey would be a good person to ask about what she'd heard regarding Ben in the diner. "Rachel told me that Ben had changed after I left. Something about dating. What was she referring to?"

"Oh. That." Casey wrinkled her nose. "Ben started dating . . . a lot . . . after you guys broke up. He explains things right up front to women, that he doesn't commit to one person, and yet still he has a long list of willing ladies to choose from."

Long list of willing ladies? "Like all three or four single women even close to his age still living here?"

"No." Casey laughed. "In Denver. He flies Dad's chopper to visit patients in the hospital all the time. But he hasn't been involved in a serious relationship since yours."

Didn't sound so different from her, except he probably slept with a lot more of his dates. The sleeping with other women part shot a little pang of jealousy to her heart that she had no right to feel anymore. Maybe that's why he hadn't fought for her. Maybe when it came right down to it, he was afraid to commit all the way and get married? Cold feet? "I haven't stayed in one place long enough to have a real relationship either."

"I imagine so much travel *would* make it difficult. And there's always the part about finding the right guy again. I wasn't sure I ever would after my divorce. You and Ben were together much longer than I was married."

Seven years counting high school. All good ones, until that last day when Ben changed his mind.

"Yeah. I guess after things fell apart with Ben, I became pretty picky."

Casey nodded. "Nothing wrong with that. But I'm curious. Have you found a place in all of your travels that makes you happy? Somewhere you feel at home?"

Had she? No one had ever asked her that before. "I guess so far, while I loved helping in developing countries, and had fun in Tahiti, I was happiest in Denver."

"When you and Ben lived together?" Casey smiled.

"Yeah." When Casey's grin turned to a smirk, Kline added, "But it wasn't because of Ben, per se. I liked the bigger-city feel of Denver, is all."

"There is that old saying that home is where the heart is . . ." Casey waved a hand. "But enough of that. Where are you off to?"

Kline hitched up her little daypack. "Birding. There are a few places I like just over there." She pointed to the meadow across the street surrounded by tall trees.

"That's where the new distillery is going to go."

Kline's spine stiffened. They were going to build a distillery, and ruin her and her dad's favorite birding spot? "Where exactly, Casey?"

"If you walk over there, you'll see the survey sticks marking the boundaries. I've got to get back to work, but can you join us for girls' night at Brewsters tomorrow evening?"

Distracted, Kline just nodded and waved a hand as she headed across the street to check out this distillery business for herself.

***

Ben sat down in his father's office and waited for him to finish his phone conversation. He had to try one last time before their council meeting later that evening to convince his father that he needed the land earmarked for the distillery for a new clinic.

While he waited, he rearranged all the crooked things on his father's desk. When he glanced up, his father held out his hand for the stapler still in Ben's and then slapped it down while he listened to the caller.

Ben really wanted to move the stapler where it belonged, but he sat back and folded his hands in his lap instead.

Once his father hung up, he leaned back in his chair and crossed his arms over his barrel chest. "What was so urgent it couldn't wait until later?"

Ben slid a piece of paper across the desk. "I ran some numbers for you. Seeing how the real estate available for commercial use is so limited around Town Square and my clinic is a one-story building with a big footprint and a large parking lot behind, you could use all that space and add higher-quality shops that would appeal to our exclusive clientele. Then it'd make more sense to move the clinic and build a two-story facility where you're proposing the distillery would go. We'd make up for the added cost by bringing in a few more docs. Dr. Richards and I can't keep up with the demand as it is and people are driving up to a hundred miles away for medical services that we could easily provide with a new facility and better equipment. There's a serious need for it, Dad."

Ben discreetly wiped his sweaty palms on his slacks and swallowed the desperation rising in his throat. He couldn't let his father see how much it meant to him. He wanted to bring the best medical care to those who didn't go to the doctor for years at a time because it was too inconvenient. His father wasn't about helping people, though. He was about the almighty dollar.

Dad studied the pages it had taken Ben hours to create. "This is a compelling argument, but you're forgetting one thing. There's no way I'm allowing Anderson Butte Whiskey to be brewed on Grant land." He slid the papers back to Ben.

"Who cares if the distillery is located just outside of town? It'd probably be better that way for the noise and traffic the facility will bring." Ben slid the papers back. "And did you see the difference in the bottom line? Moving the distillery could potentially bring double the income."

Dad picked up the papers and threw them in the trash. "*Potentially* is not the same as hard dollars, Ben. Just stick to healing people and I'll stick to what I do best. Making money!"

Ben's heart pounded as he leaned forward to make his case. "You're just feeding into your ridiculous age-old feud with the Grants instead of considering what's best for *everyone* in town. And you can't stop me from presenting this to the others tonight. Then we'll take a vote." He stood and turned to leave before he lost his temper for the second time in two days.

Dad laughed. "Go ahead, waste everyone's time and present your numbers. But no one is going to vote against me. They all know better."

Ben walked out the door and just barely refrained from slamming it. He hated that his father was right. Dad had appointed everyone on the council. They were all too afraid to do anything to cross him. Except for Ben's grandmother. And maybe he could get Fred on his side. Then they'd have a real fight.

He was in such a foul mood over Kline anyway that he looked forward to the battle.

———————

Kline walked through the tall grass and checked out the survey stakes that delineated most of the meadow as a building site. There was no way they could construct that large a building without disturbing the surrounding trees. She hated to see any part of the forest removed, but especially a quiet meadow surrounded by trees that had a river flowing a few feet nearby. It attracted all sorts of wildlife because there were no homes or humans to disturb the animals. That's what made it the best place to go birding and still be close to town.

The air grew cooler as she walked a few feet into the shadows of the forest. She found a nice spot near the river and sat down, her back against a tree. After digging her phone out from her backpack, she pulled up her birdcall app. She hoped to bring an owl to her, or maybe a male kestrel who hadn't migrated south yet. Just as she was about to play a call, she heard a monotone "Whup, hoo-hoo," followed by a nasal whistled "Toweeeeeeip." Kline quickly stood and approached the edge of the cliff that had a rushing river at the bottom of the deep ravine. Owls liked to make their nests in the rocky walls above the water. Her guess was that the call was coming from a Mexican spotted owl, or *Strix occidentalis lucida* in scientific terms. Her heart rate sped up at the thought of adding a federally threatened species to her lifetime list of identified birds.

Walking slowly and as silently as possible along the bank, she heard the call again and glanced up into a nearby tree. There sat the owl, watching her. She quickly spread her fingers on her phone's screen to zoom in and snapped a picture to confirm the species sighting. Then she slowly backed away.

She hurried to her backpack at the base of the tree and found her bird guide to double-check that she had identified the owl correctly. If she were right, they weren't going to be able to build anything the size of the distillery nearby. It was against the law to knowingly disturb the critical habitat of a bird that is covered by the Endangered Species Act.

Paging through her book, she finally found the bird. The guide said that the owl was most often found on the west coasts of the United States and Mexico, but some lived year-round in Colorado. It was large, had a round head, dense mottling on the breast and belly, and no ear tufts, so it looked like the right owl to her. Just to be sure, she sent the picture to her ex-boyfriend, Nate, who did biological assessments for the Feds now.

Ninety-nine percent sure she was right, she slung her backpack over her shoulder and headed for the mayor's office. A few people had mentioned the groundbreaking ceremony soon, so she needed to let Ben's father know he might have to wait until a biologist determined whether they could build anything near the owl's nest.

Kline trudged through the tall meadow grass until she hit Main Street again and then she quickly walked the short distance to Town Square. When her phone dinged with a text, she stopped and read the screen. Nate confirmed that it was a spotted owl she'd seen. She quickly tapped back the information about the distillery going in soon and asked what she should do before she slipped her phone back into her pocket.

After passing by the white bandstand that stood in the middle of the park, she crossed the street and went up the stone steps that led into Town Hall and the mayor's office. Just as she approached the glass doors, Ben came striding out with a fierce frown etched on his face. When he saw her he stopped, opened his mouth to say something, but then just lifted a hand and kept right on going.

Ben was one of the most easygoing guys she'd ever known. He rarely got angry. Something must be up. "Are you okay, Ben?"

He stopped, turned around, and then huffed out a breath. "I'm fine." He pointed to her backpack. "Been out birding?"

"Yeah. Found a spotted owl where the distillery is planned and I was just going to tell your dad that he'll need to wait up on building anything until a biological assessment can be done."

Ben cocked his head. "Nothing can be built there? Because of a bird?"

"I suppose you could build something there as long as it wouldn't disturb the forest area where the owls nest."

Ben's mouth slowly formed into a big smile. "So say, something smaller and two stories that would fit in the meadow area alone might work?"

"I don't know." She shrugged. "I've e-mailed someone I know in Denver who assesses areas for the Feds. Only an expert like that would know for sure. And now that I've alerted him, I'm sure he'll come check it out or send someone else. They take their threatened species pretty seriously."

Ben took hold of her arm and guided her down the steps. "This is perfect. Can you come to the council meeting tonight? So everyone can hear this? It's at seven o'clock."

She threw her thumb over her shoulder. "I was just going in to tell your dad now."

Ben kept tugging. "It'd be better to tell everyone at once. So this is serious business, right? If the Fed person says it is?"

"Yes." She had to jog to keep up with his long strides. "Your dad won't be able to get a building permit if the assessment won't allow it."

Ben stopped walking, grabbed both of her arms, and turned her to face him. "You might have just solved my biggest problem for me."

She blinked. "I thought *I* was your biggest problem. You said you didn't want to be anywhere near me."

"Only because all I can think about when you're around is how much I *want* you." He gave her a smacking kiss on the lips. "Thank you, Kline."

The quick kiss surprised her, and at the same time left her traitorous lips wanting more even though they'd set the no-touching ground rules between them. But it was nice they weren't at odds at the moment, because she really would like to be friends with Ben again, so she replied, "You're welcome. But what's going on? I don't get it."

"World War Three is probably going to break out tonight when my dad figures out he might not get his way."

That Ben's father ruled the town with an iron fist had always irritated her. "I'll be sure to wear my flak jacket." She raised her hand for a high five.

He moved his hand like he was going to slap her palm, but slowed at the last second and then weaved his fingers through hers. "It's nice to be on the same team again." He gave her hand a squeeze and then released it. "See you tonight?"

"I'll be there."

"Thanks." He smiled, then turned and walked away.

She hated to admit she'd missed being on Ben's team too. She'd felt like a lone, free agent ever since they'd broken up.

Kline let her smile bloom as she turned the opposite way to go home. Maybe the tyrannical, gruff mayor was finally going to get his due.

CHAPTER SIX

As Kline passed by her uncle Zeke's house, it reminded her that she still needed to figure out a way to charge her car, so she turned up his driveway and toward his warehouse-size shop. The familiar whir of power tools filled the air as she stepped inside. But it wasn't her uncle making all the noise; it was a tall, muscular, blond guy she'd never met. When he saw her, he swiped off his protective glasses and beamed a friendly smile. "Hi. Let me guess. Are you the infamous Kline?"

"I am. But I was expecting to see my uncle Zeke."

"He'll be right back. He just went for some donuts at the diner. I'm Josh. Meg's husband." He wiped his hand on his jeans and then stuck it out.

"Nice to meet you." She returned the shake. "You used to be in the FBI, right?"

"Yeah. I'm liking this line of work a whole lot better. Although, the grapevine around here rivals the FBI's intelligence network. It's been all lit up about you. Everyone's excited that you're back."

If she heard that one more time, she'd scream. "I appreciate it, but I'm not staying."

Her uncle called out, "We'll see about that, Kline. We're all determined to change your mind." He opened his arms for a hug as he approached.

"Believe me, I've noticed." She circled her arms around her uncle's tall, thin body and gave a hard squeeze. "You need to eat a few dozen donuts, Uncle Zeke. You're still too thin."

He patted his stomach. "You'll be happy to know I've recently gained five pounds. It's all the great dinners Ruth is feeding me these days. But not tonight. She has a council meeting, so I thought I'd grab a snack so I don't starve to death." He held up his bag of donuts and winked at her.

Her uncle had always had a crush on Ben's grandmother and an insatiable sweet tooth. She was glad to see him so happy. "I guess I'm going to that meeting tonight too. Who all is on the council these days?"

Josh answered, "The mayor, Toby, Mrs. Anderson, Fred, and Pam."

Her uncle offered her a donut, but she shook her head. "Not a single Grant?"

"Nope." Zeke stuffed a bite of powdered donut into his mouth. "You know the mayor. Wouldn't want anyone who might disagree with him on the city council."

"Figures. Hey, do you still own that big piece of land on the edge of the town limits?"

Her uncle nodded. "I'm going to let Josh use the forested portion on the far north end. He's starting up a camp for kids next summer. Why?"

"Would you be interested in parting with some of it for the distillery? It'd be a perfect place for it, especially because the strip mining that went on all those years ago has left the whole front half by the road pretty barren." She filled them in on the owl.

Uncle Zeke glanced at Josh. "Would having a distillery at the entrance to the camp road work for you?"

Josh shrugged a broad shoulder. "The camp will be way at the rear, so I don't see that being a problem. But it's your land, Zeke—do whatever you want. I just appreciate you letting me use a portion of it."

"Well then, I guess I might be interested. For the right price, of course."

"Of course." Kline smiled. "If I get a chance, I'll throw that out as an option tonight. It'd be the best place for it. But I really need your help with something else. I need a way to charge my electric car."

"No problem." He popped the last donut in his mouth and then held out the empty bag. "Write down the make and model on this." He handed her a pen from his top pocket.

After she'd written down all the information, she handed the bag and pen back. "Thanks."

"Let me get Josh to find us some parts on his fancy phone there, and I'll get you all set up. Give me a few days?"

"That'd be perfect." She stood on her tiptoes and kissed his cheek. "I'll let you know how the meeting goes. Ben said there should be fireworks tonight." She lifted a hand. "Nice to meet you, Josh."

"You too, Kline."

When she turned to go, her uncle said, "I might just have to show up to the meeting tonight. I'd love to see the mayor's face when you tell him he can't have his precious distillery because of a bird. I'm proud of you for standing up to him, Kline."

"It'd be the Feds standing up to him, not me. I just hope he doesn't shoot the messenger."

Ben caught up with his grandmother on her slow trek up the stairs to Town Hall and slipped his hand under her elbow. "Hi, Grandma. Let me help you."

She swatted his hand aside. "I can walk up the darned stairs on my own. I'm not all the way over the hill yet."

"Okay." Ben released her but stood close behind just in case. She wobbled with every step. "Hey, I need a favor tonight."

Grams huffed a little as she raised herself up the next stair. "And I need you to work things out with Kline. But you're being awful stubborn there, so why should I help *you*?"

"Because it'd be good for the town. Please just listen to what I have to say tonight with an open mind. I need your support."

Kline appeared by his side. "Mrs. Anderson, let me help you." She quickly moved in front of Ben and grabbed Gram's elbow.

"Why, thank you, Kline. You always were such a nice girl." Grandma looked over her shoulder and smirked at him.

Ben shook his head and moved around them to open the front door. Once they'd made it to the meeting hall, Kline helped his grandmother into her seat on the raised dais, so he found a seat in the front row of folding metal chairs to wait for his turn to speak. Kline walked down the steps and sat next to him.

She whispered, "Your grandmother is getting older, Ben. You guys need to help her more now."

Ben opened his mouth to explain but Kline quickly added, "Oh, and I talked to my federal biologist friend again. He said he'd try to make the end of the meeting. He had some things to tie up first and then he's driving in from Denver."

Her Fed friend was a guy? "Where is he going to stay? I thought I read on the loop the whole hotel is booked by that sheikh from Abu Dhabi."

She nodded. "Yeah, Mom mentioned that at dinner. He can stay at my house. We . . . know each other . . . well."

A pang of jealousy made Ben's fist clench around his stack of papers as he leaned so close he could smell her flowery shampoo. "How well?"

"Asks the man with"—Kline made air quotes with her fingers—"a long list of willing lady friends." She frowned and crossed her arms, which only made her breasts look even more enticing, dammit.

He hated that someone had opened their yap about his former dating habits. That made him sound like a player. Admittedly, right after she'd left he had been, but the one-night stands had gotten old quick. Nowadays he didn't sleep with a woman unless he genuinely liked spending time with her.

He whispered, "I'm just saying it might look bad if my dad thinks your *ex-boyfriend* is the one doing the evaluation."

"Nate's loyalties are to the environment before anything else. It's not going to be a problem," she said quietly.

His father cleared his throat. "Ben, if you and Kline are done bickering over there, can we begin?"

All heads in the room turned their way. While they'd been talking, a few others had joined them in the audience, which rarely happened. Ben smiled. "Sorry."

They got started with all the usual Robert's Rules that seemed never-ending, as Ben ran what he was going to say over in his head again. His phone beeped with a text so he answered it and then the three more that followed right behind. Between his family and his patients, he never got a break.

While the council droned on over miniscule details about office supply budgets, Kline leaned close. "So do you really just have one-night stands now?" Her scrunched nose indicated her disapproval.

"No. Sometimes it's just dinner. Did you date the Fed guy?"

"None of your business." She turned her attention back to the meeting.

He leaned his shoulder against hers. "Why do you get to ask and I don't?"

"Do I have a gun in my hand? No one *made* you answer my question." When Kline smiled at him, he felt it all the way to his gut. He'd missed seeing that cute grin when she teased him.

Dad cleared his throat again, so Ben lifted both palms to show they were through. But he still wanted to know. It really could affect things if Dad thought the Fed and Kline were in the owl thing together just to spite him. It was Kline's favorite birding spot. He could see her wanting to save it at all costs.

When the new topic, snow removal, was batted back and forth so long it drove him nuts, he picked at the lint on his slacks. As the discussion carried on, he alternated between straightening his stack of papers to swiping at his pants.

Kline's hand covered his, trapping it against his leg. She whispered, "Relax. It'll be fine."

He nodded, but his hands itched to straighten his papers one more time. He tried to slip his hand out from under hers, but she shook her head as she held his hand in a death grip.

Resigned to his stack remaining crooked, he focused on her warm, soft skin instead. She'd always had the prettiest hands. Long, tapering fingers and a small, delicate palm. He turned his hand over and weaved their fingers together. Her thumb slowly caressed the top of his and before long his urge to straighten melted away.

When it was time for Ben to speak, Kline gave his hand, still in hers, a quick squeeze for good luck. Holding hands in public with Ben wasn't going to help the gossip network, but it seemed to calm his restless behavior, so she'd been willing to do it. Never mind that it had felt kinda nice to simply hold hands with him again.

Kline listened as Ben presented his plan. It made a lot of sense, but the mayor's scowl proved it'd be a tough sell. Pam, the town's bombshell hairdresser, Toby, and Santa Claus Fred were the non-Andersons on the council, so Kline watched their faces carefully. Unfortunately, they kept glancing the mayor's way, presumably to see how he felt about the proposal.

The mayor was just as big a bully to the townspeople as Lisa and Rachel had been to Kline as kids. Each time the mayor glared at someone to shut them down, it brought back all the unwanted memories from her childhood. Someone needed to shut the mayor down in return, but no one had the guts to do it.

A soft kiss landed on her cheek, bringing her thoughts back from the dark place they'd wandered off to. She glanced up and smiled at Nate, the sexiest biologist she'd ever met, and had dated for many months until he'd wanted to move to the next level. She didn't trust that a player like him would ever settle down, and she didn't want to risk the heartbreak. Ben had left her with deep scars.

She moved her coat from the chair beside her. "Hi. Glad you could make it. And thanks for rushing the paperwork through. Have a seat."

"Catch me up." Nate sprawled his tall, muscled body into the metal folding chair.

Kline quietly whispered the condensed version into his ear. Then she said, "Ben might need for you to explain how this works."

Nate nodded. "No problem."

She glanced Ben's way again and was greeted with a frown. He said to the group, "But just today, Kline found something that might make building on the site across from the hotel problematic. And she's invited an expert to help explain things."

She took that as her cue, so she stood and introduced Nate.

Nate sent the council members one of his sexy smiles. Pam sat up straighter and proudly displayed her impressive cleavage as she grinned back.

Nate winked at her and then said, "Thanks for allowing me to speak. I haven't seen the Mexican spotted owl in person yet. I've only seen the picture Kline sent me today. But presuming we find a resident pair of owls, which are protected by the Endangered Species Act, they will surely nest in the same spot next spring during the breeding season. According to Section 7 of the ESA, it's unlawful to disturb their critical habitat."

As Nate explained all the technical details, Ben sat down beside her again. He leaned close and whispered, "You've definitely slept with that guy."

"I guess you'll never know for sure." She smiled. Jealous was cute on Ben.

His warm breath tickled her earlobe as he hissed, "Oh, I know. He looked at you like he was seeing his first Lamborghini . . . naked!"

"Bad analogy," she whispered behind her hand. "He drives an electric car like I do. Now stop talking before we get into trouble again."

Ben crossed his arms and turned his attention back to Nate. Right in the middle of Nate's explanation of biological site assessments, the mayor raised his palm to cut Nate off. "I have plenty of friends in state government who will be willing to work with me to get things cleared up. Thanks for your time, but I think we need to go ahead and vote."

Nate shook his head. "Sorry to disagree, Mayor, but you're dealing with the federal government on this one. There's no favor that's going to fix the situation. You have to follow proper procedure. I'll be assessing the area tomorrow and then I'll file my report. What the government does after that will dictate what you do with that land, no matter who owns it. Thanks for your time."

Nate turned and sat on the other side of Kline, making her the middle of a hunk sandwich. "Thanks, Nate."

"Welcome." He stuck his hand around her and held it out to Ben. "Hi. Nate Banks."

Ben slowly moved his hand to return the shake. "Ben Anderson. Nice to meet you."

Ben stood again and said to the council, "I think we have enough information here to propose a delay on the vote you planned to take tonight. And maybe we should form a task force to study this before we move on."

While Ben pleaded his case, Nate leaned closer. "Ben looked like he'd rather beat the crap out of me than shake my hand. You've slept with him too, right? Is he the one who ruined you for all the rest of us guys?"

Men!

"Shhh. I want to see what happens next." She was grateful she'd never told Nate that it was Ben who'd broken her heart. She should still be angry with Ben for it, but after all the years that had passed, and after being around Ben again, she realized how much she missed her best friend. She'd never had another like him.

She tuned back in just as the mayor's face turned a deep red. "I'm in charge here, Ben. And it's my property in question. We'll vote just as planned. Now, all in favor—"

"Mayor?" Pam interrupted. "We need to have a motion—"

"Nope." The mayor pointed a beefy finger at poor Pam. "I don't give a damn about all your silly rules. Now everyone shut up so we can vote!"

"Wait!" Outrage over the mayor's dictatorial ways made Kline jump from her chair. "Just because you own things doesn't give you the right to disregard the law. You've run this town so long, and bullied everyone so often, that you've forgotten there are rules outside of Anderson Butte that you have to live by just like the rest of us. If you take that vote without giving due diligence to the issue, I'll figure out a way to get you thrown out of office."

Jaws dropped on all the council members' faces.

The mayor's brows rose. "First off, Kline, you'd never stick around long enough to go through with your little threat, would you? And second, everyone here knows that area was your dad's favorite birding site. I think you're getting your emotions mixed up with logic."

Oh, she could just choke the man. It took all her resolve to speak at a somewhat normal level. "*You're* disregarding the law. You need to be stopped. Clearly you're so afraid of being overruled, you've made sure over a quarter of this town, the Grants, have no representation in your kangaroo court."

The mayor laughed. "If you think you could do a better job, then run against me. It's reelection time. Now sit down!"

She was boiling mad. So angry she was tempted to do it. To show everyone how corrupt the mayor was. Besides, she might be stuck in town for a few months anyway because of her mom. "How long is the term?"

Ben's grandmother smiled. "We just recently voted to make it two years because my son is getting older and might need to have one of the boys take over soon. But Anderson Butte has never had a mayor who wasn't an Anderson. We've always outnumbered the Grants. It'd be futile to try." Ruth winked at Kline.

She wasn't one to shy away from a challenge. Especially one thrown down at her in front of everyone. If she could endure a nasty jail cell for six weeks while waiting for justice to prevail, she could endure anything for two short years. "So all I'd need is a nomination? And then it'd be official?"

The mayor crossed his arms and scowled. "You might want to knock off the righteous indignation act, Kline, and think this through. The pay is only a stipend. I live off the businesses I own. Not this job."

Kline met Fred's amused gaze. "Will that teaching position be available if I win?"

Fred's face split into a huge grin. "Yep. It'd be all yours, win or lose, Kline."

Righteous indignation act, her ass. She'd meant every word. Her body shook with anger and outrage.

She glanced at Ben, who lifted his hands in an "it's up to you" gesture. Before she could decide what to do, her uncle Zeke's voice rang out from the back. "I nominate Kline Grant for mayor!"

The onlookers all cheered. She turned around to see who was there and it was half the town. Even her mom had come. Someone must've put something on that damned loop.

She caught her mother's eye, who gave her a thumbs-up before she called out, "And I second it!"

Pam, the secretary, said, "This is out of order and should be under new business, but who cares? Kline Grant, do you accept the nomination?"

Did she want to go up against the tyrant, a man who'd never thought she'd been good enough for his son? Oh, hell yeah! She stared into the mayor's narrowed eyes and called out, "I accept."

As a throng of people surrounded her, she shook their hands. Pats on the back, hugs, and thank yous from people she'd known from her childhood made her feel better about her rash decision. It'd be good for the town, and clearly people wanted change.

Her heart rate had finally settled a bit by the time the mayor gave up trying to calm the room and declared the meeting over.

Then reality punched her square in the gut.

What have I just done?

CHAPTER SEVEN

*B*en had waited until the crowd surrounding Kline in the meeting hall thinned before he moved by her side. Her friend Nate stood next to her, smiling and chatting up Kline's mom like they were old friends too.

Since when did biologists look like muscle-bound male models? Ben had expected a skinny guy with glasses who hugged trees like Kline did. They seemed to have a lot in common. And the guy was clearly into her.

He needed to stop thinking of Kline as his. She'd already laid down the "hands-off" law between them. They were just going to be friends.

But he needed to have a serious talk with his *friend* about what she'd just done. "Kline. Can I speak to you for a minute, please? In private?" He tilted his head toward the empty side of the room.

Kline nodded and then laid a hand on Nate's arm. "Why don't you and Mom head home, and I'll catch up in a bit? Uncle Zeke wants to talk to me too." She held up a finger to her uncle, who was talking to Josh.

Her mother slipped on her coat. "When I heard you were coming, Nate, I made you a batch of snickerdoodles. I remember how much you used to like them."

"Thanks, Betty." Nate stuck his bent arm out for Betty to lace her hand through, the suck-up. "See you around, Ben."

Ben hitched his chin and waited until they were out of earshot. "Snickerdoodles, huh?"

Kline rolled her eyes. "My mom used to send me care packages when I was in impoverished countries. Nate and I worked on a few projects together, and I shared."

"Looks to me like he's back for seconds of more than just the cookies. He must've dropped everything to get here so quick."

Kline crossed her arms. "What did you want to talk about? Besides Nate, that is."

He took her arm and led her to a chair. Then he grabbed another and turned it so they were facing each other. After they sat with their knees almost touching, he said, "You do realize that if you become the mayor you'll actually have to live here, right?"

"Of course I realize that." Kline chewed her bottom lip as she always did when she was uneasy. "If I win, I'll just stay for my term and then I'll move on. It'd do this town good to have some fresh blood in charge."

"We need someone who's dedicated to seeing Anderson Butte prosper, not someone who took the job because she won't back down from a challenge."

Kline's gaze dropped to her hands in her lap. She kneaded her fingers together for a few moments, and then finally looked him in the eye again. "You know I've never liked the way your father treats you or your brother and sisters, and the way he runs this town. He's a bully."

Ben raised a finger to stop her, so she quickly added, "I also know how strong your loyalty is to your family, so while it's the truth, I'm sorry if it offends you."

"I appreciate that. But I'm not saying you're wrong."

"Thank you. Anderson Butte is run like a dictatorship. And I truly want to end the whole Anderson-versus-Grant feud. You and I fought it when we started dating, and while I can see it's gotten a little better with time, why not wipe it out completely? So the Grants can stop feeling like second-class citizens around here. Maybe having a Grant run the town, and a few serving on the city council, would help equalize things. I'd be doing it for my family, more than to spite your dad."

"And to show Rachel and Lisa that you won't be bullied anymore?"

Kline nodded. "Maybe that too. I spent too many miserable years dealing with that to want to see an entire town living with your father's tyrannical ways."

His father had never approved of Kline. Ben had never known if it was purely because she was a Grant, or because she stopped being intimidated by him when she was in high school. "You've avoided coming home all this time. What if a few months in you get bored with life here again? Then what? It'd be worse to win and then quit, leaving us in a lurch."

Kline laid her warm hand on his knee. "I've really enjoyed exploring the world, seeing what else it has to offer, but now I'm feeling the need to be a bit more grounded. To actually own living room furniture, plant a garden, and still be around to enjoy the harvest."

"Wait, what? Kline Grant, who never cared for possessions, especially big flat-screen televisions, wants to be a homeowner?" He never thought he'd hear those words pass her lips. But it gave him hope.

She smiled. "You're still mad I wouldn't split the cost of that seventy-inch screen when thirty-six was just fine for our apartment, aren't you?"

"Damn right. Size matters. Especially when it comes to football."

"*Town* size matters. I've been looking at houses in Denver. I want to be closer to my mom as she gets older. Then I'll still travel on school breaks. It's not like I completely hate it here—although I do wish there was some decent Thai takeout. I figure if I could live in a tent in Africa for six months, then I can deal with Anderson Butte for two years. It's still close enough to Denver to get away a few weekends a month to get my city fix, which I'm sure I'll need to do to stay sane."

She'd finally admitted that she didn't hate Anderson Butte. If she could change things for the better by being mayor, maybe he really did have a chance to change her mind about staying permanently and they could resume their relationship. "Then why haven't you come home for even a visit since you left?"

She blew out a long breath. "Because of you."

While Kline had been a killer in sports and intrepid enough to travel the world, her habit had been to avoid and run away from emotional problems rather than face them.

He laid his hand over hers still on his knee. "Because you hated me that much?"

She shook her head. "No, I *loved* you that much."

Dammit. If he'd gone after her when his contract was up instead of assuming she hated him for bailing on their plans and breaking up with her, would she have forgiven him? Could she ever forgive him for it now?

She slipped her hand out from under his. "I got over you, but I never wanted to feel that kind of pain again. I didn't know what I'd feel when I saw you, so it was easier to just avoid you. If not for my mother's health issues, I wouldn't have ever come back."

So maybe this was his chance to show her they were both different now and belonged together. She'd had her adventure and he'd figured out that she was more important than any contract he'd ever sign. Or his father and family. He leaned closer and whispered, "So what *did* you feel when you saw me again?"

"Sick, if you'll recall." She smirked. "And in debt to you for a pair a shoes."

Should he push for a real answer?

All he knew for sure was that he didn't want to lose her to the Fed guy, so he needed to make his intentions clear.

He reached out and took both her hands in his. "So, now you've seen me, and it wasn't so bad. We needed to do what we had to do back then, but now we're in different places. You just admitted you don't hate it here, so I think we should try for a fresh start."

Kline blinked at him for a moment. That she didn't protest right away boded well for him. She finally said, "My time away *has* taught me to appreciate people and the little things that make up my life. I *am* a different person now. Maybe with more time we could—"

"It's been long enough, Kline. I don't want to be just your friend anymore. I want a real relationship. I won't stop until I win you back. So if that's not something you want, I'd reconsider pursuing the mayor's position in a town so small it's impossible to hide." Telling Kline that when he was the one who'd broken up with her ought to piss her off enough to make her deal with how she really felt about him.

He stood to leave, but she yanked on his hand to stop him. "Wait a minute. If *I* decide I want a relationship with you, you'll be the first to know. Otherwise, things will stay as they are and you'll have to respect my boundaries. But that will have no bearing on my run for mayor. Is that understood?"

He suppressed a grin. Yep. She was mad. But her being angry used to spur her into action and that's what they both needed. "Absolutely. But this town might not be big enough for both of us, Kline."

She scowled at him as he turned and walked away. He wasn't sure if he'd helped his case or hurt it. But second chances don't often come along in life and he needed to make sure she knew where he stood.

His footsteps on the shiny floors echoed in the quiet hallway as he made a hasty exit. When he reached the main lobby, he pushed the glass door open and headed down the steps. The cold air sent a shiver up his spine, so he pulled up the collar on his suit jacket. As he crossed by the bandstand, his grandmother, seated on the steps, called out, "'Bout time. I'm freezing my knickers off here, Ben."

"What are you doing out this late? I thought you went home an hour ago." He reached out to help her stand. "Let me walk you home."

Grams must've been tired because she actually let him help her up. Then she grabbed his arm for stability instead of her cane as they set out for her house. "I was waiting for you because it's pretty obvious that Nate fellow wants Kline. And he might even be a little better looking than you."

"Thanks a lot."

She chuckled. "Just telling it like it is. The girls asked Kline to ladies' night tomorrow night, but now that Nate is in the picture, we decided to go with plan B."

"And what would that be? Careful." He held on to her with both hands as they started down her gravel drive.

"You need to get one of your lady friends here tomorrow night instead of going to Denver on your usual night off. Take her to Brewsters so Kline can see you with her."

He already had a dinner date in Denver he'd nearly forgotten about. "What is that supposed to accomplish?"

"Kline still has feelings for you. The question is, how deep? A woman doesn't hold a man's hand to stop his compulsive habits if she doesn't care for him at least a little."

He should let it go, but he'd heard that term one too many times. "I don't have a compulsion. I'm a doctor, I know what the symptoms are."

"Well, I'm your grandmother and know you better than anyone else, and I have the Internet right on my phone now. I looked it up. It said one of the things that could trigger an episode was serious family and relationship problems. I don't think it's a coincidence you started with your strange quirks shortly after you and Kline broke up."

Thankfully, they were almost to her front steps so he could end the ridiculous conversation. "I don't know why I bothered to go to medical school. Now anyone with an Internet connection can diagnose and cure themselves."

Grandma started up the first step. "Don't use that smarty-pants tone with me. I'm just trying to help you win Kline back. Now where were we? Oh, yeah. Bring your girl here tomorrow night, and do whatever you need to do with her to make Kline jealous. I'll be sure Betty gets Kline and pretty boy to Brewsters. Your sisters will take care of the rest."

Once at the top of the stairs, Ben moved ahead and opened her front door. "Is this high school? What if it backfires and sends Kline into Nate's arms for comfort?"

Grandma shook her head. "It's amazing you ever graduated from high school. You can be so darned dense sometimes. You're going to go over to Kline's house now and tap on her bedroom window just like you did years ago when you thought I didn't know. Then you're going to ask her if she wants you to cancel your date tomorrow night. Trust me. The rest will fall into place just fine. Now get out of my hair. I'm tired."

Grandma slammed the door closed in Ben's face.

He had no clue how going over to Kline's was going to help. Or if he should even play along with the game his grandmother and sisters had cooked up. But Kline was angry with him and the Fed guy was in her house to console her, so maybe he should go talk to her. First he'd make a stop at home, though. He had just the thing to make Kline forget she was mad at him.

Kline slid under the covers and turned off her bedside lamp. The full moon made the room unusually bright, so she slipped out of bed and closed her curtains. Once settled in bed again, her brain was so full of what-ifs and whys that she couldn't sleep. Distracting her busy mind with a story on the new tablet, which she still needed to pay for, seemed like a good plan.

Just as she'd found a comfortable position on her old, lumpy mattress, a soft knock sounded on her door. She laid her tablet down and threw the covers back. When she opened the door, Nate stood before her wearing only his boxers and a grin. "Couldn't sleep. Wondered if you'd like to blow off a little steam with me?"

Nate was great in bed. No doubt he'd make her a satisfied customer for the short term with his smoking hot body. But they had a complicated past that she didn't want to make any more complicated by sleeping with him. Seeing Ben again had solidified that she hadn't loved Nate as much as she had Ben. And look how that had worked out. "Tempting, but I'm super tired. It's been a long day."

"No worries." Nate leaned closer and whispered, "Good night . . . Mayor."

"We'll see about the mayor part. Night." She should've told him that sleeping together wasn't going to happen ever again, but she just didn't have the energy after dealing with Ben earlier.

Nate calling her mayor sort of took her aback, though. Whenever she heard that title, a vision of Ben's scowling father flashed in her head.

She crawled back into bed and tried to read, but her overactive brain refused to stop asking her hard questions. Like, how was she going to win the election? What did she need to study up on to be good at running the town? And would the council help her until she learned?

Worse, what would she do about Ben if she actually won the election? It was one thing to avoid dealing with him for three weeks, but two years was a long time. He'd been right about one thing: they'd see each other often. And they *were* both in different places than they'd been before. Ben was established in his career now, and didn't seem to need his father's approval like when they were young and poor in college. And she'd learned that men she could love were few and far between. As much as she'd tried to open her heart, she'd only been able to give it to Ben.

And she knew in *theory* that love was precious and worth fighting for rather than hiding from the pain it could bring. But her heart still hadn't caught up with the idea of that. Could she let Ben back into her heart? Did she want to risk being hurt all over again?

Ben had made her so mad with his earlier "promise" of not giving up until he won her back. He was the one who'd pushed her out the door, so he'd lost the right to pursue her unless she wanted to be chased, dammit. He'd just decided they should be back together as quickly as he'd decided to end things with her. When he'd said he'd like to try again, her heart had momentarily skipped a beat. When the oxygen had returned to her brain, though, she'd realized that if they were going to be together, then this time it'd be her choice. Not his.

Reading wasn't happening either, so she turned off her tablet, punched up her pillow a couple of times until it was just right, then laid her head down and hoped for sleep.

Quiet tapping on her window, in a familiar pattern, made her huff out a breath. Ben. He was the last person she wanted to talk to. She'd just ignore him and maybe he'd go away.

The tapping sounded again, so she threw her covers back and stomped to the window. After throwing the curtains aside, she lifted the window just enough to hear him without freezing her tush off. "What?"

"Still mad, huh? Here, this is for you." He lifted the window another few inches and stuck an insulated lunch bag inside. She unzipped it and found a cellophane-wrapped bowl and a spoon. On the bottom there was a perfectly folded napkin. Of course.

"What is this, Ben?" She slowly unwrapped the bowl.

"Better than any Thai takeout in Denver. Still love tom yum goong?"

Yes! Her mouth watered at the spicy aroma. "Thanks. But I'm still mad at you."

He blew on his fisted hands for warmth as he leaned to the side, seeming to search for something. "Bet it'll be tough to stay mad after you taste that." He strained his neck farther to the other side to peer around her.

She took a step back and held a hand out toward her rumpled covers. "Not that it's any of your business, but I'm alone, if that's what you're worried about." Things could've been awkward had she taken Nate up on his offer. Not that she would have anyway.

She was freezing, and the lovely smells wafting from the bowl made her curious, so she said, "Come in out of the cold."

While Ben maneuvered himself inside, she sat on her bed and dug into the spicy dish. She closed her eyes and savored the combination of fragrant herbs and the kick at the end from the chilies. "Mmmmmm."

Ben was an awesome cook. Growing up without his mom and being the oldest, he'd had to learn how to make family meals at an early age. "This *is* better than takeout. Is it an apology for your caveman act earlier?"

"Nope." He closed the window behind him. Then he crossed the room to the bed. The mattress took a big dip with his weight, sucking her toward him, so she juggled the bowl to keep the soup from spilling.

He took out his phone and answered a text as he said, "Did you know you make the same sound for incredible food as you do for incredible sex?"

She glanced at him as she swallowed another big bite. "Pleasure is pleasure, I guess. If you're not here to apologize, then why are you bringing me yummy food this late at night?"

His lips formed into a very sexy grin as he tucked his phone away. "If I told you I hoped to seduce you with Thai, would you let me? Seduce you?"

Her mouth was full again so she just shook her head. But being seduced by Ben *was* tempting.

"Didn't think so." He laid his hand on her bare leg just below where her flannel boxers ended, and then his gaze landed on her chest. She wished she was wearing something other than a thin tank top, because the cold had made the girls stand at full attention. Ben's hungry stare made them ache for his touch.

"So why are you here, Ben?" She slipped her finger under his chin and tilted it up, until his eyes zeroed in on hers again.

"Sorry." His full lips formed a naughty, unrepentant grin. "I'm here because I need to clarify the rules of our friendship agreement."

"It's pretty straightforward. We act like friends, and we *don't* act on our baser desires."

His brows shot up. "Baser desires? That sounds kind of dirty. And fun." He ran the tip of his index finger along her collarbone and made her shiver. "Did you learn a few new interesting techniques in all your travels that you'd like to share with the class?"

She brushed his finger aside and then finished scraping the bowl clean. "If I did, I wouldn't be so foolish to tell you while you're on my bed with that predatory gleam in your eyes." She hoped he didn't see the one in hers. He looked awful cute in a pair of sweats that showed off his nicely formed butt and strong thighs. It'd just take one tug and those pants . . . she needed to knock off the naughty thoughts.

He leaned away a fraction and patted her thigh. "Actually, I just wanted to be sure you hadn't changed your mind. Because I have a date tomorrow night. I'll cancel if it makes you feel uncomfortable."

"Date?" A sharp pang shot through her chest. She was pretty sure the burn left behind wasn't from the spicy dish.

What was wrong with her? She stood and placed the empty bowl back in the bag to give herself a second to pull her thoughts together. "You don't have to ask my permission to date." Did the man have that many women clamoring for his time that he had to date on a Thursday night to squeeze them all in? "Taking her somewhere nice in Denver?"

"No." His jaw tightened as he stood. "I've asked her to come here."

"Long drive for a date. She must really like you." And she'd most likely be spending the night. That pang was back again. She rubbed her chest to ward it off.

"She's not driving. I'll pick her up in the chopper tomorrow after work and then take her back home on Friday afternoon. We're going to do some hiking Friday morning."

Hiking? She used to *love* to hike with Ben. They went whenever they could. "That sounds like a fun date."

"Yeah." He huffed out a breath. "Okay, I guess we're good here then. So I'll see you when I see you?"

"Yep." She forced a smile. "Thanks for the Thai fix."

"Welcome." He scooped up the bag, straightened the lampshade by her bed, and then headed for the window. Once he was all the way out, she started to close it but stopped. "It worked, by the way, Mr. Sneaky."

He stopped walking and turned around. "What worked?"

"Thai food. I'm not mad at you anymore." She hated that now she was jealous because he was taking someone besides her hiking. But she needed to push that aside.

He walked back to the window and whispered, "Are you sure you don't want me to cancel? You and I could go hiking on Friday instead. As friends."

Her stupid eyes burned with tears. He seemed to want her to tell him to cancel. But she couldn't have it both ways. It'd just be confusing for both of them. "Maybe another time. Bye." She quickly shut the window and drew the curtain closed before he saw the tears she couldn't hold back any longer. It made no sense that she was crying. She was over him. Had been for many years. She needed to keep her eye on the goal.

Tomorrow she'd make an appointment for her mother with a doctor in Denver. Whether she liked it or not. Then she'd figure out how to beat the mayor and become the first Grant ever to be elected in Anderson Butte. That was enough for now. She'd deal with Ben and all the messy emotions that'd surely bring after the election.

And she'd get used to seeing Ben with other women . . . eventually.

CHAPTER EIGHT

Dawn finally illuminated Kline's bedroom curtains. She'd tossed and turned all night thinking about Ben and what he'd said about the both of them living in their small town. As much as she probably needed to try to sleep a little longer, that just wasn't happening.

She dressed in sweats and pulled her hair back into a ponytail. Then she quietly slipped down the hallway, past the guest room where Nate was sleeping, and to the kitchen. She grabbed a banana from the bowl on the counter and then opened the door that led to the garage. Her old basketballs stood right where they always had on the shelf next to the pump. She chose the best looking of the worn balls and filled it with air. Maybe a little physical activity would help her out of her funk.

Her father, tired of hearing the thump of the ball when she'd practice in their driveway on early mornings, had built a court away from the house and nearer the road. After she finished off her banana, she grabbed a broom and walked down the drive to the full court built to exact NBA specs, complete with chain link surrounding it so she wouldn't have to chase after loose balls into the woods.

Basketball had been her father's second-favorite passion after birding, and he'd taught her all he knew. Having one shot at a child due to complications during her birth meant Dad was unlucky to have a girl instead of a son he could mold into an NBA player, but he'd made the best of it. And so had she.

Kline swept the court off and by the time it was clear of dirt and pine needles, she'd warmed up enough to take off her jacket. She dribbled the ball to get a feel for the bounce and then took a few simple shots. As her muscles became more fluid and loose, she began making shot after shot and was finally in her zone. She moved back to the three-point line and let the ball sail. A no-net three-pointer!

She whispered, "And the crowd goes wild," as she ran to retrieve the ball for a slam dunk. She hopped up in the air, but was short. Frustrated that she'd missed one of her signature shots in college, she lined up to do it again and again until she got it right.

By her twelfth try she was sweating in the forty-degree temperature, but pleased she'd finally made the shot. She had to stop and lay her hands on her thighs to catch her breath.

Her mom called out from the bench, "I knew you'd get it eventually."

Kline was so focused on proving to herself she still had it, she hadn't heard her mom slip inside the court. She sat on a bench bundled up in a coat and had a thermos and two mugs. "Want some hot cocoa?"

Kline shook her head and picked up the ball again. As she let it fly toward the backboard, she asked, "Why are you up so early?"

"I'm always up early these days. What's wrong, sweetheart?"

"Nothing." Kline started an approach shot again. "Just felt like getting some exercise."

Mom poured out the steaming cocoa into her mug. "So you're not having second thoughts about running for mayor, or about whatever Ben climbed into your window to talk to you about last night?"

That stopped Kline midshot. "How did you know about that?"

Mom took a sip and chuckled. "When you were in high school, your father rigged up a wire that rang a little bell in our bedroom when your window was opened. He was worried about more than just talking going on in there, so he'd always stand outside your closed door to be sure he wasn't going to have to throw Ben out."

Despite being a full-grown woman, heat crawled up Kline's neck and warmed her cheeks. "Ben and I never . . . I told him I wouldn't feel comfortable in my . . ." She gave up and threw another basket.

"I know. Your dad kept a watchful eye. And don't think I didn't know the difference back then between practice and coming out here because you were upset by the bullies at school or when you had boy trouble."

Boy trouble? Her mother had no idea what trouble Ben was causing her insides at the moment. She dribbled toward her mom and stood in front of her. Still bouncing the ball to stay warm she asked, "If you knew about the bullying, why didn't you make it stop?"

Her mom took another sip of her hot chocolate. "Your teachers kept an eye on you for us. If we'd thought you couldn't handle it, we would've stepped in. You needed to learn how to direct all that self-doubt and bad energy, Kline. Basketball was good therapy. I don't think you would've ever earned a college scholarship if we'd solved all your problems for you when you were young. I remember you spending three or four hours in a row out here throwing one basket after the next. Next thing we knew, you were a high school state champion."

Until then, memories of her school years weren't good ones. She'd been so tall and awkward and flat-chested. Glasses and braces had only made it worse. Most of the Anderson kids felt superior to the Grants and that it was their duty to stay loftier by being mean.

But never Ben.

Thankfully, puberty had been kind to her and once the boys started noticing, especially Ben, many of the popular girls suddenly wanted to be her friends. Between basketball practice and eventually dating Ben, she didn't have time for new fake girlfriends, though. "Okay, you win." She sat beside her mom and poured herself a mug of cocoa. "I'm worried about *you*. And maybe a little about living here if I beat the mayor."

"I can take care of myself, and you can do anything you put your mind to. You've proven that time and time again, sweetheart. And Ben?"

She shook her head. "Ben . . . has a date tonight. We're just friends."

Mom patted her leg. "Well, he passes by here most mornings when he jogs. If you want to avoid seeing him, I suggest you come inside now and let me make you a good breakfast."

Kline drained her mug and then hopped up again. "I'm not going to start hiding from Ben. This town is big enough for the both of us, despite what he says. What I'm going to do is throw this basketball into *my* hoop in *my* front yard until I figure out what I'm going to do with *my* damned life!" She threw a perfect half-court basket to make her point.

"Says *my* stubborn little mule." Her mom chuckled and gathered her things. "I'll make you some French toast after you figure it all out. Here comes Ben now. Good luck."

Her mother called out, "Good morning, Ben. How are you?"

The traitor.

Ben lifted a hand, and then his eyes met Kline's and his feet changed direction. He jogged up the drive and opened the gate. "You two are out early this morning."

Ben wore running tights that hugged his muscled thighs way too nicely, and his snug long-sleeve shirt highlighted his defined chest. Better not to look.

She turned away and threw the ball into the hoop. "Don't let us keep you from your run."

Ben jogged in front of her and scooped up the ball. "I always have time for some hoops. You on, or are you scared I'll beat you?"

Out of the corner of her eye, she saw her mother slink away. "Why would I be scared of a man who has never beaten me unless I let him?"

He dribbled the ball, alternating hands. "I joined a rec league after you left. I've got moves now. But if you're chicken . . ."

Kline stole the ball from his hand and landed her shot. "One, nothing." She bounce-passed the ball to him. "I'm taking you down, Anderson. First to twenty-one—street rules."

Ben crossed the half-court line, and then dribbled toward her at a full run. "Cocky, aren't you, Grant?"

She hadn't expected that kind of speed from him. A bolt of adrenalin shot through her veins as she reached in to steal the ball. Ben swiveled his back to her and stuck out his fine rear end, defending. Then he turned and, before she could block, scored.

He shot her a smug grin. "One, one." Then he passed her the ball.

She held back her smile as she dribbled back to the half-court line. Ben *had* gotten better and, oddly, it made her proud of him. She'd have to work to beat him for the first time ever. So she charged, faked right, threw him off, and then turned and threw the ball from the three-point line, earning her double the points.

"Three, one." Time for a little smack talk. "Are you sure you don't want to save up all this energy for your date tonight? Wouldn't want to poop out early and leave her unsatisfied." She passed him the ball.

He dribbled toward the basket. "Satisfaction in the sack is my trademark. Anytime you'd like a reminder of that, just let me know." He jumped up to throw, but Kline anticipated him and blocked the ball. She grabbed it and ran back to the top of the key.

"Now who's being cocky?" She'd planned to throw another three-pointer, but Ben had learned from the last time and got in her face. She made a few moves to test him and then spun around and dribbled toward the basket. Ben's hands reached in and wrapped around her breasts to stop her, giving them a good squeeze. "Hey! Foul!"

He lifted his hands palms up and plastered on an innocent expression. "I thought this was anything goes. Do street rules for women mean no chipping the other's nail polish?"

Good for him. He was smack-talking her right back.

"Not wearing any nail polish." She jabbed her elbow into his gut so hard he grunted, and then she ran to the basket to score. "Four, one."

His cell rang in his pocket so he held up a finger. He studied the screen, glanced up at her, and then back at the screen.

She said, "Oh, just take it already."

"I'll just be a second. It's Meg."

Kline dribbled the ball to keep warm as Ben talked on the phone. Another call beeped in so he hung up with his sister and spoke to what sounded like a patient. When he was done, he slipped his phone back in his pocket and said, "Sorry. Ready to get your butt kicked now?"

"I think you meant that the other way around." She passed to him with all her might.

After the ball slammed into his chest, he snagged it. "So you want to play hard now, huh?"

"I always play hard." She moved in front of him and assumed the position.

He whispered, "You're making *me* hard."

The same hunger she'd seen last night gleamed from within his steady gaze as Ben dribbled the ball. He kept his eyes locked on hers as he planned his next move. Like a lion, waiting for the right moment to pounce. Major turn-on.

But she hated to lose, so she'd just stay focused on the game.

———

Ben wiped the sweat from his face with the hem of his shirt. He hadn't had so much fun since he could remember. He tried to tell himself it'd be okay to lose to a former college basketball player. No, Kline was a national champion former collegiate player who'd been recruited to play in the pros, but a major knee injury at the end of her senior year of college had ruled that out. He was still bigger and faster than she was, though, so it grated on his ego.

She'd kept pulling out damn perfect three-pointers, so he was behind, eighteen to twenty. She only needed one more point to win. But she had to win by two, so if he could just make a long shot and earn two points he'd still be in the running.

She passed him the ball. "Getting scared?"

"No. As a matter of fact, I want to up the stakes." He moved toward her, stopping just before their chests touched. He loved how Kline stood her ground.

She raised an arrogant brow. "What did you have in mind?"

"If I win, I want a five-minute reprieve from restraining my 'baser desires' with you. Then we'll go back to being friends." He reached out and tucked a loose strand of hair behind her ear.

She swallowed. Hard. "And if I win?"

"Whatever you'd like from me."

She chewed her bottom lip as she considered, making him wish he could nibble that full lip for her.

Finally she said, "If I win, you have to loan me the keys to your office tomorrow. Just for a few minutes. You're closed, right?"

It took him a second, but then he realized what she wanted. To get a look at her mother's file. "I'd have to have a legitimate reason for loaning you my keys. So think of something else."

She moved closer and pressed her soft chest against his, the cheater. "You'll loan them to me because I'm going to forget my purse in your office this afternoon, and I'll need my EpiPen from it. You'll be busy hiking tomorrow, so you can text me and allow me to get the keys from your unlocked house." She stood on her tiptoes and whispered in his ear, "My life could depend on it."

Her warm breath caressing his ear made it hard to think. "Why do you carry an EpiPen? What are you allergic to?"

"Bee stings. I found out the hard way in Africa." She gave his earlobe a little bite that shot straight to his groin.

Her idea could plausibly work, but he couldn't do it. "Can't mess with HIPAA, Kline."

She sighed. "Had to try. Then how about the name of a doc in Denver who would know how to deal with my mom's 'particular' problem. You could give me that without telling me specifically what's wrong with her, right?"

Betty's problem was matchmaking, not medical. He should give Kline the name of a good shrink. "How about I make a nice dinner for you instead?"

Kline whispered in his ear, "Nope. But I'd gladly kick your ass for some of your world-famous chocolate-filled cannoli."

She was trying to distract him. And doing an excellent job, because a vision popped into his head of her, with just a thin sheet draped over her naked body, from when he used to serve those to her in bed. Then she'd thank him by making sweet love to him.

He slipped a hand down to her nice ass and gave it a hard pat. "You're on."

Her slowly growing grin as she pulled away made him hope she hadn't been holding back so far, or he might be in trouble.

Ben passed the ball for her to check it. Kline passed it back and then he made for the three-point line. Kline caught up and moved between him and the basket, then got a hand on the ball. It slipped from his grip so they both dove for it. Their feet tangled and she stepped on his shoelace, tripping him. He stuck out a hand to stop himself before he hit the pavement, then realized Kline was falling backward right beside him. He moved his hand behind her head to protect it as they both hit the concrete with a jarring thump that shot searing pain to his shoulder. His bottom lip was on fire, but that didn't hurt quite as badly as his knuckles under her head.

Kline winced. "You're on my hand."

He quickly rolled back so she could slip it free, hating that he'd hurt her. "Are you okay, babe?"

She squeezed her eyes closed and nodded, but the tears leaking out the edges sent a shot of guilt straight through his heart. She rolled on her side and held her wrist. "Dammit! And I was ahead."

Of course, Kline would think of that before the pain in her hand. She was the most competitive person he'd ever met. He liked that about her. "Let me see."

She slowly sat up and held out her palm. Her wrist had already started to swell. "Can you wiggle your fingers?"

"Yeah." She slowly moved them, wincing again from the pain. "Your bottom lip is bleeding. Did you bite it?"

"Yep." He prodded her hand and tried not to grimace as the movement caused pain in his own hand and shoulder. "I think it's just a sprain. You need to get this iced down right away. Then wrap it up snug."

"'Kay." She slowly stood and then held out her good hand to help him. "You sure know how to kill a mood, buddy. I guess we'll have to call that a draw. We're both down for the count."

He grabbed her hand, just to hold it, and got up on his own. "I bet I could get the mood back if you gave me my five minutes."

She slipped her hand from his and walked to the bench to grab the broom and the ball. "Kissing would be pretty painful for you at the moment. Hope it doesn't put a damper on your date tonight." She smirked, the brat.

He'd awoken to a text from his date that said she'd rather not come to Anderson Butte because she had plans on Friday evening, so he wasn't going to do any kissing anyway.

He wouldn't tell Kline that, though.

As they walked to the gate he asked, "Have you given any more thought to what we talked about last night? If you win the election and stay?"

"I'm still thinking about it." She closed the gate behind them. "But I can't win with just the Grants' votes. Can I count on yours?"

An Anderson had always run the town his relatives had founded. The tradition ran deep in his blood. And he needed his father's support to get his new clinic built.

Before he could speak, she said, "Seriously, Ben? That answer should've just popped right out. I can't believe you'd vote for your dad over me."

She turned and walked up her drive.

"Kline, wait. I just—"

"Don't bother." She let out a long sigh and then turned to face him. "Why would I ever expect you to take my side over your family's? It's never happened yet. See you."

Dammit!

He could go after her, tell her he *wanted* to vote for her. He just hadn't found a way to do that and have his clinic too. But he was still working on it.

He spit out the blood pooling in his mouth and headed back to his house. Why, when every time he thought he'd made a little progress with her, did something like that have to happen?

Ben walked up the steps to his front porch and found his dad sitting in a chair waiting for him. "Morning." It couldn't be good news. His father never just showed up on his porch.

Dad frowned. "What the hell happened to your mouth?"

"Fell. What's up?"

His father rose out of the chair and poked a beefy finger into Ben's wounded shoulder, sending searing-hot pain down his spine.

"You need to talk some sense into your damned girlfriend. She blows into town after God knows how long and starts screwing with our new distillery, one that this town desperately needs, and now she's running against me? I was going to work with you on your clinic, but I won't be able to without the sale of that land for the distillery."

Could the day get any worse? "What are you afraid of? That she might actually win?"

His father's jaw clenched. "You saw how many people jumped on her bandwagon last night. She's something shiny and new, a novelty. Just pretty fluff who spouts liberal, happy cotton candy out of her mouth. That's not what it takes to run this town. *You* need to remember your loyalties as an Anderson, Ben. That girl has always been a major pain in my ass!"

"Kline's a woman, not a girl, and whip smart, Dad. You know she's always cared deeply about the welfare of others. Whether it be animals or people. Don't disrespect her like that."

"She's never earned my respect and never will. She's always been a bad choice for you, Ben. Why you don't see that is beyond me." Dad stomped off the porch and called out, "I expect her to withdraw from the race before the election, or I'll see to it that you *never* get the new clinic you so badly want. Fix this, dammit!"

Ben sank down in a chair on the porch and closed his eyes. He wanted that clinic with all his heart. He'd been planning it and recruiting the best docs he could find for two years.

Now that he'd seen Kline again, he wanted her back just as badly.

What the hell was he going to do?

CHAPTER NINE

Kline slapped the door to the garage closed behind her and headed for the kitchen cupboard that held medical supplies. Her mom, seated in the nook, glanced up from the book she was reading. "What are you looking for?"

"Something to wrap my wrist with. Ben fell on it." Kline grabbed a bottle of pain reliever and then found what she needed.

Mom slipped in a bookmark and closed the cover. "Do you want some help?"

"No, I've got it." Kline grabbed a plastic bag, filled it with ice, and sat at the table across from her mom. "I asked Ben if he was going to vote for me, and he just stood there blinking like I'd asked him to recite the periodic table. It's a no-brainer to vote for the best candidate. Someone with an actual heart. Someone he claims to love. But he'd never go against his father. He hasn't changed a bit."

"You haven't changed either, Miss Hothead. Who do you suppose Ben has voted for every time since he's been old enough to vote?"

The cold of the ice crept into her bones and made her wrist ache even harder. She wished it'd hurry up and make things numb. "His father, obviously."

"Exactly. Like everyone else around here, we don't think, we just vote and get it over with like we do any other chore. Ben might not have even considered it yet. And I thought you said you were just friends?"

"Right now I don't know what we are. Last night he told me—didn't ask what I thought about it—just told me that if I stay, he's going to win me back. Like some Neanderthal throwing his woman over his shoulder and hauling her back to his cave. Then he said this town wouldn't be big enough for me to hide from him."

"So which is it, Kline? Friend, girlfriend, enemy?" Mom's eyes twinkled with amusement.

Kline wasn't entirely sure what she wanted Ben to be anymore.

"If he has it his way, we'll get back together. But I'm still afraid his first priority will always be his family and this damn town. It's no wonder he's never married. What woman wants to always feel like she takes a backseat in a man's life?"

"If that's his problem, then what's yours? Why haven't you had a serious relationship since Ben?" Mom's brows rose in that no-nonsense way that signaled Kline had better not try to get out of answering the question.

"I . . . just haven't fallen in love . . . like before." Kline turned her attention to her achy iced wrist. "Now that I know what it feels like, I won't settle for anything less."

Mom laid her hand over Kline's good one. "I think that's wise. But maybe your hard head just doesn't want to hear what your heart is trying to tell you."

Her heart was starting to fall for him again, but fortunately her head was still in the game reminding her to be careful. "Sometimes people hurt us so badly it can't be fixed."

"We fix what we choose to fix, honey." Mom stood and crossed to the stove. "Ready for some French toast now?"

"That'd be great. Thanks." Kline closed her eyes and sighed. Her heart and her hormones needed to come to some sort of agreement about Ben. The sooner the better.

"Good morning, ladies." Nate walked into the kitchen dressed in hiking boots, jeans, and a tight thermal Henley, ready for the cold while they checked out the owls' habitat. "What happened, Kline?"

"Basketball injury. No big deal."

Nate wandered to the coffeemaker and poured himself a mug. "How are you, Betty?"

"I'm great. Want some breakfast?"

Nate leaned his large body against the countertop and smiled at her mom. "I'd love some. You want to come owl hunting with me and Kline today?"

Mom shook her head. "No thanks, I don't have a lot of energy today. But after dinner tonight, Kline needs a man to take her to Brewsters and pay complete attention to her. Are you up for that?"

Nate turned his head and met Kline's gaze. "I'm always *up* for Kline." He hitched his brows and took a long drink from his mug.

Kline pointed to her mother's back and mouthed, "Knock it off!" Geez. Her mother wasn't dense. Surely, she knew exactly what Nate had meant.

She needed to make it clear to Nate that she wasn't going to sleep with him. It wasn't because she was still in love with Ben like her mother thought. It was because . . . hell if she knew. Nate was good-looking. Great in bed. And a fun guy. Maybe she just wasn't interested in a player like Nate, that's all.

Or Ben, with his long list of willing women.

————————

After dinner, Ben put the last of the pans in the dishwasher and turned to his best friend since their days as residents. He'd called her last minute to fill in for his date. "You sure you're up for this, Sam?"

"I'm game." The tall, blonde ER doc finished off her glass of wine. "But as many times as I've come to visit you, are you sure you've never mentioned to anyone that I'm gay?"

"Of course not. Why would something like that even come up in conversation?"

"Oh, you'd be surprised." She put her glass in the dishwasher. "But if you're sure no one knows, then let's do this. I can't wait to meet the *one* woman who's captured your heart."

Ben turned out the lights and grabbed their coats from the closet by the front door. "Okay, so to make this believable I might have to touch you . . . inappropriately. Just think of me as your ex." He helped her into her coat.

Sam pulled her long hair out from under her collar and let it cascade down her back as they walked onto the porch. "Julie didn't have stubble on her cheeks and a rock-hard chest, so that'll be a stretch, pretty boy. I'll do my best, but should we have a safe word?"

He laughed. "I'm not asking you to have kinky sex with me, Sam."

"Obviously. But look at this from my perspective. You nibbling on my earlobe while dancing would be like your brother doing the same to you."

"Point taken. No nibbling." Ben shivered at the brother image she'd just implanted in his head. "How about 'whiskey' since you don't drink that?"

"Perfect."

"Thanks, Sam. I owe you one." He held out his hand to help her down the steps.

She swatted it aside. "Just because I'm pretending to be your date doesn't suddenly make me an invalid. You should ice that hand tonight, by the way."

"Thank you, Doctor Obvious."

"Your flippant attitude just proves that doctors make the worst patients."

"It's no big deal." Ben winced as he threw his injured arm around her shoulder in a companionable way. "It's a little cold tonight."

"It's freakin' *freezing*." Sam moved against his side and wrapped her arm around his waist. Then she gave him a squeeze. "You're so tense. Let's just relax and have fun tonight like we always do."

"I'll try." As they walked to Brewsters in comfortable silence, Ben weighed the merits of his grandmother's scheme. He didn't usually go for game playing, but he wasn't sure he was making any progress with Kline. His time with her could be limited. So as long as Sam was up for it, he was willing to try, but didn't look forward to watching Kline with the bird guy.

Sam reached out to tug open the door to the bar first, so it was Ben's turn to swat her hand aside. "Nope. If we're going to look convincing, you have to let me open doors for you. Just for tonight."

"Fine." Sam rolled her eyes. "This could be a long night."

A warm wave of air washed over them, along with loud country twang. Ben searched for an empty table, but there weren't any. Then he spotted his sister sitting alone at a table big enough for six people. He didn't know who else was coming, but Sam was right. It *could* be a long night.

Ben slipped his hand to Sam's lower back and guided her to the table. When they got there, he said, "Casey, you remember Sam, right?"

"Yes. Good to see you again. Hope you're up for some darts. There's a tournament tonight so I got here early and signed us all up."

He turned to Sam and held up his swollen hand. "It's going to be up to you to save us."

"Sam isn't your partner, Ben." Casey's smile was laced with mischief. "I mixed things up a bit."

Of course she had.

Sam said, "Sounds fun. I'll go get us a pitcher of beer." Sam turned and left before Ben could tell her he was supposed to do that.

His sister waited until Sam was out of earshot. "Perfect choice. Sam is gorgeous."

"I'm still not sure about whatever this evil plan is you guys brewed up." Ben pulled out a chair and sat. "Why are there so many people here on a Thursday night?"

"Uncle Brewster got Dad to sponsor the tournament so that the drinks are all half price tonight. There was an e-mail sent out on the loop earlier."

"Since when does Dad sponsor dart tournaments?"

Casey grinned into her wineglass. "Maybe since we asked Uncle Brewster to remind Dad that he has an opponent running for mayor for the first time ever."

"Clever. Is Zane joining us?"

"No. He and the boys have planned some big video game battle after they finish their homework. I'm pretty sure he just wanted nothing to do with this. He thinks I should leave you and Kline alone to work things out."

"And that's why I like Zane." That, and because Zane was so great with his nephews and seemed to make his sister happy.

"He's a man, so he doesn't get it." Casey's eyes shifted away. "Kline and the sexy biologist just walked through the door."

Ben hated seeing them together. "His name is Nate."

"Hot Nate, if you ask me."

"You're engaged."

"I can still look." Casey smirked as she took another drink. "I've never seen you look so jealous, Ben. This ought to be fun."

Sam returned with a tray filled with beer and glasses and sat beside Ben just as Kline's gaze locked with his. When Kline noticed Sam, a little frown line formed on her forehead.

Should he whisper "whiskey" in Sam's ear and make a run for it, or would his sister's mystery ploy actually work?

Kline broke their locked stare and forced a smile. "Hey, everyone. This is my friend Nate."

After the greetings were over, Nate and Kline sat across from them. Kline kept glancing toward the door as if she wanted to escape, while Nate stared openly at Sam. Ben couldn't blame the guy. Sam was a beautiful woman, but that was disrespectful to Kline, and it pissed him off.

While Casey chatted up Kline and Nate, Sam drained her beer glass. "This is my favorite song, Ben. Let's go." She grabbed his hand and pulled him to the dance floor.

As they merged into the two-stepping traffic on the small wooden floor, Sam said, "Holy crap, Kline is hot. I'd arm wrestle you for her if I thought I could beat you."

"She's mine." Ben pulled Sam closer. "Slip your hands around my neck."

Sam complied and then glanced over his shoulder. "She looks like she's Nate's at the moment. Unfortunately, on an empirical scale, he might be even more perfect than you are. His build is larger and—"

"Can you please keep your head in the game?"

Sam laughed as he spun them around so he could see what was going on back at the table. He studied Kline's body language while sliding his hand slowly toward Sam's rear end. "Kline's not into him. She's just pretending to have fun."

When they flipped positions again, Sam's smirk grew. "I don't know, Ben. She's laughing at something Nate said. I think she might be into him."

"It doesn't matter. She's not even watching us so we need to move to plan B." When the song was over, Ben grabbed Sam's hand and tugged her back to the table. "Ask Nate for the next dance."

"Fine. But if he gets handsy, he's going to lose them."

Sam had a black belt in karate. He hoped Nate would try.

Soon after Sam and Nate left, Casey quietly slipped away, finally leaving Ben alone with Kline.

He forced his best smile. "Looking forward to the dart tournament?"

"I guess." Her gaze shifted to her fingers running up and down her chilled mug. "Sam is very pretty, Ben. She smiled at you the whole time you were dancing, so that's a good sign."

So, she'd been watching them after all. "We've been friends for a long time. Since right after you left." He straightened the display advertising the beers on tap and then centered the bowl of nuts on the table.

Kline moved her cool fingertips over his hands to stop his rearranging. Her touch sent a calming wave through him again. Just like at the council meeting.

"So then you *have* had a long-term relationship, just not a serious one?" she asked.

"Long-term friendship. Like you and Nate?"

"Except I'm not sleeping with Nate anymore. We really are just friends." Kline lifted her injured hand from the table and examined it. "Thank you for saving my head from being this swollen."

"No problem." He was happy she wasn't sleeping with Nate, but hated how quiet Kline was. Maybe bringing in Sam had been a mistake. Did it give Kline an excuse to pull further away from him emotionally? He needed to put a stop to the game playing and just have a conversation with her. "How's the wrist?"

"Hurts." She slowly slid her hand along his cheek, then ran her thumb softly over his swollen bottom lip. "So does this, I imagine."

His lip tingled under her light caress. He'd missed Kline's habit of touching him whenever they were near. Gazes still locked, he whispered, "Maybe you should kiss me and make it better."

"I doubt Sam would appreciate that." She leaned away and then drank deeply from her beer. "We found two pairs of owls today. Nate e-mailed his assessment in this afternoon. Your dad won't be able to get a building permit for the distillery now."

"So you won. Does that mean you're still running for mayor?"

"The environment won, not me. I meant what I said earlier. I'm running because this town needs a fresh point of view. Even if I don't have *your* vote, Gloria said she started a poll, and I'm getting a few votes."

Ben's stomach sank. "That's great, Kline."

He took a drink as his gut ached at the prospect of losing his clinic. Now that they had found the birds, would anything be able to be built across from the hotel? Because all of the land surrounding the town was owned by Grants, it seemed he'd never get another chance to build. There wasn't a Grant he could think of who would sell their land to an Anderson.

But he couldn't stand Kline thinking he was on a date any longer, so he leaned closer and whispered, "I need to tell you something. I'm not—"

The scrape of a chair interrupted them. Meg and Josh had arrived. His sister said, "Hi, guys. How's it going?"

Just as Ben opened his mouth, Nate and Sam returned.

Nate said, "I've finally figured out where I met Sam before. It's been driving me nuts, but I never forget a face, right, Kline?"

Dammit.

Ben cut his gaze to Sam, who mouthed, "Whiskey!"

CHAPTER TEN

Kline glanced at Ben after Nate's statement put a panicked expression on Sam's face. When Ben's eye twitched in annoyance, it confirmed Kline's suspicion. Something was going on. "It's true. Nate never forgets a face, especially if it's a pretty one."

When Sam had laid her hand on Ben's shoulder and mouthed something, another pang of unwanted jealousy had zapped Kline's heart. She'd thought she'd be fine seeing Ben with his date, but it was harder than she imagined.

Just as Kline opened her mouth to ask where Nate and Sam had met, Meg said, "So, we're in the first flight of teams tonight. Ben, it's you and Kline, Sam and Nate, Josh and me. Because Zane isn't here, Casey will play with the first guy eliminated in the round robin, and they'll go last. First up, Nate and Sam versus Kline and Ben."

Kline drew a deep breath for patience. Of course Ben's sisters had to make Ben her teammate. It was bad enough she'd have to watch him on his date all night, but now she'd have to play darts with him too. Probably best to get it over with and then go home.

The first team all stood and walked over to the dartboards. Two small tables with stools shoved against the wall were reserved for the players. Another competition was in full swing on the second board, so they claimed their spots.

Nate drained his beer, and then said to Sam, "This is going to be as close to a date as I'll get with you, huh, Sam?"

"So it seems." Sam smiled sheepishly. "Who goes first? How does this work?"

Nate turned to Ben. "I met Sam in the ER last year because I needed stiches. When I asked her out afterward, she set me straight. Who would've ever guessed Sam was into girls? It's such a waste, right?"

Into girls? What the hell was going on? Was Ben lying to her again?

Kline whipped her head in Ben's direction. "You told me last night you had a date."

"I did." Ben pinched the bridge of his nose. "That's what I was going to tell you. Mine canceled, so I asked Sam if she'd like to go hiking tomorrow instead."

"Excuse us, please." Kline didn't want to have it out in front of everyone, so she grabbed Ben's arm and tugged him toward the hallway that led to the bathrooms. When they got to the quiet corridor, she said, "What's going on, Ben?"

"My instructions from my grandmother were to bring a date here tonight. After that, I have no idea."

"To make me jealous, no doubt." She closed her eyes and leaned against the wall.

It'd worked. She hated how her stomach had clenched at the sight of Sam and Ben. "This is the perfect example of annoying, small-town life. Why can't everyone just leave us alone and mind their own business?"

Ben moved a step closer. "Gossip and nosiness weren't rampant when you lived in your cozy tent community in Africa with Nate?"

Now who was acting jealous? She ignored the question and said, "Please go call off your sisters so we can just throw some darts and get through this evening. I don't want to make a scene." She started to leave but he laid a hand on the wall beside her head, blocking her in.

"Not until we get something straight. Do you still have feelings for me, Kline?"

She sighed. "That's beside the point. It's the game playing—"

"So let's make it the point. You say your piece on the matter and then I'll say mine." He moved so close the heat from his body warmed hers in the cool, drafty hallway as he whispered, "Yes or no?"

She stared into his eyes that searched hers so intently she felt his longing deep in her soul. Where her heart, filled with her past love for him, battled against the temptation to let him back in. The deep scars still ached, reminding her to stay strong. "Let's look at the facts, Ben. Yes, we both have undeniable physical attraction for each other. And yes, I have some unresolved feelings for you. I might win the election or I might have to stay for a while until I get my mother's health issues sorted out, but I don't know what'll happen after that. It'd just make it harder if I leave and we've become involved again. The reasonable side of my brain says we should save ourselves the inevitable grief and stay friends."

"I disagree." He laid his mouth on hers and whatever chance she'd had for a logical rebuttal went straight out the back door. The man made her toes curl and her heart melt every time he kissed her. And she couldn't deny she'd been jealous seeing him with someone else earlier.

Her hands slid into his thick hair, and she pulled him closer. She wanted to make the most of their last kiss, because that's what it needed to be.

While his tongue made sweet love to hers, her hormones pulled rank on her logic and she gave in completely to the spell Ben's kiss cast over her. It *wasn't* just physical attraction. Ben took her to that familiar, happy place no other man ever had—and she missed going there with all her being.

She'd *missed him*.

Wanting more, she pressed her mouth and her needy body harder against all of his glorious muscles. When her lungs burned from the lack of air, it reminded her that she needed to end the kiss. Slowly, she leaned away and stared into his eyes. Should she take a chance with him again?

He ran his tongue over his swollen bottom lip and then whispered, "Thanks for proving my point." Ben turned and walked away, leaving her hot, bothered, and knowing full well that he was right. Her body had given him the answer he'd been looking for without her having to say a word. She still had feelings for him.

She forced her feet to follow in Ben's wake back to the dart game.

Kline made her way through the crowd watching the other dart game, surprised by all the well wishes and high fives she received from people for the upcoming election. She couldn't restrain a grin as she slapped their palms in return.

It was so unlike her childhood; everyone seemed genuinely happy to see her as they welcomed her back and wished her luck. It was . . . nice.

She sat at the small players table across from Sam. "Where did the guys go?"

Sam pointed. "Ben went to get more beer and got sidetracked by that woman, and Nate is at the bar flirting with a waitress."

"Typical Nate." She'd told him they weren't going to sleep together earlier, so he was on the prowl. "Ben is talking to my aunt Millie. She's been convinced she's on her deathbed since I was little. She'll keep him for a while."

"That's just one of the things I love about Ben. His bedside manner is stellar. If I were into men, I'd marry Ben in a heartbeat."

Kline blocked the vision of Sam and Ben in wedding garb that popped into her brain. Sam wasn't into Ben. She needed to tame the jealous thoughts. "Ben said you've been friends since residency?"

"Yeah." Sam nodded as she took a drink from her glass. "I feel I know you, because you were all he talked about for many years. So I hope you don't mind me asking, but why aren't you really mad at all of us for the 'make Kline jealous plan'?"

"I was at first, but now I'm more frustrated than angry. Clearly, you didn't grow up in a small town. This is standard operating procedure around here."

"Nope. Chicago. Only child of overachiever parents. But I'd love to live here. Everyone has been so friendly. I hope Ben gets the clinic he's been dreaming of, because he's convinced me to work there with him."

"Seriously? You work in a busy ER. Don't you think you'd get bored?"

"No." Sam's expression turned sad. "I'm so tired of seeing kids with gunshot wounds I can't save, or so high on drugs they fry their brains. Then there are the homeless so far adrift they wander in and make up symptoms so they can get out of the cold for a bit. I need a break."

"I can understand all of that, but the buttinskies and lack of entertainment here can be cloying for someone not used to it."

Sam smiled. "Ben's family makes me feel a part of them, something I never had growing up. And I can always pop into Denver when I need culture and shopping. Ben has been teaching me how to fly a chopper so I'll be able to help with transporting patients."

Kline had asked Ben to teach her to fly too, but he'd never had time while in med school. "Seriously, Sam, even everyday activities you take for granted aren't available here. The nearest movie theater is fifteen miles away, and the only place to get even plain coffee to go is the diner. You can forget about ethnic food." She'd learned to be happy with very little in her travels, but Sam was from a big city so she should be warned.

Sam shrugged. "Ben can fill that void. He's a great cook. He makes the best Thai I've ever had."

Kline's glass stopped halfway to her lips. "He makes you Thai food too?"

"I'm no threat, remember?" Sam patted Kline's hand. "Ben learned to make it because it was *your* favorite. He said you'd miss it when you finally came home. I can't imagine what took you so long."

"You and the celebrities who visit see this town as a quiet slice of paradise, a place to get away from your busy big-city lives. What's not to like about the lake, and the beautiful forest, and all the fun recreation both provide? Add in the quaint shops surrounding a town square with a bandstand in the middle, for goodness' sake, and who could resist it, right?"

"Right." Sam nodded.

"While that's all true, there's a part that's not obvious to visitors. Try growing up a Grant in a town run and dominated by Andersons. We've always been treated like the lower class with nowhere to escape the torment. I couldn't wait to leave it all behind."

"Well, I hear you're going to change all of that, right, almost Mayor-Elect?" Sam hitched her brows. "You and Ben are very similar. Both the type who feel compelled to help others, solve everyone's problems, just in different ways. And locations."

"I suppose you're right." She helped others because she felt called to it. She'd filled the hole Ben left in her heart by doing for others, but that kiss earlier proved her service hadn't worked as well as she'd thought it had. A little something had definitely seeped through the hardened wall she'd erected to protect her heart.

Sam leaned closer as if about to spill a juicy secret. "I think one of the reasons Ben is so drawn to you is that you don't need him. Unlike his siblings who he raised, and the townspeople who depend on him for their health care and more. You're a strong, independent woman, Kline."

Maybe always being on the defensive after her breakup with Ben had made her become too independent. Too ready to move on when she'd start to have feelings for men, before things could get complicated, drifting from place to place, avoiding close friendships so she wouldn't get attached to anyone or anything she'd miss when she left. Now, after being locked up in prison, she knew she didn't want that solitary life anymore. She wanted to be with people whom she cared for.

Sam knew more about Ben and Kline's past relationship than felt comfortable, but since a normally closed-mouthed person like Ben had shared so much with Sam, he probably trusted her completely.

"Everyone *does* depend on Ben; he's always played that role. He seems to thrive on that, so I'm not so sure about your theory, Sam. But I'm glad Ben has had a friend like you all these years." Kline drained her glass. "I'm dying to know something before he gets back, though. When did he start with the straightening-and-organizing thing? Is it something serious?"

"No. It's just how he deals with stress. It's not a full-blown compulsion or anything. He's had to keep things orderly and under control since I've known him." Sam chuckled. "During dinner, I could tell he was trying not to straighten everything on the table. I always threaten to write him a script and force it down his throat to prove to him that mild anxiety meds could help. Of course he insists he doesn't have any stress problems."

"Right. Because that'd be a weakness in his eyes, and he wouldn't want to have one of those." So Ben had started his straightening tendencies after she'd left? Had her leaving had anything to do with that? He used to tell her she was his true north. The only person he wanted to be with, especially after a bad day.

She glanced at Ben again. He laid a hand on her aunt's arm as he talked to her, no doubt soothing away whatever new health worry she had. Then as if he felt Kline's stare, he locked gazes with her and smiled. A smile she felt all the way to her toes.

Yeah. She was still in love with Ben, dammit. So what was she going to do about it?

Ben finally escaped Millie's latest health-scare tale and hurried back to his own table with the beer. Until Nate had joined them a moment ago,

Sam and Kline had been chatting alone, and that made Ben nervous. Sam knew too many details of his dating life post-Kline that he'd rather leave buried in the past. He'd been trying to forget Kline, and wasn't proud of his behavior.

Serial dating had reinforced there wasn't someone better than Kline out there for him. The idea of marriage held no appeal because of it. Until now. Surely if Kline stayed for any amount of time she'd see that Anderson Butte wasn't so bad now that she was a grown woman whom no one could bully. And that being near her mother as she aged would be a good thing.

Sam had recently asked him to consider being a sperm donor so she could have a child. With Kline in the picture again, he was glad he'd told Sam he'd have to think about it. If he got back together with Kline, she might not be too pleased if he had to co-parent a child who wasn't hers for the rest of their lives.

He laid the new pitcher of beer on the table. "We're holding up the show. Kline's up first."

Kline's dominant hand was uninjured, so she'd have to be the one to keep them afloat in the tournament. Just as she lifted her left hand to throw, his father's voice boomed out from the crowd. "There's my opponent now. What do you say to an impromptu debate, Kline?"

Her face clouded with fury as she hissed at Ben, "Was this part two of your family's plan? To ambush me?"

He lifted his hands in defense. "Absolutely not, Kline. I swear." He hoped he was telling the truth. He couldn't imagine his grandmother doing that on purpose.

The bar fell silent and all eyes turned to Kline. He could practically see the wheels turning in her head, deciding if she should accept the mayor's challenge.

He needed to put a stop to things. "Dad, we're having fun and playing some darts here. Pick another time and place."

His father smirked. "Will your boyfriend be doing all the talking for you during your campaign too, Kline?"

That was sure to set Kline off. "Dad, she needs time to prepare—"

"I've got this, Ben." Kline turned her attention to the people watching. "I don't want to ruin everyone's fun tonight. It's only fair we put it to a vote."

His father bellowed, "Who here would like to see what Kline knows about 401(k) plans and health care? Something that you all have because of *me*?"

Murmurs went out through the crowd at the thinly veiled threat, and hands gradually popped up as residents worried he'd find a way to revoke their benefits. After a few moments, all hands were in the air except for Ben's sisters' and Josh's.

Dad said, "Great. Looks like we got ourselves a debate, Kline. Why don't all of you go grab a drink on me, and then we'll get the show going."

His father was using bribes and threats as usual. Ben tried to figure a way to stop the debate, but nothing popped into his head short of pulling the fire alarm. He moved beside Kline and whispered, "What can I do to help?"

"You can stop coming to my rescue, please. I can handle your dad." Kline filled her beer glass and then took a long drink. "But I wouldn't mind a quick data dump of all you know about how the finances work around here."

It'd be smarter for him to feign ignorance so she wouldn't win the debate and he'd get his clinic, but he couldn't stand an unfair fight.

He glanced at the line at the bar, estimating he had maybe fifteen minutes to cram into Kline's head all he knew about the town's finances. Beyond that, there wasn't much more he could do to make it a fair playing field so he'd have to let her sink or swim on her own.

By the time he had filled Kline in, two mics had been set up on the stage, and everyone had a drink in their hands. His uncle Brewster tapped on a mic to get everyone's attention and the bar fell silent again. "Kline and Mitch, we're ready for you."

Uncle Brewster winked at Kline before he hopped off the stage. Everyone in Ben's family loved Kline except for his father. His sisters' plan to fill the bar, forcing him and Kline to sit with them so they could pull their matchmaking crap, had backfired. Instead, their father had taken the opportunity to catch Kline unprepared.

Brewster pulled a piece of paper from his back pocket. "Okay, I have a few questions here that I gathered in the last few moments—"

Dad cut his brother off and said, "I think we should first address Kline's motive for finally coming home." He turned and faced Kline. "Word is, you're pregnant and have come home to lick your wounds while hoping to win Ben's heart back so the child will have a father."

Ben hopped off his barstool to defend Kline, but stopped when she burst out laughing. "Really, Mayor? Is that what the *word* is? Because that couldn't be further from the truth. Not that it's anyone's business, but I'm not pregnant. I'm just here to visit my mom. Brewster, do you have a real question there?"

Relieved, Ben sat down again.

Sam slid her hand on his forearm and squeezed. "She's going to kick your dad's ass. Relax and enjoy the show."

The state of his clinic might be riding on the outcome of the debate, so relaxing wasn't happening. The election was just a week away.

CHAPTER ELEVEN

line forced a smile and remembered to breathe after she'd winged yet another answer. Everyone in the bar had been amazingly quiet during her debate with the mayor. The townspeople hung on her every word, as if fascinated that someone had finally challenged the mayor. Luckily, her years of teaching middle schoolers had taught her to be quick on her feet when answering embarrassing or tough questions. Kids were notorious for wanting to get a laugh out of their friends.

However, the mayor wasn't joking around. He was doing his best to make her look bad by asking her 401(k) questions. So far she'd held her own, thanks to Ben's coaching, but the questions were getting more intense.

She surreptitiously checked the time on her cell. They'd set an hour limit, so if she could get through the next ten minutes, she'd be home free.

Brewster asked, "Kline, while many other small towns rely on revenue from taxes, utilities, and the lottery, traffic tickets are the second-largest source of income for many. Since we're not on the beaten path, most of our income comes from taxes for services provided—mainly from the hotel. Seeing as Mitch Anderson owns most of the businesses in town, what could you do as mayor to increase our town's income so we can maintain our current benefits and a balanced budget?"

Crap. That was a damn good question. Ben's dad pretty much ran the show financially.

In the moments while her mind raced for an answer, the mayor said, "Kline's a teacher. She's probably never had more than two thousand dollars in her bank account at any given moment. She doesn't have a clue how many millions it takes to run and maintain this town."

She had more than two thousand dollars, but she'd just bought a new car, so not enough more to disprove his overall point. Because of their town benefits, and based on what Wayne had said their teachers made, most everyone in town probably did have more money in savings than she had. She'd quickly googled similar-size towns right before the debate and looked at their budgets, but Anderson Butte was unique in the way it was run.

Panic set in.

As Kline's mind raced for how many millions it might take to run Anderson Butte, Meg coughed and then tapped three fingers against her cheek.

Thank you, Meg!

Kline reeled in her anxiety and said, "Obviously I've not been privy to the town's financial reports like you all have, but I'd have to think a town this size would have upward of a three-million-dollar budget."

The mayor's jaw clenched. "Yes. But you still haven't answered the initial question."

Phew. Now the tough part. How could she bring in more revenue?

Something Nate had said earlier, and then the results of her research popped into her head. "Most small resort towns in Colorado make a good portion of their money from real estate transfer taxes. Since Mr. Anderson rarely sells property to outsiders, and then sells to his own family at severely reduced rates, that's not an option for us. I'd do my best to lobby for more government funds and tax credits for all the open space we naturally maintain around here. On both Anderson, and even more so, on the Grant lands in our county. There is federal money to be had; we just have to jump through hoops to get it. I'd be more than willing to do that. It could be millions."

She turned and smiled at the mayor.

Take that, you big bully!

Ben's father shook his head. "That's all conjecture on Kline's part. My point stands. She doesn't know how to handle millions."

Nate called out from the rear. "It's not conjecture, it's true. I'd help her find the money. And I'm sure the council has plenty of experience spending money. Ultimately, they are the ones who control the funds anyway. Not the mayor."

Thank goodness for Nate, whose father was in politics, so he knew of what he spoke.

The mayor said, "Moving on, Brew. It looks like we have time for one *last* question."

Ben's father sneered at Kline as Brewster read from the paper in his hand. "Kline, the distillery opening up would help the town financially. Do you really think saving one owl is more important than securing the future of our town?"

Of course, that would be the *last* question asked. The mayor had primed that pump. "It isn't one owl at stake, it's at least one breeding pair of *endangered* birds." She glanced around the room. The blank expressions on most of their faces proved she wasn't getting her point across. "Zeke's land just outside of town was used for strip mining before people woke up and realized it needed to stop. It's clear to see that parcel of land has been left permanently damaged, and because of that, it's the perfect location for the distillery."

A wave of low murmurs swept across the crowd. Most were Andersons, as many of the hard-core Anderson-hating Grants hung out at another bar just outside of town. Kline quickly added, "Uncle Zeke is open to selling that land. I know it's technically Grant land, but Zeke's grandfather won it in a poker game from an Anderson." She turned to Ben's father. "I'm sure the mayor will confirm that particular portion of Zeke's land lies within Anderson Butte's town limits." Kline was grateful her uncle had shared that with her after the council meeting the other night.

The whispers grew louder among the people so the mayor held up his hand. "Hold on. While technically that's true, there's no need to change the location. I made some phone calls today and the clearing crew is on its way. We're moving up the groundbreaking to tomorrow afternoon. The crew plans to work through the weekend clearing the land so we can get started. I hope you'll all take a few minutes to stop by at five tomorrow for a sample of the best whiskey you've ever tasted and to celebrate our new distillery!"

Loud clapping made it hard to hear, so Nate moved to just in front of the stage and said to the mayor, "You've been made aware of my findings. If you disturb that forest land surrounding the meadow, be prepared for heavy fines and even jail time under Section Eleven of the Endangered Species Act, Mayor."

The mayor cupped a hand around his ear and yelled, "Sorry, can't hear you. This debate is over. See you all tomorrow." Then he walked off the stage.

Dammit!

He'd probably won round one, but two could play that game. Kline needed to talk to Tara's father, the man responsible for building the distillery, and put a stop to the mayor's plan. Those birds needed protecting and Anderson Butte needed a new mayor who cared about people and the environment, not money. She was even more determined to figure out how to win the election now.

On the chilly walk home with Casey and Sam, Ben warred with being incredibly proud of Kline for holding her own at the debate against the worry of his father's threat to the new clinic if Kline didn't drop out of the race.

Casey gave him a shoulder bump. "Why so quiet?"

"Ben!" His father's voice boomed behind them. "I need a word."

Ben whispered, "You're about to see why." They stopped walking and waited for his father to catch up.

Dad started right in. "Are you an idiot? I saw you talking to Kline before the debate. No doubt helping her. Do you want your clinic or not?"

"Yes. But Kline's idea of moving the distillery to Zeke's land is a good one. Then we might be able to save the owls and have my clinic too. Assuming the footprint will work with the new restrictions."

"New restrictions Kline made happen! If she gets her way, that land will stand empty forever. You need to figure out how to make her drop out of this race!"

Ben dug deep for patience. "Would it really be so bad if she won, Dad? With your heart problems, you need to slow down. And none of us are interested in taking your place. Ever. Brewster is in about the same shape physically as you, so that doesn't leave too many other willing and capable Andersons."

"That's why I have no choice but to keep at this. I won't consider stepping down unless an Anderson replaces me. Make. Kline. Go. Away!" Dad spun on his heels and left.

Sam whispered, "What are you going to do?"

They started walking again. "I'm trying to find a way to have both, but those odds aren't looking so hot."

Casey said, "Whatever you do, figure out what will make *you* happiest, not Dad or the town. Because at the end of the day, that's all that counts."

"I've never had the luxury of putting myself first until now. Meg only just recently got her head on straight. I always worried for Haley the way Meg lost jobs because of Haley's asthma. I bailed them out more than I should have, but Dad would've never done it."

Casey rolled her eyes. "And you worried when I was dating a rock star, and you were afraid Ryan wasn't happy and would leave town for the wrong reasons until he met Tara. One of these days you'll figure out we're all grown up, Ben, and don't need you like we did when we were younger. Here's my stop. Good night, guys." Casey started down the long driveway to the hotel.

Casey claimed they didn't need him anymore, and yet they all still ran to him to solve their problems. It'd be a miracle if at least one of his siblings didn't call or text him at least once a day. But he'd concede that now the problems were more about town issues or their father. Maybe he shouldn't be so quick to give them advice anymore. Maybe then they'd learn to solve their problems on their own.

Once his sister was inside he and Sam continued on to his house.

Sam broke through his thoughts when she said, "Casey is right, you know. There's no one else to rescue but yourself, Ben."

"There will always be someone to save. That's why we need a new clinic with better equipment. My father and grandmother currently top that list with their health issues." They walked up his front steps and he pushed the door open for her to enter first.

"You know that's not what I meant." Sam slipped out of her coat. "So are you trying to save Kline from something too?"

"I don't want to discuss that." He hung up their coats, and then rearranged the others in the closet by color.

"It's way too late to pull that card with me, Ben. You dragged me into all this drama tonight, now stop all that organizing and go talk to Kline. Get to the bottom of what you're saving her from and sort things out."

That wasn't a bad idea. He still wasn't sure Kline had come to terms with living in town if she won. "Okay. I'll be back in a bit."

Ben zipped up his jacket and jogged to Kline's house. He wanted to catch her before she went to sleep. He tapped on her window, while shifting his weight from foot to foot to stay warm. After the curtains drew apart, she slid the window open for him to crawl through. "What? No food delivery this time?"

"Nope. Wanted to talk to you about something." He slid the window shut behind him.

"Okay. Talk." Kline sat on her bed. She wore an oversize T-shirt that left her sexy legs bare and made it hard to concentrate.

He wanted to tell her about the clinic and his father, but he feared she'd drop out of the race if he told her what was riding on the election for him. And then leave town before he had a chance to win her back.

He sat beside her. "Now that you're back and can see things have changed, would you consider staying in Anderson Butte even if you lost the election?"

Kline shook her head. "I've told you, I'll stay if my mom needs me. But I was happiest in Denver, and plan to live there."

He picked up her hand and weaved his fingers through hers. "Don't you think part of that happiness was because we lived there *together*?"

"I suppose that was part of it at the time." Kline pulled her hand away and stood. "Denver has so much more to offer. It's hard to be bored there." Her tone sounded as if she was still trying to convince herself of that.

"And yet, when we lived there, I'd offer to take you out on a Friday night, but you preferred my cooking, or Thai takeout, and a movie on the couch rather than a real date."

Kline opened her mouth to argue, and then snapped it shut. "We were poor back then. It made more sense to stay in."

She wasn't being honest with herself. "Okay, then explain something to me. In all your travels, you could have settled anywhere, so why did you always end up in small towns or makeshift villages?"

Kline's forehead scrunched. "How do you know where I've lived all these years?"

"Your mom. And I know the answer, but I'd like to hear it from you."

"You may think you know the answer, but my goal was to help impoverished people. I was sent by my job to small villages and poor communities in developing countries. It's not that I purposely chose small towns over larger ones."

He kicked off his shoes and settled against Kline's headboard while she paced nervously around her bedroom. He was rattling her, so he poked a little harder. "What about Tahiti? You were teaching in a regular school in a resort town there, weren't you?"

"Yes." She threw her hands up in frustration. "But there's a whole long story behind why I ended up there. It's getting late. Maybe you should get back to your houseguest?"

"Sam makes herself at home." He wasn't going anywhere until they got to the heart of the matter. "I'd rather talk about what you figured out by living so many other places. Was the grass really so different and so much greener out there, Kline?"

"No." Kline closed her eyes and huffed out a breath. "Maybe I just needed the *option* to live elsewhere. I'd felt so trapped here."

He folded his hands behind his head. "Because of the inequity and the bullying. I know. I was here too, remember? Rachel and Lisa had you convinced you were unattractive and unlikable, when that was the furthest thing from the truth. Admit it. That's what you were running from. And me."

Kline studied her feet, avoiding his gaze. "Yeah. I suppose that's true."

"I'm sorry I bailed on our plans. I wish I'd handled that differently. And that we'd found a way to be together. Can we leave the past in the past and live in the present?"

"Easy for the town's golden boy to say. You're still everyone's hero."

He sat up and put his shoes back on. "Your opinion of me is the only one that matters. I don't know what else I can do to prove that to you so we can get past the hurt, embrace the new people we both are, and try again."

She finally met his gaze again. Her eyes pleaded with his and she whispered, "I'm afraid of being hurt again, Ben. Can't we just stay friends?"

When her eyes misted with tears, he wanted to hug her, but the way she'd wrapped her arms tightly around her middle, as if protecting herself, showed she clearly didn't want to be touched. Yet her uncertainty gave him hope she was considering a fresh start. "You don't kiss me like you just want to be my friend. I hope you'll stay and do what you really love to do. Teach. And save people. In this case from my dad. Please think about it." He opened the window and climbed out. "Good night."

———

Kline closed the drapes and then crawled under the covers. She hated that Ben knew her so well. She *had* chosen smaller towns when given a choice, because she'd been more comfortable in them. She'd been all alone, for goodness' sake. It'd made it easy to settle in because it was what she knew. And after being in that damned jail cell that she thought she'd die in before she'd been released, she chose Tahiti because it was a safer place for her to be the last months of her contract.

Had Ben asked her mother, or had Mom volunteered all that personal information on where she'd been? And if Ben knew where she was, and wanted her back that badly, why hadn't he tracked her down and told her?

She punched up her pillow that now annoyingly smelled like Ben's sexy aftershave. She tried to push all the thoughts out of her mind that Ben had put there, but it was futile. He was right; she didn't hate

Anderson Butte, per se. It was a great little town. Since she'd been back, people had been kind and welcoming to her. She hadn't run into Lisa Anderson, but Rachel had treated her nicely that first day in the diner. It was the few mean people and the politics that she didn't like.

If she won the election, she'd try to get rid of the things that had made it so challenging to live there. By having a Grant in charge, maybe things would even out and the power that Andersons held would lessen. But then what would she do about Ben? He'd been right. She'd stayed away partly because of her childhood circumstances. She *had* been trying to bury those memories by staying busy in challenging places so she wouldn't have time to think about them—and Ben.

She closed her eyes and huffed out a breath. It was going to be another long, sleepless night. If the man was going to sneak into her bedroom and stir her up like that, he should've at least had the decency to bring her food. Now all she could think about was Thai food and how she couldn't have it in Anderson Butte unless Ben made it for her.

Looked like she'd just have to learn to cook it herself. Or try a relationship with the new and improved Ben.

———

When Ben walked through his front door, Sam was on the couch in the living room, sipping wine and reading a book. She looked up and said, "How'd it go?"

He shucked off his coat and hung it up. "Kline is so damn stubborn. I don't know if she'll consider a thing I said tonight." He sat beside Sam and put his feet up on the coffee table. "Getting Kline to trust me again, and actually consider a relationship with me, is going to be the toughest hurdle."

Sam stood and poured him a glass of wine. When she returned she asked, "So what is it about Kline that you love, Ben?"

He accepted the glass Sam held out and took a long drink, pondering her question. "I don't think it's one thing. Kline and I have known each other our whole lives. In school, Kline made an easy target for the other girls because she was good at sports, tall and skinny with glasses and braces, although I never saw her like that. She was always just . . . Kline. I think that's when I first knew she meant something to me, because it hurt to see her treated that way."

Sam nodded. "And then hormones kicked in and you saw her as a woman? How did that go?"

"Badly." He laughed. "Kline was convinced the mean girls and I were pulling a prank on her. That I couldn't possibly like her more than the 'much prettier girls' in town. It took perseverance to make her understand that I would love her no matter how she looked, and that she was beautiful on the outside too was just a bonus."

"Did you tell her all of that tonight?"

"No. And she wouldn't want to hear it. She's still unsure about having another relationship with me."

"You're definitely between a rock and a hard place here. I don't envy your decision about the clinic and Kline." Sam leaned over and kissed him on the cheek. "For the record, I'd still love you too, even if you were ugly. Good night."

"Smartass." As she walked away chuckling, he threw a pillow at her back. "You were supposed to help me figure out what to do!"

Sam's voice called out from the hallway. "You know what to do. So just do it."

He knew what he wanted. But he truly didn't know how to get them both, so he stood and went to the kitchen to rearrange all the things Sam had moved while she'd helped him cook dinner. He'd been dying to do it since they'd been home.

As he put his kitchen back in order, a plan began to form. First he'd come clean with Kline about why he'd had to stay in Anderson Butte.

Then if he could get Kline to stop overthinking and listen to her heart, maybe she'd realize how much they were still meant to be together.

The way she'd kissed him back earlier proved she wanted him as much as he wanted her.

———

The next morning, Kline tapped lightly on her mother's bedroom door. After some rustling around, a quiet "Come in," sounded, so Kline stepped inside. Her mom sat propped up in bed reading on the tablet Kline had given her. "Good morning, Mom. How are you feeling today?"

Her mom smiled and laid down her story. "Morning, sweetheart. I'm about the same. How are you?"

"Great." Kline sat on the side of the bed. "I found a doctor in Denver for you to see. We have an appointment next Monday afternoon."

Her mother picked up her mug of coffee from the nightstand and frowned into it. "No, Monday afternoon doesn't work. I have a . . . thing with Ruth." She quickly looked away.

"A thing?" Her mom was making excuses again.

"Uh-huh. Ruth and I are planning a surprise."

"No worries. I'll talk to Ruth and clear you. I'm sure she'll understand that your health is more important than your 'thing.'" Kline stood to go. "But first I have an appointment with Tara. I need to get ahold of her father to put a stop to the mayor's latest antics. Can I get you anything before I go?"

Her mom laid down her mug and grabbed Kline's hand. "How about I promise to go to the doctor after the election on Thursday? I didn't want to say, but Ruth's and my plans are to work to get you elected. We're going to make banners and talk to everyone we can, personally, to make this happen. We only have a few days, so I don't want to waste a whole day and a half going to Denver right now."

Ruth wasn't going to vote for her own son? That Ruth would back Kline made her chest warm. Maybe with Ruth's help, a few more Andersons might vote for Kline too.

She'd been doing her own research on how small towns were run. And Nate's father had suggested a few sites and books for her to read, and he'd given her tips for the next debate. She was getting excited at the prospect of a win.

Kline took a serious tone. "Okay. We'll hold off until after the election. And only if you're sure you're feeling up to doing all of that campaigning."

Her mom's head bobbed. "I'm sure!"

"Okay. And I'll go along and stump for myself as soon as I finish up with Tara. But you have to promise me, Mom. No more excuses about seeing the doctor after that."

"Promise." Her mom made a crisscross across her chest with her finger. "I just wish your father could be here to see you become the first Grant to run our town. He'd be so proud of you. And honestly, Kline, just having you here has made me feel so much better."

Her mother did seem better than she had those first few days—other than being tired all the time and staying in bed a good part of the day. Maybe she was just getting older, as she'd pointed out. "I'll change your appointment and let you know. Then I'll catch up with you guys after my meeting."

"Perfect!" Mom threw her covers back and was, oddly, fully dressed as she scurried to her bathroom. Kline would add that to the list of the other weird things her mother had done lately. She shook her head and headed for the door, calling out, "Don't overdo, please."

When she stepped off the front porch, she spotted Nate packing up his car to leave, so she joined him. "Hey there. Guess you found somewhere else to bunk last night, huh?"

Nate grinned as he slapped the rear door closed on his SUV. "Missy and I had a lovely evening." He gave Kline a hug. "I'll walk the paperwork through myself today to stop the mayor. Call you later." Nate got behind the wheel and started the engine.

Hopefully, he'd get the Feds involved in time.

Kline lifted a hand and waited until Nate's car rolled down the drive before she set out to Tara's office. On the short walk there, she noted the mayor's new campaign signs sprouting up on some of the lawns. She'd better get herself some of those too.

Kline reached for the door to Tara's office, but Missy, Tara's assistant, appeared out of nowhere and tugged first. "I'm late. Tara's going to kill me!" Missy let the door close in Kline's face.

Missy being late was as sure as the sun rising every morning. But Nate spending the night couldn't have helped. Funny how she didn't feel a bit jealous about Nate sleeping with other women, like she had with Ben.

After running the options around in her head after Ben had crawled out of her window the night before, she'd come to the conclusion that the possibility of happiness with Ben again should outweigh her fear of being hurt by him. And maybe if she won the election, Anderson Butte would be a better place. One she'd consider living in long term. But that was still a *big* maybe.

But then, no risk, no gain. She'd sworn to live her life to the fullest after she'd gotten out of jail, so no time like the present. She hoped Ben was free to go to dinner with her later so they could discuss things. Run all the possibilities and weigh the risks to their hearts.

Smiling, Kline pulled the door open again, then walked into the reception area. The air smelled too flowery and clean, like most of the dentists' offices she'd been in. Like they were trying to hide the smell of antiseptic and pain. She was glad she was just there for a chat.

Missy joined her again as she slipped into her white lab coat. "Tara said to go on back to her office. Right down that hallway. Sorry about that earlier, I should've said welcome back. It's nice to see you again, Kline."

"You too, Missy." Kline followed the hallway Missy indicated and stopped just outside the open office door. Inside, a blonde woman tapped keys on her computer. "Tara?"

The woman lifted her gaze from the computer screen and smiled. "Hi, Kline. Nice to meet you. Ryan has told me all about you." She stood and held out a hand toward the guest chairs in front of her wide desk. "Have a seat."

Kline was tall, but Tara was even taller—and intimidatingly beautiful. Women like that always made Kline feel frumpy. "Thanks."

Tara's eyes twinkled with amusement as she studied Kline. It was hard to resist the urge to squirm under the scrutiny.

Tara finally said, "Ryan tells me you and he used to talk for hours when he was a kid. Ryan speaking more than ten words in a row was rare when we first met. Now I can't shut the man up sometimes. I realized you might be the only other person who would believe that."

"Yes. I know exactly what you mean." Kline's anxiety melted away as she and Tara laughed. "Ruth was the only one who ever believed *me*."

"Speaking of Mrs. Anderson, she stopped by to campaign for you this morning. She said she's going to make up signs that say, 'Vote for Kline, or find a bullet in your behind.'"

Kline stopped laughing. "She was kidding, right?"

Tara shrugged. "Who knows with Mrs. Anderson. She might just do it."

Ben's sharpshooting grandmother had a reputation for firing first and asking questions later. But she'd never killed anyone—mostly just nicked them. "Maybe I'd better have a chat with her about that, just to be sure. Anyway, I know you're busy so I won't keep you. Were you able to get ahold of your father?"

Tara shook her head. "No. He and my mother are traveling home from Europe today. They'd planned to be at the groundbreaking ceremony next week, but the mayor changing things last night means they'll miss it. My dad won't be happy about that."

Crap! That meant she'd have to go with plan B. "Thanks for checking. I'll have to find another way to fix this."

"Sorry about that. But I wanted to tell you that you have my vote, Kline. I hate how Ryan's father operates. I'll do anything I can to help you get elected." Tara stood and held out her hand for a shake. "Either way, I hope you'll take the teaching job and stay. I have a feeling anyone who can make Ryan talk must be destined to be my friend."

Tara's warm words melted Kline's heart as she returned the handshake. "Thanks. I guess we'll have to wait and see what happens." Kline started to leave but stopped in the doorway. "You moved here from Denver, right? Aren't you missing city life?"

"My mother asks me that all the time." Tara's smile turned dreamy. "I don't miss Denver a bit. I've come to love all the nosy, kind people here. Especially Ryan, of course. He makes me feel like the luckiest woman alive. I'd be happy wherever I lived as long as we're together."

"I have a feeling Ryan would say the same of you." Ryan seemed happier than she'd ever seen him. Could she be happy anywhere if she were with Ben again? "See you at the groundbreaking?"

"I wouldn't miss it. Good luck stopping it."

"Thanks. I'm going to need it." Kline waved and then walked out the door. A stomachache formed at the prospect of what was now her only course of action to stop the digging. After Tara's office door closed behind her, Kline headed for the general store for supplies.

Hopefully, Nate would come through and stop the mayor so she wouldn't have to do it her way.

CHAPTER TWELVE

en tied down the chopper behind the clinic after his flight from
Denver to drop off Sam, and then made his way toward the groundbreaking ceremony across from the hotel. He looked forward to finally
tasting the world-famous whiskey that his grandfather had raved about.

As dusk began to fall, forming long shadows between the trees, his
father's voice rang out over a PA system, outlining all the benefits the
new distillery would bring to the town. Ben weaved through the big
spotlights set up on the ground and the people milling around with
plastic cups of whiskey in their hands. He found the line to get his own
taste and joined the queue. "Hey, Zeke. How are you?"

Kline's uncle turned around. "'Bout time you got here, Ben. You're
probably the only one who can talk Kline out of her crazy plan."

After Zeke got his drink, he stepped aside and waited for Ben to
grab his from the table.

He scooped up a cup and then joined Zeke. "So, what's Kline's
crazy plan?" Ben took a sip of the smooth, dry, woody liquid. If they
could replicate that flavor, no doubt they'd have a hit on their hands.

Zeke lifted his cup in the direction of the huge bulldozer that sat
loudly idling. "See for yourself."

Ben glanced to his right and saw Kline blocking the path of the huge machine. "Seriously?" Ben drained his plastic cup as he moved through the crowd to talk some sense into her. He tossed his cup into a trash bin and then hurried in her direction.

When he reached her, the bulldozer operator was yelling for Kline to step away from the front blade. Kline shook her head and wrapped a long length of heavy chain around the implement. Then she wrapped the chain around her waist and called out, "I can't let you destroy protected land."

Ben leaned over her shoulder and said, "This isn't going to work, Kline."

She turned and lifted her stubborn chin. "If you're not here to be supportive then leave."

"Maybe this is just a symbolic gesture for the crowd, a little scoop, and nothing will be harmed. Have you considered that?"

Kline shook her head. "Your father moved up the groundbreaking before they could pull the building permit. I confirmed with the operator, and he said he was going for the surrounding trees first. But if you'd rather support the actions of a lying, cheating politician, then go on and leave me to this."

Ben glanced up at the huge yellow bulldozer as he debated what to do. The chances of the situation ending well were almost nil. Protesting against his father would practically guarantee the clinic would never be built, but Kline came first and needed his support. "Wouldn't it have been better to have Nate put a stop to this? Legally?"

A loud click sounded as Kline closed a large combination padlock woven through the chain links at her waist. "He's been working on it all day. He called a few minutes ago and asked me to stall."

His grandmother hobbled over and cocked her head. "What have we here? A real live sit-in? I haven't done something like this since the sixties. Chain me in too."

"Nope." Ben clasped his grandmother's arm to stop her. "Don't even think about it." That'd be all he needed. His grandmother was even more stubborn than Kline. "You know you can't stand for long."

Grandma jerked her arm from his grasp. "Well, then get me a chair, Benjamin, and we'll chain it in too. I agree with what Kline's doing here."

He wanted to punch something. "I'm not chaining my grandmother to a bulldozer—"

"What the hell is going on?" his father bellowed from the street as his face turned a concerning deep red. "Mother, get away from there right now. And Kline, get off my land!"

Most of the town had moved closer to see who was going to win the standoff.

Ben leaned close to Kline and whispered, "Call Nate and see how much more time you need." Then he straightened and said loudly so everyone could hear, "Dad, let's just enjoy the whiskey tonight and leave the bulldozing until we know it'll be legal."

His father slipped his hand into his coat pocket and produced a piece of paper as he approached. Waving it in Ben's face, he shouted, "This building permit says it's legal. Until I hear otherwise, we're moving along with our plans. Talk some sense into your girlfriend or I'll have her arrested for trespassing."

Ben pulled his father to the side. "Having Kline arrested might be bad for your reelection. It makes you look like a bully."

"I'm not letting her ruin this for us. Take her and go or I'll have you both thrown in jail."

"Dad, you need to calm down. Your blood pressure is probably through the roof right now. Give me a few minutes and I'll—"

"Nope. I want the both of you gone right now."

"Fine." Ben slowly walked back to Kline and his grandmother. "We're out of time. Let's go, Kline."

She shook her head. "Not until the state troopers arrive. Nate said they're almost here."

"My father's serious." Ben glanced back at his dad, who stood off to the side, screaming something at Ryan. The deep frown on Ryan's face didn't bode well for them. "Let the troopers handle this."

Ryan joined them. "Kline and Ben, I'll need to ask you to move to the street or I'll have to arrest you. You're both trespassing."

"Dad really told you to arrest me?"

Ryan nodded. "So don't make me."

Now it was Ben's blood pressure that spiked to dangerous levels. He held out his hands. "Cuff me, then."

Kline's eyes grew wide. "Ryan, Ben had nothing to do with this. He was trying to talk me into leaving."

His father rejoined them. "I want them both arrested. Now, Ryan!"

Ryan ran a hand down his face. "Dad, let's be reasonable here."

"Arrest them now!"

Ryan stared into Ben's eyes as he slowly removed the cuffs from his belt. "We'll sort this all out at the station. Sorry, bud."

The cold metal slowly cinched around Ben's wrists. He couldn't believe his father had done that.

Ryan turned to Kline. "Will you please leave on your own, Kline? For me?"

Kline pursed her lips and shook her head. Ben had to admire her passion.

She said, "You're going to have to arrest me too. What the mayor is doing is wrong."

Ryan lifted the lock and examined it. "I can have my deputy bring me a set of loppers that will take care of this, or you can give me the combination."

Grandma said, "Don't give it to him, Kline. Make him lop that chain off!"

When a loud commotion sounded, Ben turned his head to investigate. He called out, "The troopers are here."

"Great!" Kline quickly entered the combination and then slipped out of the chains. "We'll be on our way then. Let Ben go, Ryan."

Dad shook his head. "Nope. I'm still pressing charges, Ryan. Take them away."

After their grandmother whispered something in Ryan's ear, he huffed out a breath and slipped his hand around Kline's arm. "Let's go, you two."

Kline threw her big purse over her shoulder, then kept looking back to see what was going on until they were too far away to see anymore. "I hope the Feds arrest the mayor."

Ryan said. "Thanks to you, my dad didn't get the chance to do anything wrong—yet."

Ben stopped and held out his cuffed hands for release. "Then let us go. We'll both just go home and stay out of things. Right, Kline?"

She shrugged. "Fine."

"Nope." Ryan hauled them both toward Town Hall. "Ben's not on call so you two aren't going anywhere but jail tonight. If you're good, I'll let you out in the morning. Grandma said it'd give you guys a chance to quit dancing around your situation and work things out."

"Seriously, Ryan?" Kline's voice rose two octaves.

"Yep. And you'll get another hour for every protest. I'll have Gloria bring you some breakfast in the morning." Ryan opened the front door to Town Hall and waited for them to pass by. "We just got new mattresses so the beds should be nice and comfy. The second cell is being painted, so you'll both have to share."

Ben exchanged a look with Ryan. When his brother's lips formed a slight grin, Ben had his answer. Ryan was putting them in the same cell on purpose. Probably part of Gram's idea to help them work things out. Fine by him, but he wasn't sure if Kline would be okay with that.

After they made their way to the back of the police station in silence, Ryan opened up the cage and held out a hand in invitation. "Welcome to the drunk tank." Ryan unlocked Ben's handcuffs and then closed the metal door shut with a loud clank. "Enjoy your evening." Ryan turned and walked away. A few minutes later, all the lights went out. The barred window allowed stingy streaks from the rising moon to illuminate the concrete floor.

Kline sat on one of the two cots lined up on either side of the cell. She bounced up and down and made the springs squeak. "Not so bad, I guess." She frowned as she examined the sink and toilet. "Although that's a little like a men's room . . . exposed. Maybe I can hold out until morning."

"Seriously? Even after living in a tent in Africa?"

"Especially after living in a tent in Africa."

He sat on the opposite mattress. "For the sake of your bladder, I promise not to look." He dug his phone from his pocket to check his messages and distract himself.

Being trapped in a cage was making him sweat. He had a certain routine before he went to sleep at night.

Kline stood and then crossed the cell and sat next to him. She dug through her purse. "Let's take inventory of the food supply."

In an attempt to stave off his growing anxiety, he drew a deep breath and closed his eyes, trying to visualize something pleasant. Like a wide-open beach with waves crashing against the shore. "I don't think we'll starve to death before morning," he snapped, instantly regretting it.

"No, but I haven't been sent to bed without my dinner in a long time. You must be hungry too." She laid a cool hand on his cheek. When he opened his eyes, she frowned. "Are you okay, Ben?"

"I'm fine." He was more focused on taking deep breaths and remaining calm than eating.

She leaned her back against the cinder block as she pulled something from her purse. "I have part of a candy bar in here. It'll make a good appetizer." She handed the loose wrapper to him.

"Who leaves a quarter of a half a stick of chocolate? Why didn't you just eat all four sticks?"

"More precisely, that'd be an eighth. You've obviously never had to ration your chocolate while living in a tent. Habits die hard."

He rolled his eyes. "*Fred* never runs out of chocolate. My grandma would shoot him if he did. She's the only one I've met who hoards chocolate like you do." He popped the tiny square of candy bar into his mouth. Maybe he *was* hungry. "What other partially consumed food do you have in there, hoarder?"

"Keep up the attitude and you'll go hungry, Mr. Cranky." She found her phone and turned on the flashlight app. "Ah. Here's a—never mind. You'll hate this one." She went back to digging and then pulled out a different breakfast bar. "Your main course. I'll eat the other."

"Wait!" He grabbed her hand to stop her. "What's the other? You got me into this mess, so I should get first pick." He needed to quit barking at Kline, but anxiety swept through him like a rising flood.

"Fine. But you won't like it when you see what it's made of." She handed over the little package and shivered. "It's getting cold in here." Kline scooted closer to his side and shone her light so he could see what was in his makeshift dinner.

Her warm body against his made it a bit easier to draw a deep breath. He read the label. "It has chocolate, so far so good. Coconut and . . . caramel? No thanks."

"Told you. I've never met anyone who so freakishly hates caramel." She switched out their bars, then Kline opened hers and took a bite. "You wouldn't even kiss me unless I brushed my teeth after eating it."

When she shivered again, he wrapped his arm around her and pulled her close. "Caramel is sticky. Maybe I was just looking out for your oral health."

"Nice try." She turned and blew a big puff of air in his face. It nearly gagged him.

Kline chuckled. "You clearly just had a visceral reaction to the scent of caramel assaulting your olfactory system. As predicted."

"Did other guys find your constant need to prove your little hypotheses correct annoying or cute?" He slowly chewed his peanut-butter-and-chocolate breakfast bar to make his meager dinner last longer.

"You're the only one who's ever been annoyed by it. Which made doing that just now so much fun." She finished off her bar and then started digging in her purse again. "Here. I found another one, sans caramel. You can have it."

He split it in half and then handed over her piece. "Why do you have so many breakfast bars in your purse? Do you ration these like you do chocolate?"

"No. My other purses are still in moving boxes until I find a house. I had this one on the plane ride home from Tahiti and just haven't ever cleaned it out. The probability of missed flights or lost luggage is on the rise these days, so I carry all the basics with me."

"Hence the need for a purse big enough to carry a bowling ball." Kline was just like her mother that way.

"Be glad I do, or you'd be starving. It pays to be prepared."

"I'd agree if you had some power tools in there to bust us out." He finished off his half a bar and then slowly folded the wrapper. Maybe teaching himself origami for the next few hours would keep his mind off things. Until they went to sleep, anyway. Then he wasn't sure what he'd do.

While Kline busied herself digging around in her purse looking for God knew what next, he grabbed another used wrapper and started folding.

As he attempted to make a duck, he said, "You don't happen to have some bottled water in there, do you?" The thought of drinking from the sink didn't appeal, but he might have to risk it. The peanut butter made him thirsty.

"No. But I do have these from the airplane." She withdrew six little bottles of alcohol.

"I'm starting to see the benefits of the giant purse." He opened two little bottles and handed her one. "Cheers." He clinked his minibar drink against hers.

"Cheers." She took a swallow and one of her eyes squinted. "That packed a punch."

"Yeah. Good stuff for airplane booze." He slowly drank from his little bottle, savoring the long, slow burn traveling down his throat.

"The older guy sitting next to me on the plane kept pulling out his black credit card—you know, the kind only rich people have?—and insisted on buying me drinks. I repeatedly told him I didn't want any, but he wouldn't take no for an answer. I stashed all of them in my purse and then just drank the soda mixer. He got so drunk he could barely make a pass at me by the time we landed, so that was good."

Anger, and maybe a good dose of jealousy, made Ben crush the wrapper in his hand. He growled, "Ask to be moved next time."

"Calm down. The guy was a married, harmless flirt. He wasn't *really* interested in me."

"You still don't have any clue how beautiful you are." He finished off his drink, hoping it'd help with his still-growing anxiety. "It drives me nuts when you belittle yourself like that. Of course he wanted you. Any guy with a pulse would. Like your *bird* friend."

"Okaaaay, still grumpy, I see." Kline produced a roll of candy from the depths of her magic Mary Poppins purse. "And now for the dessert course. Your favorite. Cherry. A little sugar might brighten up the gloomy cloud in here named Ben."

"Thanks." He accepted one and popped it into his mouth. "You should have one too, caramel breath."

Kline gave him a shoulder bump. "Lucky for you, I have a travel toothbrush and toothpaste in here that should make me kiss-worthy once more." She grabbed her little kit and walked toward the sink.

Was that an invitation to kiss her? He folded his wrapper while pondering the kiss-worthy part. Then he sent a text to his brother asking him to turn up the heat.

Ryan wrote back, "Nope. Body heat is your only option."

He was going to kill his brother the next time he saw him.

When Kline rejoined him, she switched off the light on her phone. "Better conserve my battery. I'll just send a quick text to my mom and then shut my phone off."

He blinked to let his eyes adjust to the dark while Kline tapped on her phone, and then he started messing with the wrapper again. Luckily, the moon was almost full, and there was a dim green safety light that shone out in the hallway so they weren't in complete darkness.

She whispered, "You never used to stay mad at me for this long, Ben. Especially when I cooked for you." Kline's soft hand reached out and covered his. "I'm truly sorry you got dragged into this with me."

"What makes you think I'm mad at you?" He weaved his fingers through hers and gave a quick squeeze. "It's not like we've really been arrested. Ryan did this to get my father off everyone's back."

"So what's making you so cranky? Is being locked up in here stressing you out?"

He hated to admit it. "I just have routines that I like to do . . ."

She nodded. "Like your straightening habit?"

"Yeah." He stood to pace. "But it's not a compulsion or anything. I'll be fine."

"Okay." Kline opened up her purse and dumped everything out on the bed. "Do you want to help me organize all of this?"

He smiled and sat beside her again. "That's a lot of crap, Kline." But he was grateful for the distraction. As he started in on the pile, he whispered, "Thank you."

She leaned over and kissed his cheek. "If you do a good job with this I'll let you organize my bedroom closet when we get out."

"Deal!"

CHAPTER THIRTEEN

With her purse as organized as it had ever been, Kline shivered on the bunk and watched as her cellmate paced back and forth like a caged animal. After explaining again that what he had was just normal anxiety and not anything serious, Ben finished off his fourth little bottle of liquor.

She understood the unease that being in a locked cage could cause some people. She'd overcome that while spending six long weeks in a foreign jail waiting for justice to be served. She hadn't been sure she'd ever get out of that hellhole. Luckily Nate had been relentless in his efforts to get her out. She'd be in debt to him forever for it.

One night in Anderson Butte's pokey was like staying in a five-star hotel compared to that dank, stinky jail cell. Except using a pot to go to the bathroom in front of other female prisoners was still easier than the thought of using the toilet in front of Ben. She'd never done that while they lived together and she didn't want to start now. Some things just needed to remain private between men and women.

Worried about Ben, she stood and intercepted him by slipping her arms around his waist. "Hey. Stop. Maybe we should just go to bed."

She hoped that last drink he'd slammed would start to catch up with him and make him calm down.

"Good idea." He pulled her against his warm body, buried his face in her neck, and whispered, "I need you, Kline."

Needed her? Like sex? Or to help with his anxiety?

His mouth landed on hers and answered that question.

The kiss was hard, urgent, and downright sexy. He ran his hands along her cheeks and tilted her head the way he wanted it so he could take more. His usual slow, sweet kisses were great but whatever had him so wound up was *really* working for her.

Maybe he was the one who'd learned new tricks in their years apart. She really shouldn't be so eager to sign up for his class. She'd vowed to stay strong and not sleep with Ben until they'd talked, but she was too intrigued to stop as he backed her toward the cot.

By the time her knees hit the bed, he'd unzipped her jacket and tossed it aside. His warm mouth on hers made her spine go weak and her knees wobble. They really needed to have a serious conversation before they did this.

Her fingers, on the other hand, had a mind of their own and had unzipped his coat. Without breaking their kiss, her busy hands ignored her brain's warning to stop and started on the buttons of his shirt. It was a race to see who could undress the other quicker. No time for doubts or regrets because his hands roaming her body turned her hormones up to DEFCON 1 and they were holding steady. She had no intention of stopping now, even though they should.

Seconds later, after they were both stripped to their underwear, Ben scooped her up and laid her gently on the bed. Instead of diving right in like her hormones voted for, he whispered, "God, you're even more beautiful than I remembered."

Her heart threatened to ooze right past her ribcage until she reminded herself to stay strong. They were just going to have sex. To put out the fire that burned between them, that's all. There were to be no feelings rekindled yet until they made a few things clear between them. They had never been good at communicating and that needed to change if they were going to resume their relationship. She needed to come to terms with living in Anderson Butte or it'd never work.

But then he laid his lips on hers again and everything inside went right back to goo. The kiss was so tender and sweet. As if she were suddenly fragile and precious. How was it possible that this kiss was even sexier than the rough ones earlier that had driven her wild?

He slowly lifted his mouth from hers and said, "I love you, Kline."

She froze as he rained kisses up and down the sides of her neck. She should say something, but what? Her mind raced for a response. She was afraid to tell him how she felt because they hadn't resolved their issues. If they couldn't do that, then why make it worse by declaring her love for him too?

But the rough stubble on his cheeks kept sending delicious tingles up her spine, making it hard to concentrate. Ben had her breathless and weak even before he whispered, "I missed you so much I thought I'd die from it."

Hot tears stung her eyes. She'd felt that same familiar ache. One that explained where the expression "brokenhearted" must have originated. A pain and longing so deep, it felt like her soul being ripped from her body.

"Ben, I—"

He cut her off with another kiss so long and deep she couldn't think or feel anything other than the hot lust coursing through her body. Taking his time to please her like he'd always done before, he slowly unclasped the front of her bra, his fingers softly caressing the valley between her breasts. When both of his palms cupped her aching flesh, he groaned. She wanted to touch him too, so she ran her hands down the hard ridges of his broad back, welcoming the heat radiating from him like a furnace. Ben still had the most beautiful body—lean muscles covered with smooth, olive skin.

She sighed at the familiar pleasure as he took the time to explore and caress her skin with his hands and mouth on his southward journey down her body. Everywhere he touched made her skin feel alive with heat and desire. Her heart pounded so hard in anticipation it was hard to draw a full breath. Would it be like before? Or had her memories over the years enhanced the way Ben made love to her, never failing to leave her sated and satisfied? No other man had been able to replicate the feeling.

After Ben had removed her panties, her hands dove to his boxers and inched them off, finding him hard and ready. Both naked now, with their chests heaving, hands exploring each other, kissing each other, desperately searching for more . . . this was *just* how she'd remembered Ben. They could never get enough of each other.

It became harder to hold any thoughts other than *yes, like that,* and *more* as he slid his fingers inside her. He remembered just how she liked to be touched and made her back arch as she cried out in grateful pleasure. "Now, now, now, Ben!" Everything inside her quivered for release.

"Still so demanding." Ben chuckled as he rummaged around for the condom in his wallet. After what felt like an eternity, his warm body covered hers again. He took her face in his hands and stared into her eyes. His lips tilted into a sexy, sin-filled smile that made her shudder in anticipation. Gazes still locked, he slowly entered her. She wrapped her legs around his waist and moved her hips in time with the steady rhythm he set. He lowered his mouth and kissed her, dissolving every bone she had left. When he stilled, her body continued to clench relentlessly around his.

His stopping tortured her, and at the same time made her want him even more. Ben knew just what he was doing and thankfully did it so damn well.

Staring into his heavy-lidded eyes, she smiled. "Still so mean."

"Mean, just the way you like it." He leaned down and kissed her as he drove his point home.

Each hard thrust sent her closer to the place she craved, holding her captive under his spell, making her want to beg for more. She gasped for enough air as Ben finally delivered her to that place only he ever had. One filled with such intense pleasure that she finally gave in to the sweet pain and let go a moment before he did.

Breathless and perfectly sated, she lay under him on the small bunk, lightly raking her fingers through his thick hair just as she always did after he made love to her. She didn't have that familiar need to leave as fast as she could like she had with other men. She was happy right where she was. As happy as she could remember being in a very long time.

When realization hit, a wave of panic filled her.

Had she just made the biggest mistake of her life by sleeping with him before they'd worked things out? She had plans to live in Denver in the long run. Maybe after her time in Anderson Butte was up, she could convince him to move away with her. Then they could be together like before without all of his family distractions. But he'd be miserable without his family.

Oh God, what had she just done? Could she live in Anderson Butte long term? Her heart couldn't bear to be broken all over again if things didn't work out with Ben.

Ben rolled off of Kline as much as he could on the tiny bed. He'd missed the way her fingers lightly combed through his hair and her warm, soft body under him. Kline had a way of making him feel whole and content. All the anxiety he'd felt earlier was gone.

He finally cracked an eye open just as a single tear leaked out of the corner of Kline's closed eyes. "What's wrong?"

"Nothing," she whispered. "I just . . . missed you too."

Nice to hear, but she didn't say she loved him back. Baby steps. "It's getting colder." He wrestled the blankets out from under them until they were covered.

When they were settled, Kline whispered, "After I left, I kept thinking that any day you'd show up. You said you loved me, and yet you never came after me."

"Because I couldn't at first. And when you never came home, I figured you still hated me for bailing on our plans." He didn't want to ruin the great moment they'd just shared by telling her the whole ugly truth, but it looked like he had no choice. Although he wouldn't go so far as to tell her that losing the election was the only way for him to get his clinic. She'd throw the election in a heartbeat rather than deny him his dream. And if she did that, she might not have a reason to stay once she discovered her mother was fine. He needed to figure out how to convince Kline she belonged in Anderson Butte with him.

A line creased her forehead. "What stopped you from coming after me?"

He paused to get the words just right. "Do you remember that crappy old apartment we had sophomore year of college?"

"Who could forget roaches as big as the mice? Thank God for that scholarship you got so we could move."

"It wasn't exactly a scholarship. I wanted a better place for us so I asked my dad for a loan. I figured I'd make plenty after I graduated and could pay him back over time."

Kline's eyes grew wide. "You knew I'd never agree to borrow money from your father. So you lied to me?"

"I didn't want you to have to live like that." Why couldn't she see that he'd done it all for her? He would have done anything to get her out of that hellhole.

She huffed out a breath. "So you justified lying to me because you were saving me? If I thought it was so bad, I could have always moved to the dorms. The point was that we were together and that's all that mattered."

"Technically, I never told you it was a scholarship; you assumed that. But it gets worse."

"I'm still having a hard time with the lie, but go on."

Crap. She was really going to be mad when she heard the rest. But he'd already stepped in it and there was no escape. Literally. "Every semester I'd tell my dad how much money I thought we'd need, and then he'd write up a new agreement. I read the first one all the way through, but after that I just signed where he pointed when we were home for school breaks. By the time I figured out what he'd changed, it was too late. I had unknowingly already agreed to his terms."

Kline groaned. "What did he slip in there?"

"That after med school I had to stay here and work for five years at a reduced salary. I should have known better, and felt like an idiot when I figured it out. I didn't tell you because I was afraid you'd put your plans on hold and wait for me."

"So you did what you thought was best for me, without asking, as usual? And you didn't trust me enough to be honest with me?" She pulled away and reached for her clothes. Calmly, because Kline hated to fight, she said, "I was entitled to make my own choice. I'm not one of your siblings who you still feel the need to parent, Ben. And you broke my heart on top of it."

"Wait, Kline." He reached out to pull her back into bed, but she danced out of the way as she slipped into her jeans. "I wanted you to have your adventures. And after that, I hoped you'd finally realize that you actually prefer small-town life. I was afraid you'd resent me if you stayed. That would have been worse than letting you go."

Kline zipped up her jacket and crossed to the other bed. After she burrowed under the covers, she said, "This isn't about me; it's about you. I think you actually thrive on people needing you. You need to focus on your own happiness and quit saving people who don't need saving."

"And you need to stop running away from and avoiding the problems in your life." He regretted his words as soon as they'd left his lips. He should've just let her go process things on the other bunk. She probably would've come around eventually. Now she'd get quiet and avoid dealing with it. As usual.

"Good night, Ben," she said as polite as could be.

"Night." All Kline could focus on was the lie, not his good intentions. But then, he should've never lied to her in the first place. He should've stood up to his father and refused the terms of his underhanded contract.

After he'd used the facilities and dressed again, he climbed back into bed, tucked his hands under his head, and stared at the ceiling. He'd prefer Kline yell at him or take a swipe at him rather than withdraw into herself. The only time she'd ever raised her voice to him was at the end of their relationship. When she'd thrown her ring at him.

Kline suddenly threw her covers back. "Dammit. I can't hold it. Put your pillow over your head, please."

"That's ridiculous. Just go."

"Please, Ben?"

"Fine." He pulled his pillow over his face and continued stewing over her.

Kline was wrong about one thing. He didn't thrive on being needed. He just *was* . . . needed. Did she honestly think he enjoyed being a buffer between his father and his family, not to mention most of the town? He did it to keep peace. Of course he'd change his plans in a heartbeat if one of his sisters needed him. They were both single mothers. Or, they had been until recently. And Ryan? He needed his ass kicked to yank him out of that shell he tended to retreat into. Until he'd met Tara, anyway.

But then, Casey had said some of the same things to him the night before. That he needed to quit worrying about his adult siblings and make himself happy. Maybe he *had* treated Kline like he did his brother and sisters rather than as his equal. He moved the pillow from his face and saw she was back in bed. "I think I screwed up one more thing. I arranged a little surprise get-together for your birthday tomorrow night. Sorry, I should have asked you first."

"Thank you, but I don't know if my mom has plans for me." She rolled over and faced the block wall.

"I invited her too."

Kline sighed. "Naturally."

Yeah. Maybe he needed to work on that. He'd stop organizing her life like he did all the other parts of his. And he'd be more honest with her in the future. "If I promise to stop making decisions for you without asking, will you come back over here and sleep with me?"

She didn't answer for a moment, but then finally said, "I think it's best if I stay over here."

"It's awful cold in my bunk. How's yours?"

"Freezing. But I'm still so mad at you. If you had just trusted me enough to tell me the truth, we could've worked things out."

"You mean like we'd be married with two kids by now, worked it out? Or you would've hated me for making you stay and have two kids, worked it out?"

She rolled over and faced him again. "I thought having to raise your brother and sisters made you never want kids of your own."

"My niece and nephews changed my mind. You'll meet them tomorrow night—if you choose to come."

"Like I'd be that big of a jerk to not come after everyone is expecting me." She punched up the pillow under her head. After a few moments, she said, "And I think I might want kids now too."

His heart nearly soared out of his chest. She'd been staunchly against bringing any more children into the world when so many needed a good home. So, they both had changed. "Sam asked me to be a sperm donor for her."

"Seriously?" Kline sat straight up. "But . . ."

"I'm still thinking about it." He suppressed his grin at her strong reaction. Maybe she did still love him enough to want to have kids with him. "But it's hard to concentrate when my teeth are chattering. I need your body heat to make a sound decision."

"Fine. But only because I'm freezing too. We probably won't get any sleep otherwise." Kline threw her covers back. "But now is no time to make that big of a decision."

"Okay. I'll think about it later." He moved over so she could slide in beside him, then pulled her close. "Much better."

She nodded against his chest. "I haven't had a birthday party since I left. My mom always sent a gift and called if I had access to a phone, but I never mentioned it to anyone. Didn't want to make a big deal out of it. So, thank you for that, Ben."

"Welcome. Sweet dreams." He'd show her what she'd been missing. Family and real friends who loved her.

"You too." She slid closer.

Hopefully, she'd forget how mad she was at him when she saw the party he'd planned for her. Well, his sisters were doing most of the work, but it'd been his idea. Maybe it would end up doubling as a welcome-home-to-stay party.

CHAPTER FOURTEEN

As they snuggled together on the small jailhouse cot, Kline's back was frozen in all the spots Ben's arms left uncovered, but her front was nice and toasty. Morning—when they'd turn up the heat again in Town Hall—couldn't come quick enough. Along with Gloria and their breakfast. All Kline could think about was Gloria's French toast. Made with thick-sliced bread, drenched with melted butter and warm syrup, and topped off with powdered sugar . . . she needed to stop.

It was already hard enough to sleep with her stomach growling, her back freezing, and Ben's earlier revelation still pinging about her brain. She'd never known him to lie before. Especially to her.

It hurt.

And made her question how many other things he might have lied to her about when they'd been together.

Lying was a deal-breaker with her. All those girls in school who pretended to be her friends so they could get closer to her guy friends had taught her early on to be wary of people. She'd caught these same girls laughing behind her back about how skinny and gangly she'd been in middle school. It was probably why her current circle of close friends wasn't a big one, and mostly consisted of men like Nate who she wasn't interested in dating.

How different might her and Ben's lives be if only he'd told the truth? She definitely would have waited for him. There was no doubt about that. But if she had, would she have ever been able to help the kids in Africa? Learned about so much culture in Europe and had the opportunity to teach all over the world? She'd loved it all, but now it was time to grow up and be an adult. Buy a house and car and settle down like most others her age had.

Would she have resented Ben if she hadn't been able to see the world? If she had stayed and started a family with him she certainly wouldn't have been able to travel. If they'd had a couple of kids would that have made the sacrifice worth it? She hadn't had any idea how much she'd come to love kids. Teaching them had made her want one or two of her own.

Ben always meant well. He'd proved that through the years as he came to the rescue of his brother and sisters all their lives, but she needed to be with a man who treated her as a partner and a full-grown woman. One who would be a top priority in his life, not just one more person to take care of. She didn't need a protector, dammit!

She rolled over to get her back warm for a few minutes and made Ben shiver.

"You're a block of ice." He sat up and took off his jacket, balling it up against the cold cinder block wall behind him. "Trade places with me so you can be warm on both sides."

"Thanks. But only if we take turns to be fair." She scooted between the warm jacket and his chest, nuzzling her face into the crook of his neck. He smelled like shaving cream and . . . sexy Ben.

When she'd been missing chocolate and her mom while staring at the cracks in that jail cell years ago, trying to block out the stifling heat and pungent odors, she'd close her eyes and recall the familiar scent of pine trees and cool lake water. Inevitably, Ben's unique scent would sneak its way in too before she'd push it away, along with all the memories of him. Thankfully, Nate's politically powerful father had been able to bust her out, or who knew how long she'd have had to stay in that awful place. She hated to even think about those six weeks of her life, so she focused on Ben again.

They used to tell each other everything, or so she thought. She'd never kept anything from him. It made her mad all over again.

After a few minutes, she was finally warm on both sides and trying her best to keep her anger at Ben alive, but just couldn't muster the energy. She'd revisit it tomorrow after she'd slept on it. And had some food. For the moment, it was awful nice to cuddle.

The next morning, when the overhead lights switched on above their bunk, Kline blinked her eyes open and lifted her head to see if Ben was awake. She was in the same position as she'd been when she'd fallen asleep.

Her hormones weren't the least bit angry at Ben, and they were happy to remind her of that. His hair was rumpled and his full lips were tilted into a cute grin. His five o'clock shadow made him even more irresistible.

He whispered, "Happy birthday."

She'd almost forgotten. "Thank you. But how come you didn't wake me to trade places?"

He pulled her closer and laid a kiss on top of her head. "Because I was fine. But now I'm starving." He leaned his head back and yelled, "Ryan!"

There was no answer.

Ben said, "I forgot. It's Saturday. No one comes in unless they have to. Maybe a janitor turned on the lights. I hope we're not stuck in here all day. Let me text Ryan."

As Ben tapped his phone, Gloria appeared with her hands full of to-go boxes. "Looks like you two had a cozy night." It must've been Gloria who'd turned on the lights.

Ben jumped up and approached the door. "We froze. And we're starving. Thanks."

"Morning, Gloria." Kline threw the covers back and joined Ben at the door so Gloria could see she was dressed too. Otherwise, the news that they were back together would be all over town within the hour, but that wasn't true because they had things to work out. Well, except for the sleeping together again part. That had gone just right.

Gloria chuckled. "If that's your story. Help me with the door there, will you, Ben?"

Ben turned the handle and then swung open the heavy bars. "My brother is a dead man."

What? The door hadn't even been locked?

Gloria handed over the boxes with a smirk. "Bet you two worked up quite the appetite last night . . . trying to stay warm."

Kline wanted to crawl under the bunk in embarrassment. They'd definitely burned the few calories they'd had for dinner as they ravished each other. Thoughts of that part of their evening made her want to grin—until she recalled the rest of the night. Ignoring Gloria's comment, Kline said, "I hope whatever is in here involves syrup."

"Of course it does." Gloria laid her hands on her wide, uniformed hips. "You'll have to take me out back and let Ruth shoot me the day I can't remember a regular's favorite order. Happy birthday, by the way. Eat up, and then Ryan says you can go on home."

Kline peeked inside her box, thrilled to see the French toast she'd craved all night. She wrapped her free arm around Gloria and hugged her. "Best birthday present ever. Thank you!" It melted her heart that Gloria remembered even after all the years that had passed. Kline sat on the bunk and dug in.

Ben sat beside her. "Thanks, Gloria. See you later tonight?" He dove into his cheese omelet with hash browns on the side.

Gloria's beehive hairdo, filled with pens, bobbed. "Wouldn't miss it for the world. Gotta get back now, though. Bye."

Kline mumbled around her buttery, sweet bite, "Bye."

Ben, sated from their hearty breakfast, walked beside Kline as they headed home. She'd become quiet again.

Just as he was going to ask what she was thinking, his phone hummed in his pocket. He pulled it out and noted the long list of texts and e-mails.

Kline said, "Let me guess. Your dad called, and at least one of your siblings needs something from you right away."

He hated to admit she was right. "I'm planning a big party tonight, remember? People probably have questions. Like what's Kline's favorite flavor of cake these days, chocolate or vanilla?"

"Chocolate, of course. What does your dad want?"

He had a good idea what his dad wanted, but didn't want to open the e-mail in front of Kline. "Don't know. So, the party is at my house. Does six work for you?"

"Yes, I'm looking forward to it." Kline led the way up the steps of her mom's front porch. "Can I do anything to help?"

"Nope. Just show up." He laid his hands on her arms and gave them a light squeeze. "Are we okay?"

Kline's forehead rumpled. "I don't know. I'm still trying to wrap my head around what you told me last night. Moving out of the friend zone was probably a mistake."

"How can you say that?" He leaned closer. "The sleeping together part was *fantastic*."

"Yeah. That much hasn't changed. But have we? Changed enough so that we don't make the same mistakes all over again?" She crossed her arms and glanced at her feet. Never a good sign when she wouldn't look him in the eyes.

"I think we have." He laid a finger under her chin and slowly tilted her gaze back to his. "I'm sorry I lied to you, Kline. And I'm sorry I let my father manipulate me like that. I promise I'll never let that happen again." He stared into her eyes, hating the uncertainty there. "But you still need a little time to work out your feelings, right?"

Her eyes misted as she nodded. He hated to see her cry. She so rarely did that it ripped his guts out. "I'm not going anywhere."

He laid a kiss on her soft lips. She tasted sweet. Like maple syrup and powdered sugar.

He ended their kiss and opened his eyes, but didn't pull away. Kline stared right back, as if searching for something in him.

He wanted to lighten the mood, so he leaned his forehead against hers and said, "You don't have to worry about last night. I promise not to press charges against you for getting me drunk and then taking advantage of me."

She chuckled. "Gee, thanks. You're so much more understanding than my last cellmates."

"Cellmates?" He leaned back so he could see her face. "Were you arrested—"

"Not telling." When he started to ask again, she laid a finger across his lips. "Maybe you don't know me as well as you think you do? I'm not the same woman I was when I left."

It was probably just another protesting thing. "You know *me* well enough to know it's going to drive me nuts until you fill in the blanks."

"Yep." She hitched her brows. "See you later."

"I'm going to get it out of you tonight, one way or another." He leaned back and stuffed his hands in his pockets to squelch the urge to scoop her up and take her home with him. She needed space.

After the front door closed behind Kline, he turned and slowly walked down the steps. Being patient was damn near killing him after last night. Especially when she'd finally smiled at him like she used to.

His phone vibrated in his pocket again, so he took it out and checked the display. His father. He was probably calling because he hadn't gotten an instant answer to his e-mail. His father's house was Ben's next stop anyway. He wanted to see if his chances were any better for getting his clinic now that the Feds had shut the bulldozing down. He ignored the ringing cell and scrolled through his texts. After getting thrown in jail, it took all Ben had not to answer that call and tell his father to go to hell. But he wanted his clinic more than he wanted vindication.

For now, anyway.

As he walked the short distance to his father's house, he answered Casey's text about Kline's preference in cake. Then he put his phone away, drew a deep breath for patience, and climbed his father's porch stairs. Ben knocked, and then returned his hands to his jacket pockets to keep them warm.

After a few moments, his stepmother, Sue Ann, who was only a few years older than him, swung the door open. She slapped her hands on her recently liposuctioned hips and pursed her red, artificially plumped-up lips. "'Bout time you got in touch. Your daddy was screaming like a howler monkey with a splinter in his butt." The former beauty queen from Texas stepped aside to let him pass.

"Good morning to you too, Sue Ann. Is he in the study?"

"Where else? That man spends more time in there than is healthy. You should get on him again for working too much, Ben."

"It all falls on deaf ears."

"Tell me about it." She walked beside him down the long hall. "I told him he needs to lose a few pounds too, but he has to have his daily sweets."

Said the woman who ate whatever she wanted, and instead of dieting, flew to Denver and had all her extra fat sucked out. Probably best to stay silent.

As usual, Sue Ann filled the void. "I'm thinking I might just have a few more headaches at night if he doesn't start listening to me. If you know what I mean?"

He remained silent on that matter too. The last thing he wanted to talk about was their sex life. Thank goodness Kline wasn't the type of woman who played games like that to get what she wanted.

The study door stood open so Sue Ann knocked on the frame. "Ben is finally here, so you can stop your bellyaching." She turned to Ben. "I might have to come see you for that headache medicine real soon. Bye now." Then she sashayed away.

His father's hard gaze didn't bode well.

"You looking for me?" Ben crossed the room and sat in front of the big oak desk stacked high with piles of papers.

His father's face turned a deep shade of red. "Did you listen to my voicemail?"

Ben shook his head. "I was busy busting out of jail. What do you need?"

"For Kline to get the hell out of town." His father's eyes narrowed. "Not for you to be throwing birthday parties for her and making her feel welcome here."

"I love Kline. It'd be easier for all of us if you'd just accept that." Ben stood to leave. It was clearly not a good time to talk about his clinic. "I think your time would be better spent figuring out how to beat Kline on Thursday instead of worrying about how welcome she feels."

"I'm not nearly as worried about beating Kline now that I have the results of her background check." His father leaned back in his chair and crossed his arms over his chest. "Not too many around here'll be willing to vote for an ex-con. I don't suppose the love of your life mentioned that she's spent time in jail, has she?"

Of course his father would dig for dirt on Kline. Ben wished he knew exactly what she'd done, but wouldn't give his dad the satisfaction of asking.

"You mean besides last night because of you? Yeah. She mentioned it to me."

"Really? Did she tell you how many weeks she was in?"

Weeks? What the hell? He couldn't think of anything Kline would do to end up in jail for more than a day. He'd assumed she'd been arrested for another protest of some sort, but that wouldn't result in real jail time. "What's your point, Dad?"

"That I'm going to drag Kline's name through the mud with this new information unless you can convince her to go back to whatever jungle she came from. I've been talking to some people in Denver. I think I've found a way to get my building permit back before the sale falls through with Tara's father. But I can't make all that happen with Kline around sticking her nose into my business."

Crap. If Kline's integrity came under fire it might give her an excuse to leave town rather than deal with his father's bullying. He wanted to show her how different it'd be to live in Anderson Butte now. That it wasn't high school any longer and people would treat her with nothing but kindness—for the most part, anyway. His father would never change his mind about her.

"I think the better plan is to move the distillery to Zeke's land. Then we can design a clinic that'll work under the new restrictions."

"If I don't get the money the land sale brings, I can't fund a new clinic for you. It's your choice. I'll give you the weekend to change her mind about sticking around, or you can kiss both Kline's reputation and your precious clinic goodbye."

Ben's heart pounded as he withheld the biting words he wanted to spew at his father. Instead he said, "Maybe you should take a hard look in the mirror and see what you're doing is wrong. You could've gone to jail too if Kline hadn't stopped things yesterday. Quit blaming her for your own shortcomings." Ben turned and walked down the hallway and through the front door, ignoring his father's cursing and bellowing behind him.

Once outside, he sank down on the top porch step and held his head in his hands.

What was he going to do? The new clinic could potentially save so many lives. Ones he'd come to care for deeply. The residents of Anderson Butte weren't just patients like Sam's were to her in Denver. They were all like family to him. More so than his own father.

His dad refused to see that the clinic could also provide skilled jobs for some of the local graduates to come back to after college, solving another problem the town had of losing its young people. He'd worked too hard to let it slip away now. It'd take millions he didn't have to fund it himself, even if he could build it on Zeke's land instead. He had to come up with another plan.

But first, he needed to figure out what Kline had done. What if she hadn't even told her mother? He had to warn Kline before his father revealed her secret.

Damn. Just when it looked like things were going to work out, his father had to go and ruin his life. Again.

Kline closed the front door softly behind her in case her mom was still sleeping. Unable to keep her bladder waiting much longer, she tossed her purse onto the couch, dodging bundles of campaign signs her mother had made, as she ran for the bathroom. She'd held on to her dignity in front of Ben, but just barely.

After taking a shower and drying her hair, she felt a little more human again. Wrapped up in her robe, Kline walked toward her bedroom to change into fresh clothes. Her mother's voice softly called out, "Kline? I need some help."

Alarmed, Kline changed direction and headed down the hall. Her mom's door stood open, her bed made, but it was empty, so she jogged toward the bathroom. It was empty too. "Mom?"

"I'm over here. On the other side of the bed."

Kline raced out of the bathroom and scooted around the bed. Her mom was on her back on the carpeted floor. "Are you hurt? How did this happen?"

"Just my pride." Her mom smiled. "I tripped over the comforter when I was making the bed and fell. I heard you come in so I was waiting until you were out of the shower. I can't seem to get up."

"I'm so sorry you had to wait, Mom." Kline knelt over her mom and helped her to her knees and then helped her stand. "Maybe I should call Ben to check you out?"

Her mother waved a hand. "No, I'm fine now."

"What would you have done if I hadn't been here?"

Her mom shrugged. "I'm not sure. But I'm glad you're here now, sweetheart."

Kline's heart still raced. "I think you need to start carrying your phone in your pocket so you can call for help next time."

"That's a good idea." Mom sat down heavily on the side of the bed. "I'll try to remember to do that after you leave."

A stab of guilt and worry pierced Kline's heart. What would've become of her mom if she'd been alone? Maybe winning the election and staying in Anderson Butte with her mom for a few years would be a good thing. Leaving her on her own might not be an option anymore.

CHAPTER FIFTEEN

etermined to enjoy her birthday party later that evening, Kline drew in the scent of the cold, pine-scented air and cleared her mind as she and her mom walked down the front porch steps.

She'd spent the day talking to people in town and asking if she could put her sign in their yards. It was interesting to hear what people would like to see change in Anderson Butte. For the most part, they were happy with their benefits that the mayor had set up. The changes they wanted to see weren't anything big, but little things it seemed the mayor could easily have given them if he'd cared enough to listen.

Kline shortened her stride as she walked alongside her mom on their way to Ben's house. He'd called and asked if they could come a little early because he had something important about the election to discuss. They probably had a lot of things they needed to talk about.

Mom said, "You've been quiet all day. Did something happen between you and Ben last night?"

Besides the mind-blowing sex?

"He told me how his father tricked him into staying here after college. And why he lied about it. Did you know about that?"

Her mom cringed. "It came out a few years after you left."

"And you didn't think to share that with me?" Her mom's betrayal was another pinch to her heart. First Ben had lied and now her mom had hidden the truth too?

Mom stopped walking and faced her. "I went back and forth about telling you. But then, all you ever told me after you left was how happy you were to never return to Anderson Butte, so what was the point?"

Kline didn't buy that answer. "Then why did you drop hints about how nice it'd be if I moved home every time I called?"

"Well, um . . ." Mom blinked rapidly. "Oh, I'm just going to say it. We both know the real reason you never came home was that you were avoiding Ben. If I had told you that he'd lied to you on top of everything else, I would've never gotten you home."

"Gotten me home?" That was an odd way to put it.

"I meant that it would've made things worse if you ever did come home." Mom waved a hand. "Anyway, it doesn't matter now because confessing he lied will give you the perfect excuse to push him away. Avoidance is your soup du jour."

Kline crossed her arms as her mind raced for a proper defense. Why was everyone still accusing her of that? Maybe because she did tend to shy away from talking about emotions. She needed to get better about that. "I've been trying to come to grips with why Ben lied to me all day. The best I can come up with is that we were young and immature. Neither of us handled that breakup well. And I told you in high school that I'd never live here after I graduated."

Her mom sighed. "That's what all kids say who grow up in small towns. But you've seen what else is out there now. Where would you rather raise a child? Here, where they'd be safe and surrounded by loving relatives, or a big city?"

She'd never thought of it from a having-kids perspective. "What if I had kids who looked like me? A skyscraper with zits and braces? The teasing I endured from the Anderson kids was horrific. No thanks."

"And you don't think that would've happened if you'd lived anywhere else? You've taught all over the world, so you have to know kids are kids. If anything, it gave you the opportunity to figure out how to shine, and look what you did with that. Dad nearly burst with pride when you got that basketball scholarship. And he always wished you'd have looked in the mirror and seen what a beautiful woman you became."

"He had to think that because he was my dad." Memories of her father threatened to make her sad again. She still missed him so much. "I don't want to argue with you, Mom. Let's go eat cake and have some fun."

They started walking again and her mom whispered, "Avoidance in the form of cake and fun."

Kline wrapped her arm around her mother's shoulder and pulled her close. Maybe it was time to start working on her avoidance issue and come clean. "No, avoidance because not only did I spend the night with Ben last night, I *slept* with him. It left me feeling confused, happy, and incredibly sad all at the same time."

Mom tilted her head. "Why sad?"

"Because I realized last night how much I've missed him, and how I should have done things differently when we broke up. I ran as fast as I could rather than fight for what I wanted. We've both changed some during our years apart, and I'm wondering if we can ever get back to that time when we were so happy, or if it'll just never be that good again."

Mom nodded. "Only one way to find out."

"I know. I'm going to try again. But I'm equal parts excited and afraid of the answer. So now, because it's my birthday and Ben is throwing me a party, I'm going to eat cake and drink lots of alcohol because they are guaranteed to make me forget my worries and feel better, even if just temporarily."

Mom slipped her arm around Kline's waist and squeezed. "Maybe you should spend the night with Ben after the party. That'd probably make you feel better too."

"I never thought I'd see the day you'd tell me to sleep with a man to make myself feel better."

"I didn't tell you to sleep with just any man. I told you to sleep with Ben. If I'd told you to sleep with Nate, may God strike me dead. He'd never make you happy."

It was true—she wouldn't have been happy with Nate. How did her mom know that about him? Spidey sense was the only thing that Kline could think of. "But I can't spend the night with Ben, leaving you to walk home in the cold and dark after the party. So no more nagging."

"Mothers don't nag. They just suggest things for your own good."

"Call it what you'd like. But no more talk about my sex life at the party, please."

"Deal. But if I find a man to walk me to my doorstep tonight, promise you'll give me an hour before you come home, okay?"

"What?" Kline stopped dead in her tracks.

"Gotcha." Her mother laughed and led the way up Ben's walk.

"Funny, Mom." Kline shook her head as they approached Ben's front door. He had comfy-looking outdoor furniture, and even a swing. Very cute. Had a woman helped him pick it all out? Ben loved fancy shoes, but his usual taste in furniture ran more toward man cave than good design.

Her mom opened Ben's front door and hung up her coat as if she lived there. Ben stood just inside the foyer putting someone else's coat on the rack next to her mom's. When his stunning blue eyes locked with Kline's, she smiled. He was dressed in nicely fitting designer jeans, equally fancy new loafers, probably to replace the ones she'd ruined for him that first day, and a shirt she'd given him the last Christmas they'd been together. It looked brand new, as if he had never worn it. Maybe he hadn't because it'd been a tad big on him then. But now the perfect fit across his muscled chest and biceps made the shirt look as if it were tailored for him.

After staring at each other for what seemed like a full minute while her mom masterfully disappeared, he finally moved closer. "You look beautiful, Kline." He helped her out of her coat.

She hadn't known why she'd packed the jeans her last boyfriend had said made her butt look nice, a silk shirt that showed off the girls a bit, a leather jacket, and high-heeled boots, because usually she'd have nowhere to wear them in Anderson Butte, but she was glad she had. "You clean up pretty nice too. I especially like the shirt."

He moved his mouth near her ear and whispered, "I especially like the person who gave it to me."

That shouldn't have moved her so much, for goodness' sake. The man had confessed his love for her just the night before *while* making love to her, but that he'd kept the shirt made her heart all gooey. "I'm surprised you still have it."

He nibbled on her earlobe and made her knees go a little weak. "I kept your ring too."

Ben still had her engagement ring? He could have sold it and bought fifty pairs of fancy shoes with that money. "About that. I'm sorry I threw it at you."

"It was better than throwing one of the bats I had by the front door at me."

She used to hate how he'd dump his softball bag just inside the front door after his games. She'd asked him to put the bats away, but they never seemed to make it to the closet unless she put them there. She'd finally given up the battle and learned to step over the bag.

She leaned away and studied his foyer. It had a low table with a pretty glass bowl that held his keys, a freestanding wooden coatrack, a live potted plant on a rustic stand, and an area rug. Not a piece of sports equipment in sight. "So did you put your softball bag away tonight on my account?"

He shook his head and opened a closet door. There, on the top shelf, was a softball bag. "You aren't the only one who's changed. Let me show you around before the rest get here."

His polished wood floors looked new, and the sage-colored walls and white, three-inch-tall trim appeared freshly painted. She'd never have pictured Ben's house to be so well put together.

She followed behind him to a formal living room with soft, inviting, fawn-colored upholstered chairs and couches, but the star of the room was the baby grand piano.

"Wow. That's pretty. You still play, then?"

"Yeah. But nowhere near as well as I used to."

He'd all but given up music because they hadn't been able to have a real piano in their apartment, just his electronic one. He'd said it wasn't the same. "I'm sure you're still better than anyone else in town."

He smiled. "Choosing medicine over music worked out for the best." He took her hand and led her farther down the hallway. "You were always my biggest, and *only*, fan."

"Maybe for music, but you've got a whole town full of fans now."

"I love what I do."

Yes, that much was clear, and she was glad to see him so happy. He loved the people in town like family and it wouldn't be fair of her to ask him to leave them. She used to have to compete for his attention with just his needy family. Now, if they resumed their relationship, she'd probably have to compete for his time with a whole town.

Next, they landed in a huge den with raised ceilings, wood windows, and French doors that looked out onto a deck with tall space heaters churning away for the few brave enough to bear the cold. On the opposite wall hung the biggest television she'd ever seen, and nearby sectional couches were placed for optimum football viewing, no doubt.

"I think your television could be a tad bigger, don't you?"

"Always. I have my eye on a new one."

"I was kidding!"

"I wasn't." He gave her hand a squeeze.

The den felt more like the Ben she'd known. He had a bar set up in the corner with a popcorn machine filling the air with a buttery scent and spilling out warm kernels. Three boys and a little girl were gathered around waiting to fill the red-and-white-striped paper bags in their hands. Josh and the rock star, Zane Steele, were busy playing foosball. Ben's sisters and Kline's mom were in the kitchen—one equipped with stainless steel appliances and lots of granite countertops—talking and drinking wine. When they noticed her they waved. It was all very homey and . . . nice.

Ben led her down a short hall with three bedrooms and a bath. One bedroom was a home office, then next a gym, and the other, a guest room that any woman would want to move into. It had a cheery queen-size bed with a white iron headboard, flowery bedspread, and walls painted a happy yellow. There was even a vanity with a chair to put makeup on beside the jet tub in the attached private bath. "You've managed to fill up four bedrooms all on your own?"

"Only because I could. But wait until you see my room."

His excitement was cute and kind of contagious as he dragged her along behind him. They crossed the den again to the other side of the house where his room was.

He stepped aside and held out his hand for her to enter first. "What do you think?"

"I think this is incredible." She meant it. Ben had a beautiful king-size sleigh bed and matching cherry wood dressers and nightstands. Pretty, yet not too frilly for a man. Maybe she'd get something like it for herself one day.

Then he led her into his bathroom and her jaw dropped. "Are you kidding me?"

"I figured this is something a person who lived in a tent and a jail cell would appreciate."

Ben was obviously digging for the scoop on her time in jail. She needed to tell him at some point, but now wasn't the time. She didn't want to spoil the good mood.

The bathroom, complete with travertine tile and granite countertops, a steam shower, his and hers water closets, a large jet tub, and matching vanities, was big enough to hold a party in. She didn't want to think about all the women who had probably been invited to share it with him.

"This is fantastic. I'm very impressed."

He nodded. "Sam helped me renovate and decorate over the years. It's sort of a hobby of hers."

Sam. Of course. That probably explained the pretty guest room. Hers when she came to stay, most likely. That pang of jealousy was back again, but quickly disappeared. Seems Sam had walked right into Kline's shoes after she'd left and she was grateful Ben had such a great friend. "It's just beautiful."

"I was really hoping you'd like it." Ben pulled her into a hug. "Could I talk you into a steam shower with me after the party?"

She wrapped her arms around his neck and snuggled close. She'd loved seeing Ben's house and how eager he was for her to like it too. It was cute. She laid a soft kiss on his lips. "Steam and getting naked sounds—"

"Ben?" A knock sounded on the bedroom door. "Sorry to interrupt, but can I talk to you, please?"

Kline turned to see her very pregnant cousin standing in the doorway. "Hi, Barb. I'm sorry I haven't been to see you yet." Kline crossed the room and gave her a hug.

Barb leaned back and smiled. "I forgive you. I hear you've been busy crusading for birds and running for mayor." Barb's smile turned to a wince, and she turned to Ben. "I'm having contractions. That's not normal this soon, right?"

Ben quickly moved to Barb's side and helped her onto his bed. "Probably just Braxton-Hicks, but let's keep an eye on them." Ben stacked pillows behind her head and laid his hand on her belly. "Kline, will you go find Tim and send him in, please?"

"Sure." Kline hurried down the hall to find her cousin's husband. She'd only seen pictures of the tall, lanky redhead after the fact because she'd been in jail when they got married. She found him talking with Meg's husband, Josh, at the bar. "Hi, guys. Sorry to interrupt, but Ben would like to see you in his bedroom, Tim. Barb's having contractions."

Tim's eyes grew wide. "Already?" Before Kline could even introduce herself, he was gone.

Josh smiled. "Happy birthday. Can I get you a drink?" He circled around the bar and stood on the other side.

"A glass of white wine would be great, thanks."

A soft pat on her leg made her look down. The little blonde girl raised her arms to be picked up. She held an empty bag in one hand. "More popcorn, please."

"Sure. If it's okay with your parents." She lifted the girl up on a barstool. "I'm Kline. Who are you?"

"Haley." She pointed. "And you can ask my daddy, Josh. Joshua Charles Granger if Mommy is mad."

Josh handed over a glass of wine. "Which obviously *never* happens." He took the bag and scooped more popcorn into it. "This is the last one, Haley, or your mom is going to start using your middle name too."

"'Kay." Haley held out the full bag. "Want some?"

"Thanks." Kline took a handful. "How old are you, Haley?"

"Three. How old are you?"

"Lots older than that." Meg's precocious daughter was adorable.

Josh cleared his throat. "That's not a polite question to ask an adult, Haley. Why don't you go see if the boys will let you play foosball?"

Haley frowned. "But I want to talk to Uncle Ben's girlfriend."

Meg appeared from behind them and slipped her hand over Haley's mouth. "Sorry, Kline. This one came out of the womb talking and hasn't stopped." Meg whispered something in Haley's ear before she lifted her to the floor. "Aunt Casey is waiting for you in the kitchen."

"'Kay. Bye, Kline." Haley started to run away, but then stopped. "Kline is a funny name."

Meg and Josh both said, "Goodbye, Haley!"

Haley shrugged and then trotted off toward the kitchen.

Meg slipped onto Haley's vacant stool and said to Josh, "And you want two more of those?"

"Yes." Josh leaned over the bar and kissed Meg so tenderly it sent a pang to Kline's heart. Ben kissed her like that.

A big hand landed on her shoulder. "You must be Kline. Happy birthday. I'm Zane." The rock star needed no introduction. And he was even more handsome in person.

She stuck out her hand. "It's very nice to meet you, Zane. Congratulations on your engagement."

"Thanks." Zane returned the shake and sat on the other barstool beside her. "So how's the campaign going?"

"My mom, Mrs. Anderson, and I have made signs and have been out stumping all day again. But I know it'll be tough to beat the mayor. There just aren't enough Grants to do it alone."

Zane nodded. "You're running neck and neck, according to Gloria's poll at the diner. It's hard to get more scientific data than that around here."

Kline chuckled. "I suppose you're right." Casey had been right too. Zane seemed like a regular guy, not one of the most famous people in the world.

He said, "Want to play some foosball? The boys need a fourth and I'm tired of getting my butt kicked."

"I'd love to. Thanks." She hopped off the stool and joined the boys. The only entertainment in many of the smaller villages where she'd stayed were Ping-Pong and foosball tables set up for the American workers. She used to play for hours in the evenings to kill time.

"Hi, guys. I'm Kline."

The tallest kid said, "I'm Eric. These are my cousins Caleb and Ty."

"Nice to meet you all." Caleb and Ty looked just like Casey.

Eric said, "Do you want to be on Ty's team to make it even?"

Ty, clearly the youngest, pouted a bit. He was at the age when girls still had cooties.

"I'd love to be on Ty's team. But I have to warn you guys, I'm pretty good at this."

Ty's face lit up and he held up a hand for a high five. "Let's kick their butts!"

The ball dropped and the battle began. Kline quickly scored, but then backed off a bit and let Ty have the ball until they'd start to fall behind. She let the other two boys score on her a few times, but it didn't seem to fool them. It just made them work harder, which was a good thing.

When she and Ty were ahead by a few, Kline put on the gas again and she and Ty won by a healthy margin.

Caleb grinned and said, "Rematch!"

"Bring it." She liked his competitive spirit.

She could see why Ben's niece and nephews had changed his mind about having kids. They were pretty great.

She turned to Ty, who was busting at the seams with pride, clearly not used to beating his bigger brother and cousin, and gave him a high five. "Let's toast these two."

Just as she and Ty were about to win again, Ben appeared. "Sorry, guys, but I need to borrow Kline." He whispered in her ear, "Barb would like to ask you a favor."

"Sure. Can you take my place?"

"Absolutely. But just for this one game. Then I need to get back to Barb." Ben moved into position. "You guys are going down."

Kline walked into Ben's room, wondering if they got back together would she be having parties by herself while he was with patients? And if they had kids would she have to be in charge of all of their activities for the same reason?

Kline sat on the edge of Ben's bed next to her cousin. Tim was on his cell pacing back and forth. Something was clearly wrong. "Hey. How are you feeling?"

Barb laid a hand on her big belly. "I'm okay for now, but I have some other health issues besides the baby so Ben wants me to see a specialist in Denver on Monday morning." Barb took Kline's hand. "You're still certified to teach in Colorado, right? Could you take my classes for me on Monday? Depending on my test results, maybe Tuesday as well?"

Concerned for her cousin, Kline nodded. "Of course. Do you have lesson plans?"

"Yes. Thank you." Barb squeezed Kline's hand. "Prep on Monday for the test on Tuesday. It's an important one for their grades, so having an actual science teacher rather than a PE coach to sub helps. I really appreciate it, Kline."

"Absolutely. Don't worry about a thing. I got this."

Barb sighed and closed her eyes. "Pregnancy isn't for wimps."

No, it clearly wasn't. Would Barb have to spend the rest of hers in bed?

Maybe substituting for a few days was a good thing. It'd be the perfect opportunity to see what she'd get herself into if she took the job.

Ben walked through his front door after getting Barb settled at her house. He'd wanted to stay until the contractions completely ceased, just in case. It was almost midnight and the birthday party had wound down. He searched for Kline, and found her laughing in the kitchen with their last guests, Tara and Ryan.

"Hey." He poured himself a glass of water when he'd rather have had a beer, just in case he got called back to Barb's house later. "Where's your mom, Kline?"

"She talked Wayne into walking her home so I could stay and enjoy the party." She drained what was left in her wineglass and placed it on the counter. "Tara and Ryan were keeping me company until you got back. And now that everyone has gone, Tara showed me her new ring."

Ben took Tara's outstretched hand. "That looks suspiciously like an engagement ring."

Ryan grinned. "It is, but we didn't want to take away from Kline's party. We'll tell everyone tomorrow."

"Congratulations!" Ben kissed Tara's cheek as happiness and pride swelled in his chest. He gave his brother a fist bump. "I'm impressed, Ry. Didn't think you'd ever get around to it."

Tara laughed. "He wouldn't have without some well-placed clues. Lucky for the sheriff, he was able to solve the crime—before I had to resort to committing one to get his attention."

Ben said, "Smart move, Tara. So how was the party, Kline?"

"Awesome." Kline's lips tilted into a slow smile. "The best birthday I've had since I was a kid. I caught up with everyone and had a wonderful time. Thank you." She stepped up on her tiptoes, pressed her body against his, and kissed him. Her doing that in front of his brother and Tara gave him hope for that steam shower.

When they finally broke the kiss, they were alone in the kitchen.

Ryan and Tara called out, "Good night." Then the front door closed behind them.

Kline smiled. "Whoops. Guess we scared them off."

Her goofy smile made him ask, "So the wine was to your liking, huh?"

"Yes! It was fabulous." She took his hand and towed him toward his bedroom. "I might have had just a splash too much, but not so much that I forgot about that steam shower. Can't wait to get you naked. But I think I'd rather sleep with you first and then steam. Sex in the shower is overrated."

Fine by him.

He kicked the door closed behind them as Kline made a beeline for the bed and started taking off her clothes. When she slowly unzipped her sexy boots, his mouth went dry.

Unfortunately, he'd just been with a patient and needed to clean up before he could do all the things he'd fantasized about doing to Kline all day. "Be right back."

"Make it quick." She slipped under the covers.

He debated taking a shower—it'd be the best way to be all the way clean—but he was in a hurry, so he scrubbed his hands and arms. Then he spotted all of his toiletries lined up out of order because his cleaning lady had been there earlier. He resisted the urge to straighten them. Kline was waiting.

He brushed his teeth, put in some eyedrops, and rubbed lotion onto his hands, which were chapped from washing them so much. Then he splashed water on his face and ran his fingers through his hair. He needed a shave, but he'd already taken more time than he'd planned, so he skipped that, along with the urge to go out and be sure the stove was off and the lights all out. He could do that afterward.

But those dammed crooked bottles were still bugging him. He had to make them right, so he quickly reorganized the jars and bottles to be sure they were all in their proper place. Only then could he draw a full breath.

He turned out the bathroom light and padded across the carpet to his side of the bed. When he slipped under the covers, Kline's quiet snoring put the kibosh on his plans for her.

He rolled to his back and sighed. He'd meant to take a minute, but it had turned into fifteen. Might have been twenty. Maybe he did have anxiety issues. It was probably time he admitted it.

Turning to face Kline, he smiled as he watched her sleep. What he wouldn't give to be able to share his bed with her every night again. He slid closer and wrapped her up in his arms. "I love you, Kline."

She slid closer and he could have sworn she'd mumbled something that sounded like, "Love you too."

Maybe he'd won her back. She just hadn't figured that out yet.

CHAPTER SIXTEEN

*K*line blinked her eyes open. She was naked and alone in Ben's big bed. And how was it morning already? The last she remembered, she'd been waiting for Ben while listening to rustling noises coming from the bathroom.

She slid her hand over to Ben's side. It was slightly warm, so maybe he was still around and hadn't been called away by some emergency.

When memories from the evening before filled her mind, Kline rolled onto her back and grinned at the ceiling. She hadn't had that much fun since she could remember. Everyone seemed genuinely happy she'd come home. She'd actually felt . . . happy to *be* home.

Then she remembered she'd also agreed to another debate with the mayor. Her mother and Mrs. Anderson had arranged to have an informal question-and-answer session later in the high school gym. She needed to do some major cramming beforehand.

Mom was making her famous snickerdoodle cookies, so there was that, at least. Speaking of cookies, she was starving.

Just as she was about to throw the covers back, Ben appeared with a tray. "Morning. How's the head?" he asked with a smirk.

"Fine. Sorry I couldn't stay awake long enough for you to alphabetize or whatever you were doing in there."

"Because you'd had a lot to drink?" Ben laid the tray on the nightstand.

"Because it was late. What's your excuse, Mr. Neat?" She chuckled as she propped herself against the headboard and pulled the sheet up to cover herself.

"I had a lot to organize." Ben joined her in bed and then handed her a plate with a bagel and schmear. "Your favorite."

"Thank you." She leaned over and kissed him. "The whipped cream cheese is a nice touch."

"It's healthier. You use less when it's whipped."

"Don't ruin my fun." She bit into her warm, onion-crusted, cheesy delight and moaned. "Perfect. But I really think we should talk about your straightening obsessions."

"Maybe you should go first and tell me about the jail time thing." Ben shoved a humongous bite of bagel into his mouth and mumbled, "It's not polite to talk with my mouth full."

"Clever." She leaned across him to grab one of the coffee cups he'd brought on the tray. "But I can wait." Draped over his lap, she slowly sipped her coffee.

Ben's gaze ran up and down her exposed skin as he chewed. After he swallowed he said, "Maybe we could talk after . . ."

"Nope. You first." She sat up and covered herself again.

Ben huffed out a breath, then set his plate on the nightstand. "Stress triggers it. Between you coming back and trying to start my new clinic, I *have* been having a harder time controlling it. Normally, it's just double-checking things and organizing. Nothing bad enough to be medicated."

She finished off her bagel and laid her plate aside too. "I hate that I'm adding stress to your life, Ben."

"I didn't mean now. Weirdly, when I touch you, I don't have any symptoms at all." He rolled on top of her. "Why don't I show you?

You could write one of your scientific papers on the phenomenon." He kissed her as his hands got busy removing the sheet between them.

"No changing the subject." She laughed and squirmed away. "Seriously, Ben, when tidying up is more important than a willing, naked woman, maybe it's time to try a pill?"

"I realized that last night while I listened to you snore. I'll have Sam prescribe me something mild. Now onto you." Ben slowly peeled the sheet away from her body. "My dad ran a background check and is threatening to use your jail time against you in the election. But you can tell me about that later if you'd rather have sex first."

Kline saw red. "Damn him! He dug into my past?"

"I guess that's a no to the sex first plan?" Ben settled against the headboard while she did the same.

"That son of a—sorry." She struggled to reel in her temper. The mayor was an ass, but he was still Ben's father. "It isn't at all what it looks like on paper. But in a foreign country, I could have been put to death for it."

Ben sat up straighter as concern furrowed his brow. "What happened?"

She hated thinking about that time in her life. It was what had made her return to the US for good. She never wanted to be that scared and vulnerable again.

"About a year and a half ago, my relief group had been assigned to work in this tiny village. We were there to help show them how to clean up their water supply and cook sanitary food. They'd had some missionaries come through before us, so some of the kids could speak a little English and had learned rudimentary math skills. I offered classes part of the day, and I had this small group of kids who sporadically came by the school hut for lessons. That's when my troubles started."

Ben's head tilted. "You were arrested for teaching kids?"

"Well, come to find out, not all of the kids told their parents. Particularly one boy. His father barged into the classroom and grabbed his kid by the arm and dragged him outside. Then he started beating the poor child."

"For going to school?"

"From what I could understand of their language, it was for not doing his chores. But no matter how hard the child begged, his father wouldn't stop hitting him. The kid was bleeding from his nose and mouth so I stepped in to stop it. I couldn't just stand there and watch."

Ben slipped his arm around her shoulder and pulled her close. "Of course not. So then what happened?"

She wrapped her arms around Ben, thankful he seemed to understand she could use a hug before she told the rest of the story.

"The man started beating *me*. The guy was a good six inches shorter, but he hit like a linebacker, so the self-defense classes we all had to take kicked in." She shivered at the memory of fighting with the man. "I shut the guy down. What I didn't know was that he was related to the leader of their clan. Later that night, four men came into my tent. They gagged me, bound my hands and feet, and threw me into the back of a truck. We drove for hours, and finally stopped in a small town. They cut me free and then threw me into a nasty jail cell with ten other women."

"God, I'm so sorry, Kline." Ben laid a kiss on the top of her head and wrapped her up tighter. "Were you able to let anyone know where you were?"

"No. And that was the scariest part. Luckily Nate tracked me down. I told him to tell my mom I was in a remote place for a while. I didn't want her to worry."

"Have you ever told her?"

"Just the basics. Only Nate knows the whole story." She blinked back the tears that burned in her eyes. She'd buried that time in her life so deeply, to tell the story brought back all the raw pain.

Ben whispered, "If it's too upsetting, you don't have to tell me the rest."

"No, it's okay." Oddly, for the first time, she wanted to tell her story. "I didn't know if I'd ever get out. Nate told me I was lucky I was an American, because the tribesmen realized they might be able to trade me for something. Nate's father was in Congress at the time, so he promised he'd get the embassy involved, but it took weeks. As the days passed, the number of women in the jail grew smaller and smaller. My cellmates ignored me when I tried to ask what was happening to them. Then one day, when the guards came to take the only other prisoner left, an older woman, she finally spoke to me. She said something like, 'To live, you have to run.'"

"Escape or be killed?"

Kline nodded against Ben's chest. "But I'd searched and couldn't find a way out. So, that night, alone in the cell, I lay in that filthy, rat-invested box and wondered who would care if they killed me? My mom, sure, but I hadn't stayed in one place long enough to make good friends after I left Denver. My old college teammates drifted out of my life because I went long stretches of time without Internet. I vowed if I ever got out of that jail, I'd get back to the US and make a normal life for myself."

Ben slid a hand across her cheek and tilted her face up. "Didn't the party last night show you how wrong you were, Kline? You were never alone."

She wiped away her tears. "Yeah, I know that now, but I let the bad memories from when I was a kid get in the way. After Nate's father finally arranged my release, I still had over a year's commitment to my group, so I looked for safer teaching jobs closer and closer to home, the last in Tahiti. So now I'm a free agent."

Ben whispered, "Anyone else would've bagged that last year and come straight home."

"You know I never go back on my word." She gave him a squeeze. "I thought about you a lot in that jail cell. Mostly, that I hoped you were happy."

Ben ran his hand up and down her back. "I haven't been truly happy since the day you left."

His words hit her straight in the heart. She buried her face in the crook of his neck and whispered, "Me either. No more lies between us, okay?"

"Absolutely."

———————

Ben rubbed Kline's back as guilt weighed heavy in his chest. If he hadn't lied to her, they wouldn't have broken up. It was his own fault he'd lost the love of his life. And if she'd stayed in Anderson Butte with him, she would never have had to go through such a horrific experience. The vision in his head of a man hitting her, and then of her being thrown in the back of a truck gagged and bound, killed him. He wished he could go back in time and do things differently.

His phone buzzed on the nightstand beside him, drawing him out of the dark space in his head. The screen showed it was his father. Ben was tempted to let it go, but maybe it'd give him a chance to tell his dad about Kline's arrest. So he'd back the hell off. "Hello?"

Sue Ann yelled, "Something's not right with your daddy!"

"Calm down and tell me what's wrong." Ben laid a kiss on the top of Kline's head and then slipped out of her embrace.

"His color isn't right, and he's having a hard time breathing."

"I'm on my way." He'd warned his father to slow down. His heart wasn't healthy enough to handle his perpetually stressed-out life. But the man was as stubborn as a two-year-old.

He grabbed a pair of jeans and the first shirt his hand landed on in the closet. He called out to Kline, "It's my dad. I'll be back as soon as I can."

When he stepped out of the closet, Kline was dressed too. She asked, "Is there something I can do to help?"

"Call Ryan and ask him to pre-flight the chopper. Just in case." Ben didn't wait for an answer. He grabbed his medical bag and car keys, and flew out the door. In less than two minutes he was in front of his father's house.

Ben took the porch steps two at a time and raced through the front door. "Sue Ann?"

"We're in the kitchen."

One look at his father and Ben's suspicions were proved correct. Blue-tinged lips told him his dad wasn't getting enough oxygen. "Tell me how you feel, Dad."

His father struggled to draw enough air to speak. "Like a damn elephant is sitting on my chest."

Ben handed his father aspirin to chew and then called Kline as he wrapped the blood pressure cuff on his dad's arm. She was closer and faster than Joyce. When Kline answered, he said, "Can you go by my office and grab two of the rolling canisters of oxygen from the storage room behind Joyce's desk? There are masks and tubing in a box just above. My spare office keys are in the bowl by my front door. Have Ryan load everything in the back of the chopper and be ready to take off."

"Okay. I hope he'll be all right."

"Thanks." Ben hung up and tried to stay calm and detached, as he would with any other patient who was probably having a heart attack. After taking his father's pulse, Ben reached inside his bag and filled a syringe. "Just going to give you a little something to ease the pressure, Dad. And then Sue Ann is going to drive us to the chopper. We need to get you to Denver." Ben was grateful for the equipment they kept permanently on the chopper. He hoped he wouldn't have to use the paddles.

Sue Ann said, "Oh, then I need to pack a few things." She started for the hallway.

"No time. Pull the car as close as you can to the front porch."

Sue Ann stopped her retreat. "Are you sure—"

"For the love of God, woman. Get the damn car!" his father hissed. The meds had started working, thankfully. Dad's color was better, but not great. Hopefully Ben could keep him stable until they got to the emergency room. He'd call Sam from the chopper and have her meet them at the ER.

Feeling helpless, Ben took to pacing in the waiting area of the busy emergency room. Sue Ann seemed oblivious to the fact that her husband had probably had a heart attack and played games on her cell phone to pass the time. It made Ben question which Sue Ann loved more—his father or his money.

Ryan had gone to get coffee for everyone half an hour ago. He must've walked down the street to get them the better stuff.

Ben sat again and took to alphabetizing the stack of magazines beside him.

"What are you doing?" Sam stood before him with her arms crossed.

Dammit. She'd caught him. "Nothing. How's my dad?"

Sam sat next to him and pulled out her prescription pad. As she scribbled she said, "Cranky, but stable. Go get this filled for yourself, and by the time you get back I should have his test results."

Ben read the script. It was for an anxiety med. "I guess it'd give me something to do other than sit here."

Sam's right brow spiked. "Really? I thought you'd just tear it up like the last one."

"Then why did you bother giving it to me?"

Sam's lips tilted into an annoyingly smug grin. "Kline talked you into it, didn't she?"

"You probably put her up to it." Ben stood to go.

Sam laid her hand on his arm to stop him. "Sorry. I was just trying to lighten the mood. I'll go see if the labs are in yet. Be right back."

Ryan finally came back and handed out coffee, just as Sam appeared again and held a swinging door open to invite them all inside. "You can see him now, but not too long. He needs to rest."

Dad sat propped up in the bed, hooked up to machines and with a scowl on his face. He looked a whole lot better than he had in the chopper. Ben asked, "So what did you figure out, Sam?"

Dad said, "I'm sitting right here. You can ask me."

"I don't know if you'll tell us the truth. I'd rather hear from Sam."

Ryan and Sue Ann both nodded in agreement.

Sam said, "If it's okay with you, Mr. Anderson?"

Dad waved his hand. "Go ahead."

Sam picked up the chart at the end of the bed and handed it to Ben to read for himself as she addressed Sue Ann and Ryan. "Mr. Anderson had a heart attack. Lucky for him it was mild, and seems to have left minimal damage. We've prescribed some meds that should keep things under control for now, but Mr. Anderson needs to see a cardiologist and begin a treatment to clear the blockage from his arteries, and a diet program to prevent this from happening again anytime soon."

Sue Ann asked, "So he shouldn't be running for mayor now, should he?"

Sam shook her head. "Mr. Anderson needs to relax and take it easy. When he feels up to it, he needs to start exercising daily. Walks at least."

His father's jaw clenched. "My kids won't step up, so I have no choice. If anyone asks about this today, we had business to attend to in Denver. Is that clear?"

Sam said, "Mr. Anderson, is being mayor worth dying for?"

"Yes! An Anderson has always run our town. That can't change."

Ben put his father's chart back in the holder. "Is dropping dead in the middle of your term going to do any good? Because there's a decent chance that could happen if you ignore Sam's advice."

His father shrugged. "Over my dead body is the only way I'll ever let a Grant run my town."

Ryan said, "Kline helped with the oxygen tanks this morning, so she knows you had a medical issue. If she tells anyone, then you'll just be proved a liar."

Dad pointed his finger at Ben. "Then you better make sure that doesn't happen. I can't have people voting for her just because they think it'll be best for my health. Tell her our debate is called off tonight. And don't tell your sisters about this." He moved his finger Ryan's direction. "You can come pick me up tomorrow at one. I need to be back before my four o'clock appointment with Joe McDaniel. Tara's father better not hear about this either, Ryan, or we could lose the distillery to Denver."

Ryan turned to Sam. "Will he be released tomorrow?"

Sam sighed. "If he remains stable for twenty-four hours, then yes."

Dad said, "Good. Now all of you go on home and keep your mouths shut about this."

Ben locked gazes with Sam, who shook her head in exasperation. "I'll keep an eye on him. Call you later."

"Okay. Get some rest, Dad. And if I have to ask Kline to keep this under wraps, then you'd better not mention Kline's background check information either."

His father frowned, but nodded.

Sue Ann wiped away a tear and then laid a kiss on his dad's forehead. "You're a stubborn old mule, but I love you anyway."

Maybe she did care.

As they walked out the sliding doors to the parking lot, Ben dialed his phone to ask Kline not to mention his father's illness. She didn't have to comply with HIPAA rules the way Ben did, but he hated to ask her to lie. Especially when she could possibly use it against his dad to prove he wasn't physically fit to be the mayor.

She had to have figured out his father's medical issues might be serious when she saw him being loaded into the chopper behind the clinic. And he'd asked her to grab the oxygen to save a few precious minutes.

Thinking of the oxygen made him stop dead in his tracks. Kline had been alone in his office. Had she snuck a peek in her mother's file? Worse, what would she do if she found out she'd been tricked into coming home by a lie?

CHAPTER SEVENTEEN

K line settled in with her laptop on her mother's living room couch to go over Barb's lesson plans and then to continue her research for the debate later that night. When her phone vibrated and danced across the coffee table, she snatched it up.

Ben. About time. "Hi, how's your father?"

"They're keeping him overnight for observation. He should be back tomorrow. Did you mention any of this to your mom?"

"No. She wasn't home when I got here. Some fundraiser at church."

"Good. Please don't say anything to anyone."

"Why?"

"A favor to me?"

"Okay. I'm sure no one will notice that I'm the only one at the debate tonight. Should be an easy win for me."

Ben didn't laugh at her joke. "He said he needed to cancel." The strain in Ben's voice worried Kline.

"That's fine. Are you okay?"

"Yeah." He was quiet for a moment, then said, "So did you look?"

She knew exactly what he meant. She'd rushed the oxygen out to the chopper just moments before they all arrived in Sue Ann's car. After the chopper took off, she was sorely tempted to go back inside and snoop through her mother's file. "No. I wanted to, but just couldn't bear the thought of lying to you about it afterward."

He let out a long breath. "Thank you."

Ben seemed so stressed out. Maybe she could lighten his mood. "As a reward for my gallant restraint, maybe you could bring the file home with you and leave it open on the kitchen counter?"

"Nope. But I can think of something much more fun to do on the kitchen counter."

In her best Marilyn Monroe sexy whisper voice, she said, "Make love?"

"If you come for dinner tonight I'll make something you'll love."

She chuckled. Ben used to get skeeved out at the idea of sex in the kitchen—way too unsanitary for him. "Okay. But I have school tomorrow, so I have to be in bed early."

"Taking you to bed early works for me."

"Then it's a date. What time?"

"Six. And it is a real date. I'm hoping if all goes well tonight, you'll finally admit how you feel about me."

"I can tell you right now. When you push me for things before I'm ready, I feel annoyed with you. But when you make me dinner, I feel very favorable toward you. See you later." She quickly hung up.

Still smiling, she went back to her lesson plans. Could be fun to see how hard he'd work for it. As much as she'd tried to bury her feelings for him for so many years, she loved Ben—she'd apparently never stopped. Hopefully, love would be enough this time around.

Ben chopped fresh herbs as he made one of Kline's favorite dishes, determined to bust through the wall around her stubborn heart. He needed to get her to commit to him and to staying in Anderson Butte before the election in four days. So no matter the outcome, she'd stay.

He had the one piece of information Kline needed to be sure she won—his dad's poor health. If people in town knew how bad his father's heart problems were, and that holding office could literally lead to his death, they'd elect Kline without hesitation. As much as his father was a bully, he did a good job running the town. People respected him for that. They'd want him to take the time away to rest, have the treatment he needed, and then get better.

By asking Kline to keep what she'd seen about his father to herself, he had effectively taken away Kline's biggest weapon. That she'd agreed so readily as a favor to him, and without question, pounded on his conscience.

Technically, he couldn't share information with Kline about his father's health because he was a patient, but it still wasn't sitting right in his gut. On the other hand, if she lost the election, the new clinic would be built. Then the next time his father had heart issues, it could save his life to have the equipment and care he'd need right in town. Ben needed to focus on that part.

Maybe he'd join his father when he met with Tara's dad tomorrow, to make sure his clinic was going to be part of the plan and hold his dad to his word. He'd thought of a new plan for the clinic that included plastic surgery offerings and wanted to run it by them.

A knock sounded, drawing him out of his deep musings. Kline was right on time, as always.

He opened the door, and she smiled as she passed him a pie box. "I brought dessert."

"Thanks, but I made you chocolate cannoli, even though we never had that rematch on the court."

"Smart man." Kline laid a quick kiss on his lips. "Because I would've won anyway. Saves you the humiliation."

"So sure about that, huh?" Ben handed her back the pie box. "Then you can eat your own dessert and I'll eat mine until I get my rematch."

Kline laughed and closed the door behind her. "I guess I'll have to choke down Gloria's awesome peach cobbler crumble all by myself then."

Dammit. That was *his* favorite treat from the diner.

He threw an arm around her shoulder and led her toward the kitchen. "You play dirty."

"I play smart. Smells wonderful in here. What are we having?"

"Brains and entrails," he teased as his phone vibrated in his pocket. He glanced at the screen. "It's Sam. I have to take this. Can you please drain the pasta when the timer rings?" He walked outside to the back deck to gain some privacy.

———————

Ben had joked with her when she'd arrived, but something was still bothering him. His jaw had been set and his slight frown told her something was up. He mentioned a talk about feelings later, so that could be it.

Kline laid the dessert box down and then plucked a chocolate cannoli from the countertop, just to be sure she got one. He might have been serious and there was no way she was leaving without having one of her favorite things in the entire world. A fair tradeoff for his talking to another woman while on a real date. Even if it was his best friend and probably the one taking care of his father in Denver.

The gooey chocolate and mascarpone melted on her tongue. Yum.

It looked like they were having Ben's famous lobster-filled ravioli. The aroma of crispy sourdough garlic bread made her mouth water.

The bread smelled done, so she took it out of the oven before it burned. Then the timer rang, so she gently poured the ravioli into the drainer in the sink, so as not to break any, as she'd seen Ben do. Then she tossed the salad with the vinaigrette that stood nearby the bowl.

The cream sauce simmering on the stove looked done so she plated the pasta, poured the rich sauce over it, and sprinkled grated Parmesan cheese and chopped herbs on top. Next she set everything on the table in the nook. He'd be proud that she'd paid attention all those years ago while she pretended not to be able to cook so he'd do it for her. She wasn't stupid, after all.

It was dark outside, so she found the light switch for the deck and flipped it on. Then she stood in front of the French doors, grabbed her stomach, and pretended to swoon from hunger. He forced a smile and lifted a finger to show he'd be right there.

Still not a happy camper. Maybe his father was sicker than Ben was letting on.

When he finally came back inside, she pulled out a chair for him. "Dinner is served."

He glanced at his plate and smiled. "You even remembered the herbs? I'm impressed."

After he was seated, she laid a cloth napkin across his lap and poured him a glass of wine. "We aim to please. Everything okay?"

"Yes. Thanks for putting this all together, Kline. So how was your day?"

He obviously didn't want to talk about his dad. "Good. I'm actually looking forward to checking out Barb's classes tomorrow. She left me detailed test content for the kids to study, so maybe I can trick them into learning while we have some fun."

He took a big bite of pasta and frowned. "I can't remember middle school science ever being fun."

She hitched her brows. "That's because I wasn't old enough to teach the class yet. Mr. Randall and the big stick up his—"

Ben's phone rang and he cut her off.

"Sorry." He glanced at the screen. "I need to talk to Casey about something."

When he rose and walked outside in the freezing night air, Kline shook her head and dug into her food before it got cold. Not much had changed in that department. His family still managed to interrupt their meals.

Ben was gone so long that Kline had finished eating and had put the leftovers away when he finally came back inside, accompanied by a cool gust of air. "Sorry, Meg called after Casey. I just needed to tell them that Dad is fine."

So maybe it wasn't his father Ben was worried about? "Finish your dinner, and then I thought maybe we could soak in that big tub of yours for a bit?" Heaven knew the man needed to relax.

He genuinely smiled for the first time all night. "You read my mind. Let me go set things up first." He finished his meal in four humongous bites and then took off at a jog.

The cannoli at her elbow called her name, so she had another as she waited. Finally he called out, "All set."

The thought of getting naked made her put the third cannoli back. She wasn't twenty-four like she was the last time he'd made them for her.

When she crossed the threshold into Ben's room, it was dark but for the flicker of candlelight bouncing off the walls in the bathroom. She stepped farther inside and smiled. Ben had placed candles around the jet tub. Rose petals and bubbles churned along the water's surface, making the room smell heavenly. It was so romantic it made her eyes mist.

Ben stood before her in a white, thick terry cloth robe. He handed her one just like it. "I couldn't give you your birthday present last night with all the people here, so happy birthday a day late."

She hugged the soft robe and laughed. "I can't believe you remembered." Back in college, when they were dirt poor, she'd told him that after he finished med school, she'd just once like to spend her birthday in one of those expensive spa hotels with little guest houses right on the ocean. One that offered couples massages on their private beach, where people sat on their patios overlooking an infinity-edged pool, listening to waves crashing while eating gourmet room service dressed in luxurious robes. Complete with hot cabana boys to bring all the drinks they wanted.

He said, "Unfortunately, I couldn't find any cabana boys on such short notice, so you'll have to settle for just me."

"I'll suffer through it." She leaned up on her tiptoes and kissed him. "Thank you, Ben."

"Welcome. But you can wear that later. Now, I want to help you out of all those clothes." He took the robe from her hand. That he'd even thought to have her name embroidered on it made her stupidly happy.

They stared into each other's eyes as he removed his robe first and then slowly removed all of her clothes. Ben's hands roamed her flesh, caressing and kneading as they explored her body. It made everything inside quiver with need.

But she could see in his eyes that something was still bothering Ben. So maybe he was the one who needed to be pampered a bit.

He took her hand and helped her up the steps and into the deep, bubbling tub, and then he slipped beside her. The soothing jets seemed to come from all directions and instantly made her muscles turn to a happy mush.

After yanking a bottle of champagne from an ice bucket, Ben poured them each a glass. "Happy birthday. I'm glad you're back." He tapped his glass against hers.

"Thanks. Me too." She took a sip, and then quickly laid her glass down. "Remember you asked if I had learned any new tricks in my travels?"

Ben's lips tilted into a naughty grin. "Yeah?"

She plucked the glass from his hand and laid it beside hers. "I've been dying to show you this one." She slid behind Ben, made him scoot down in the water a bit, and then laid her hands on his shoulders, using her thumbs to knead the pressure points in his neck. "There was this tribeswoman I met who could get rid of my migraines with just her hands."

"Mmmm." Ben closed his eyes and let his head fall back against her shoulder. "You still get migraines?"

She whispered in his ear, "Only when I'm super stressed. I guess it's my version of straightening stuff." She lightly nipped his earlobe and made him moan.

After a few minutes, Ben's shoulders and neck muscles became putty in her hands. So it was time to move on to the rest of his magnificent body. She laid kisses on his neck as she slid her hands slowly up and down his muscled arms, purely for her own pleasure, before she moved to his solid pecs and squeezed. She loved all the hard steel covered by soft skin. Ready to get things a little more heated, her hands dove under the bubbles. She traced her fingers over the dents and valleys of his abs. They twitched under her light touch as she made her way lower.

"Wait." Ben's hand covered hers to stop her progress. "I have a few new tricks I wanted to show you too. So unless you want this over quick—"

"I do. You can show me later." Touching Ben had made her unbearably turned on. She slipped from behind and then straddled his lap. She took his face in her hands and said, "I want to make love to *you* this time, Ben."

"I'm all yours." He kissed her long, slow, and deep. Then he leaned back and whispered, "Condoms are over—"

"I'm on the pill and was just tested. How about you?"

"Squeaky clean." His eyes darkened with desire as he caressed her needy breasts. When he switched to using his mouth and tongue she slid her hand behind his neck and leaned back to enjoy the hot desire forming low in her belly. When she couldn't take any more, she slowly lowered herself onto him and closed her eyes as she relished the feel of him. She hadn't had sex without a condom since Ben and she'd almost forgotten how good he felt inside of her.

His large hands cupped her bottom and moved at the fast pace they both wanted. She was supposed to be in charge but it felt too good to complain as his hips thrust under her, harder and faster until he had her begging for more. But it was supposed to be about him this time, and she couldn't hang on much longer. She wanted to give him what he'd crave most, so she leaned her mouth next to his ear and whispered, "I love you, Ben."

He took her face between his hands as he filled her with harder, faster strokes that took her to that place between sweet pleasure and pain, and said, "Look at me and say it."

Panting for release, she stared into his beseeching eyes and said, "I love you." Then they both went over the edge together.

Later that night, after they'd dried off from their bath, and he'd made long, slow love to Kline, he lay next to her, unable to sleep. He should have been elated that Kline had finally admitted she loved him, but instead he was wracked with guilt. He needed her to lose the election to get what he wanted. At the same time, he wanted his father to slow down and take care of himself.

He'd been toying some more with the new plan to fund a new clinic, even if they had to expand upward in their current location. His idea would cater to the celebrities who already supported their town, but it'd feel like selling out to him if they did it. But if it would get him the staff and equipment they needed along with it, he'd suck it up and stomach it. And maybe it'd get him out from under his father's iron fist.

He glanced over at Kline, who slept soundly at his side. Could he have everything he wanted, but be certain he wouldn't lose her? If he could convince Tara's wealthy father to back the new venture, then it wouldn't matter who won the election.

Kline asked for no more lies—he'd made that mistake the last time—so maybe after the meeting with Joe McDaniel and his father tomorrow, he'd tell her the truth about the threat his father had made and that he'd never ask her to pull out of the election. He wanted to show her that he had changed for the better, and that meant he'd tell her the whole truth and let her make her own decision to stay in the race or not.

CHAPTER EIGHTEEN

Kline had planned to get to school early, but Ben talked her into showering with him and messed up her schedule. Not that she was complaining; it just meant she'd have to hurry. She had come home and dressed in record time, but she would drive to school to save a precious ten minutes.

She couldn't be late on her first day.

Kline threw her laptop and a container of her mom's snickerdoodles onto the seat beside her and then pressed the button to start her car. Nothing. No light saying it was good to go.

Her battery must have lost its charge. And Uncle Zeke hadn't called to say the parts had come in to make her a charging station. She quickly grabbed her things and ran back inside. She called out, "Mom? I'm going to borrow your car, okay?" Kline grabbed the keys from the hook by the garage door.

"That's fine, honey."

Kline jogged to the garage and slipped behind the wheel of her mother's ten-year-old SUV that had a whopping twenty thousand miles on it. Because there was little need to drive in Anderson Butte, cars lasted forever.

She pulled out of the long drive and then gunned it toward Main Street. Her mother had mentioned that the mayor had donated land on the very outskirts of town to build a newer high school and that he'd remodeled the middle school. Kids were bused in now from far and wide.

As she got closer, that familiar queasy feeling she'd had most mornings before middle school came back. How excluded she used to feel sometimes by the other girls, and how hurtful it had been when they'd laugh at her behind her back and call her names. But that was ridiculous; she was the teacher now, not that picked-on girl.

When she turned into the parking lot, she blinked in surprise. The old single-story middle school was three stories high. She got out of the car and glanced across the street at the new huge high school. It even had its own football stadium. No wonder Wayne was happy to move back home to teach in such shiny new facilities.

Barb's e-mail said to check in at the front desk and then go straight to her classroom. The principal would probably stop by later to see if Kline had everything she needed.

Kline hardly recognized her old school as she dodged kids milling in the hallways in clusters around their lockers. After she'd checked in and received a temporary badge, multiple sets of eyes tracked her progress to Barb's classroom. Some were surely plotting how they could have fun with the substitute teacher, but this wasn't her first rodeo. She'd throw in a little twist first and make sure the kids were the ones off-kilter.

She quickly laid her laptop on the teacher's desk in front of Barb's classroom and then started rearranging the students' desks into a baseball diamond, complete with dugout sections. A glance at the clock on the wall showed she had four minutes before the kids got there.

As she worked, Kline studied the shelves filled with equipment. The experiments and project possibilities would be endless with materials like those. Along the back wall stood shelves filled with textbooks and reference materials that would put a college biology classroom to shame. So different from her past teaching experiences where she was lucky to have the bare minimum.

Kids wandered in with bewildered looks on their faces as they studied the room setup. One boy asked, "What's the deal? Did Mrs. Wilson pop out her kid early?"

"Nope. She'll be back Wednesday. I'm Ms. Grant. Take a seat anywhere."

Kline found some stickers in Barb's desk, and as the kids filed in she handed them out. When the bell rang, she did the introductions and roll call, then set up her laptop and the projector. "All of you who have a red sticker please go to the window side of the room, and blue to the other. We're going to play some baseball."

The kids quickly split into two teams while Kline laid out the rules. They especially seemed to like being able to earn snickerdoodles after crossing home plate. But if her game went as planned, not too many would get the chance for a cookie, because "stealing" bases after a wrong answer always made the game more fun and harder to score a run.

Kline pointed her remote at the laptop and called up the first image. "All the questions today *might* show up on the test tomorrow, so paying attention could pay off. And earn you cookies too. Red team, you have twenty seconds to answer. If you're wrong, the blue team can steal and all of your runners lose their bases."

The question about cell structure popped up and the kids dug into their textbooks for the answers. All except one girl who had her head down on her desk, her closed book beside her. Kline sat in an empty desk next to her. "Not a baseball fan?"

The pretty blonde girl jumped as if startled. The cute redheaded girl who sat on the other side said, "Ally stutters so she doesn't like games like this where she has to talk in front of the class."

Ally nodded.

An arrow of familiar pain went straight through Kline's heart for Ally. Kline knew full well what it was like to want to hide and just get through the day without anyone noticing, so she handed Ally the remote control. "I was just going to ask for a volunteer to change the questions and keep score. Could you do that for me instead?"

Ally smiled and nodded again.

Kline leaned closer. "Do you know the answer to the question?"

Ally whispered, "N-n-n-nucleus."

"Very good." Kline stood up and said to the class, "Ally was the first to answer correctly with nucleus so she gets to be our score keeper. Red team, take your base. Next question, please, Ally."

With all the kids engaged and having fun, Kline wandered around the room. The blue team started calling out the answers unusually quickly, so Kline quietly slipped behind their dugout to see what was up. One kid was using his phone under the desk to google the answers. Not a stupid move, but unfair to the others. Just as she was going to take the phone away, the blue team blurted out a wrong answer. Kline moved next to the kid with the phone and said, "Close, but incorrect."

"No way!" The kid thrust his cell her direction. "It says it right—ah, never mind."

Kline called out, "Who can tell me what your *textbook* says?" Then she held out her hand and waggled her fingers at cell phone boy. "Hand it over. You can pick it up from my desk after class."

The kids on the red team answered correctly and then gave the cell phone kid such a hard time for cheating that Kline didn't have to say another word. She moved to the front of the room and laid the phone down. "Red team steals. Next question, please, Ally."

As the game progressed, the kids got louder and louder, but they were having fun, so Kline ignored the noise. It would probably send her home with a splitting headache by the end of the day if all the classes were as loud. She was pleased to see most of the kids taking notes as she wandered the classroom.

Ally's friend, the redheaded girl named Shelly, appeared at Kline's side. "Did you know Principal Ellis has been standing in the back for like five minutes?"

"Oh. Thanks, Shelly."

Kline turned around and her stomach dropped. Lisa Anderson, the bane of Kline's existence growing up, was Principal Ellis? Why the hell hadn't Barb said something?

Kline was just starting to picture herself teaching in Anderson Butte, but there was no way she'd ever work for that dragon queen.

The same sick-to-her-stomach feeling Kline had through most of middle school reared to the surface as she slowly walked to the back of the room. "Hello, Lisa. I didn't notice you standing there." Lisa was still pretty and well put together. That hadn't changed.

"Hi, Kline." Lisa's eyes did the familiar sweep up and down Kline's body as if assessing Kline's poor wardrobe choices. "Some of the surrounding teachers called because there was so much noise. I thought maybe you needed a hand, but I see everything is under control."

Kline tamped down all her old insecurities that tried to fill her with familiar self-doubt. "I'll keep it down if it's bothering the other classrooms."

Lisa waved a hand. "No. You're fine. And thank you for being sensitive to Ally. The kids give her a hard time."

Kline chewed her bottom lip. Should she say it? Why not? She had nothing to lose because there was no way she'd take Barb's job now. "Bullying and teasing? Like you did to me when we were this age?"

Lisa crossed her arms. "I owe you an apology, Kline. I honestly regret being so horrible to you. I just hope that won't stop you from taking Barb's place. You're clearly a fantastic teacher and we could use someone like you on our staff."

A few kind words now couldn't erase the years of pain she'd caused Kline. "We'll see after the election on Thursday."

"Okay." Lisa pointed to the front of the classroom. "Just pick up the phone there if you need anything. It goes straight to the main office. Whoever answers will be happy to help you." Lisa abruptly turned and walked away.

After the door closed behind Lisa, Kline shook her head and tuned back in to the game. She drew a deep breath and willed her system to settle. Seeing Lisa again had been an unpleasant shock to Kline's system.

Was Lisa sincerely sorry, or was that a ploy to fill a teaching void? Lisa had been a world-class bitch back in the day.

Surprised to see the class period was almost over, Kline sat in the empty desk next to Ally. "So, who's ahead?"

Ally smiled. "R-r-red. Did my m-m-mother get mad at you about the n-noise?"

Her mother?

"Principal Ellis is your mom?"

Ally nodded.

Shelly added, "Principal Ellis is so much better than Mr. Richards was. That guy was mean."

Kline was still processing the news that Ally was Lisa's daughter. Ally seemed like a nice kid. Not at all the type Kline would picture Lisa having.

She and Lisa were the same age. If Kline had stayed with Ben, she might have a kid in middle school too. "No, your mom wasn't mad. And Mr. Richards *was* mean. He was the principal when I went here too."

Both girls' eyes widened as they seemed to be trying to do the math.

That made Kline's inner clock strike midnight. She needed to get on the baby train pronto, before it passed her by.

After the bell rang and the winner was announced, Kline braced herself to do it all again.

As the day progressed, Kline realized how much she wanted to teach in such a well-equipped school. She loved teaching underprivileged kids, but she could help the kids here too. Barb had left notes about the ones who might need some extra support and Kline had enjoyed visiting with them and seeing how many were actually eager to learn. Funny, Barb's notes didn't include Ally.

But the students had all behaved for the most part, and were all well ahead of the state minimum requirements. It'd be a good school to send her own kid to one day.

Barb's last class period was a planning one, so Kline took the opportunity to track Lisa down. She needed to see if the new principal was being sincere or not when she'd asked Kline to stay on. And maybe she'd get to the bottom of a few things that had been bugging her all day since running into Lisa. They were both adults now, on even ground. Maybe it was time to stand up to the bully.

The secretary at the main office told Kline to go on back. Lisa's door was open, and she was tapping away on a computer.

Kline rapped a knuckle on the doorjamb. "Hi. Do you have a minute?"

Lisa looked up from her computer. "Of course. How'd it go today?" She stopped typing and folded her hands on top of her desk, giving Kline her full attention.

"Great." Kline sat in one of the guest chairs. "But I didn't realize Ally was your daughter until after you left."

Lisa nodded. "Thank you again for working with her."

Kline mustered up her nerve and asked, "Is it hard watching the bullying from the other side?"

Lisa looked Kline straight in the eyes and said softly, "It rips my heart out every day. Ally doesn't stutter nearly as much at home. The anxiety of speaking in front of others and the prospect of being teased for it makes her worse. That's why we recently moved back here, so she could be in a smaller school. I thought maybe it'd be easier, but kids can be so cruel no matter where you live, right?"

Kline nodded. She was going to ask the one question that she wished she'd been brave enough to ask as a kid. She'd seen enough bullying while teaching to have eventually put what happened to her as a kid into better perspective. "What did I do to make you and Rachel treat me so badly?"

"You didn't do anything, Kline." Lisa's gaze dropped to her hands. "I was the classic-case bully, full of insecurities I was hiding. My bad home life, which as you might remember came out much later, combined with the way all the boys adored you and not me, made me petty and mean. You never fought back, so it made you the easiest target. Then high school came along and all of that changed, didn't it?"

"It's never been in my nature to fight with people. But I eventually learned to stand up for myself. Playing sports helped me do that. Maybe Ally will find something she excels at to help her find some more confidence."

Lisa nodded. "I can only hope. And then maybe she'll be the one all the boys adore, like you were."

Kline smiled. "The boys thought of me as one of their own. They used to talk about how pretty you and Rachel were most of the time, by the way. I was glad I had basketball and my parents to get me through all those tough years."

"And you had Ben. He was always your champion. No one dared speak a bad word about you when he was around."

Ben *had* always been her champion. Even when he was making decisions for her. And Lisa seemed to be genuinely repentant. So maybe it was time to give Anderson Butte another chance.

———

Ben finished up early for the day and grabbed his notes for the new clinic idea from his desk. He waved to Joyce on his way out. "I'll be at my dad's office if anyone needs me."

She said, "Good luck, Ben."

"Thanks. You can call it a day, when you're done with the filing."

"Will do."

Ben hurried down the street and then across Town Square. He regretted forgetting his coat in his haste to get to the meeting. They'd already started without him and he hoped to catch Joe McDaniel before he left. A loud clap of thunder sounded as fat, gray clouds formed above his head. Could be a cold, wet walk home later.

He took the stone steps into Town Hall two at a time, slowing at the top to hold the door open for the Three Amigos, head of the church council and spreaders of all gossip in town, to pass before him. "Ladies. How are we today?"

Mrs. Johnson, leader of the grannies, said, "Every day we're able to get out of bed is a good one. Want to buy a knickknack for Kline?" She thrust knit-covered things his way.

"Not today. I'm late for a meeting. Behave now."

"What fun would that be?" The three giggled as they made their way to their usual table by the door, ready to pounce on any unlucky victims who walked by.

Ben hurried down the hall to his father's office. His father's assistant was on vacation, so Ben passed by the empty desk and went straight back. Dad looked tired, but back to his usual self.

"Sorry I'm late."

Joe McDaniel stood and shook Ben's hand. "No problem. You father was just telling me how he plans to get the building permit back so we can get started on the distillery."

They both sat down as Ben glanced at his father, who had a "Don't say a word" glare on his face. Whatever Dad told Joe had probably been more a hope than the truth. Not his problem at the moment, however.

Ben cleared his throat. "I wanted to talk to you, Joe, about possible funding for the expansion of the clinic. My thought is to offer the celebrities who come here one more reason to stay a few days. I'd like to add two floors to the current structure and expand the bottom floor. The third floor would have a separate entrance and private elevator that would serve a top-notch plastic surgery center, the second floor could offer more basic services like Botox and fillers, and the bottom floor could be expanded to provide emergency and hospital-stay services."

His dad asked, "So what makes you think we could attract plastic surgeons of that level to come live here?"

"They don't have to live here. We could fly the best plastic surgeons in from Denver, each only taking one day a week, and then hire one or two full-time docs for the emergency and hospital-stay portions. Plastic surgeons from Denver would jump at the chance to get their hands on those celebrities that all the California docs get now."

Joe's mouth tilted into a slow smile. "Plastic surgery brings in a fortune. And this would be the perfect place to recover afterward so celebrities can avoid paparazzi. And to be able to get all that filler and Botox crap while I'm out skiing or hiking would make sense to *my* wife. I like this idea, Ben. Put some numbers together and I'll take a look."

"Thanks, Joe." Relief washed through Ben as he shook Tara's father's hand. Ben hated that he'd be running a glorified spa, but could live with that for the upgraded equipment and surgical suites that he'd be sure came along with it.

Joe stood. "Well, looks like you have things under control here, Mitch. Guess we'll be business partners and in-laws too, now."

Dad nodded and shook Joe's hand. "We're glad to make Tara an Anderson."

Joe chuckled. "Tara might have something to say about another name change. Should be interesting. See you gentlemen later."

As soon as Joe left, Dad said, "I made some big promises today, Ben. And one of those was that I was going to be reelected. I'm all for this new clinic idea, but not unless I'm still mayor and in control of this town."

It was time to take a stand on Kline's behalf. His father wasn't going to like what Ben was about to say, but he wasn't going to back down.

────────

The rain pelted Kline as she ran up the slippery stone steps of Town Hall. Joyce said Ben had been in a meeting, but maybe he was almost done. She couldn't wait to tell him she'd decided to take the teaching job. No matter if she won the election or not. She was going to stay. And be with Ben.

Kline's shoes squeaked so loudly there was no sneaking past the Three Amigos, so she headed their way. "Hi, ladies. How are you all?"

Mrs. Johnson, the former high school principal, cracked a smile. "We're great. Heard you were a hit at school today."

"How could you have heard that already?"

Her wrinkled hand held up a cell phone. "Got a text from my great-grandson. Said you were pretty cool not to keep his phone today."

Cell phone boy from first period.

"I hadn't looked up the school's policy yet, so he got lucky. Next time it's mine for the whole week. You can tell him that. See you ladies later."

"That a girl, Kline. Gotta keep those kids in line or they'll walk all over you."

Kline chuckled as she squeaked her way to the mayor's office. Raised voices were echoing down the hall. Ben was in a full-out fight with his dad. She was about to turn back around and wait in the lobby when the mayor said, "Your cute little plan to make sure everyone in town made Kline feel welcome isn't going to be enough, Ben. She left because she never fit in around here and you know it."

Kline's stomach dropped. So there was a *plan* to make her feel welcome? None of the kindness she'd received had been sincere? Had they *all* been lying to her? God, had nothing really changed? Were they all conspiring behind her back?

Ben started to answer, but the mayor cut him off. "And why have you put off telling her to drop out of the race like we'd agreed?"

Kline laid a hand on her stomach as the mayor's words punched her in the gut. Ben had agreed to ask her to drop out of the race? Was he doing it all over again? Making plans or decisions behind her back and calling it for her own good?

The mayor added, "Kline drops out of the race or you can kiss your new clinic goodbye."

Ben replied, "Joe McDaniel and I—"

Tears filled her eyes when Ben didn't even fight back after being told to choose. Had he already made up his mind? Was she going to be thrown under the bus for a new clinic?

The mayor said, "I'll convince Joe it's a bad decision, and I won't stop at making up my own numbers to do it. You need to talk to Kline today, before she gets too settled in that cozy teaching job, because none of the Andersons want her here. All it'll take is one word from me to Lisa and Kline's out. Lisa is a *loyal* Anderson, and you need to be too."

"Dad, your heart attack alone is enough—"

"You tell Kline about that, and I'll lose for sure."

Kline's feet started moving backward in retreat. He'd had a heart attack? And Ben hadn't told her about it because of the election? So his father would win and Ben would get his clinic?

Her hand went to her chest as the pain of Ben's betrayal sliced her heart in two.

Ben appeared in the doorway as he called out, "I'm done with you, Dad. You can just go—" When he saw her he stopped dead in his tracks. "Kline?" He threw a thumb over his shoulder. "Don't listen to any of that."

Kline didn't want to hear any more lies. Her heart still bore the bruises from Ben's earlier revelation. He promised her there'd be no more lies between them. She couldn't be with a man who wasn't capable of telling the simple truth. She turned and ran down the hall, past the Three Amigos, who called out to her, but she was too angry to hear their words.

She shoved the glass door open and ran into the pouring rain. Ben was right behind her, shouting her name, but he was the last person she wanted to talk to. She needed to see for herself what had been said on the town loop behind her back. Were they all laughing at her for running for mayor too? That familiar sickness from her middle school days sat like a lead ball in her gut.

She beeped the locks on her mother's car and got in. Before she could start the engine, Ben caught up and banged his fist on the window. She ignored him and took off. When she glanced in the rearview mirror Ben kicked a puddle, sending water everywhere and probably ruining another pair of fancy shoes.

Good. The traitor. And to think she was just about to tell him she wanted to stay and try again with him. But he hadn't changed a bit. Telling lies and always catering to his father no matter what it cost her.

Tears blurred her vision, forcing her to slow down. When she got home and inside, she found a note from her mother on the kitchen table. "Be back in time to cook a celebration dinner for your first day of school."

Damn. Now Kline felt even worse for making her mom walk wherever she'd gone in the rain. That probably wouldn't help whatever ailed her.

Kline jogged to the study and powered up her mom's computer. It asked for a password, but her mom used "Kline" for everything so she got right in. She hit the icon to pull up her mother's e-mail and started reading.

Sure enough, Meg had sent an e-mail asking everyone to "make Kline feel welcome." So it'd all been fake? The free meals, the tablet, the gym membership. Just to please their favorite son, Ben? Had he begged people to come to her birthday party too? To make her stay and feel like she fit in? Because the mayor hadn't lied about that. She *hadn't* fit in before.

Scrolling further, she found an e-mail between her mother and Ben's grandmother. As she read, her already achy heart threatened to just stop beating and put her out of her misery. She laid her head in her hands and let her tears fall.

Her own mother?

The one person Kline trusted completely had betrayed her too.

The e-mail conversation about how Ben knew her mom was faking her illness was the final blow. But to get the whole truth, she forced herself to keep reading.

With each new e-mail she read, Kline felt more nauseated. When she couldn't take it anymore, she shut down the computer and went to her room to pack.

She was through with Anderson freakin' Butte and everyone in it. She should have never come back.

CHAPTER NINETEEN

*B*en stood in the rain as Kline raced away in her mother's car. Not knowing how much she'd heard, he had to assume the worst. She probably thought he'd chosen his father and the town over her. Again. Why hadn't he come clean with her sooner?

Soaked to the bone and freezing, Ben slowly walked to the hotel. He needed to talk to Casey. Get a woman's take on things before he talked to Kline. That is, if Kline would ever talk to him again. He'd never seen her so mad. Not even when they'd broken up the last time.

The thought of losing her again made his chest ache.

He pulled out his cell and dialed Betty's number. He needed Kline's mom to be sure Kline didn't leave town before he got a chance to talk to her, because there was no doubt in his mind that's what she'd do. He got Betty's voicemail so he left a message.

As he approached the hotel, the automatic doors slid open. Before he could take two steps inside, his sister called out, "Stop! Don't drip all over my wood floors."

Ben glanced at his feet. A puddle had formed on the mat under his ruined shoes. "Sorry."

"I'll get you some towels, then you can tell me why you're wandering around in the rain like a crazy person."

His sister disappeared behind the front desk for a moment and then joined him again with a stack of white fluffy towels. "What's wrong, Ben?"

He slipped out of his shoes and left them by the front door. "I really screwed things up with Kline." He dried himself off as he told her what happened.

When he was deemed suitable to enter, Casey led him down the hallway to her office and closed the door behind them. "You're sleeping with Kline, right?"

He nodded.

"Then that just made what you did ten times worse. Why didn't you just tell her that Dad was pressuring you? It wouldn't have come as any big shock."

He lifted his hands in frustration. "Because I knew she'd throw the election if she thought it would cost me my clinic. And why would I want to put even more strain on Dad and Kline's relationship? It's bad enough as it is."

Casey rolled her eyes. "And yet now, by not telling her, you've put an even bigger strain on your and Kline's relationship. When are you going to learn?"

He opened his mouth to reply, but snapped it shut. She was right. But he couldn't lose Kline again. And the way she refused to talk to him made him realize he needed help this time. "Please tell me what to do to win her back."

Casey huffed out a breath. "Kline is a full-grown woman. She doesn't need you to shield her from the truth. It's what you still do to Ryan and Meg, and even me, sometimes. You're not responsible for anyone's happiness but your own."

Hell. Kline had said almost the same thing to him. Why was it so bad to try to make life easier for the people he loved if he could?

He straightened Casey's nameplate. "Okay. I'll concede that. But how do I fix things with Kline?"

"You might only have one chance at this, so you need to decide what's more important to you. Kline, or your new clinic. Because Dad owns the building you're in, you'll always have to deal with him. And you'll never be able to please both of them."

Lose his new clinic? After coming so close by having Joe McDaniel finance a new one? But Casey was right. Even if Joe put up the money, the building wasn't Ben's to alter. Dammit.

"There has to be a way to do both. Kline and Dad need to bury the hatchet. Maybe if I could sit them both down, they could find a way to coexist?"

"Stop trying to fix them." Casey crossed her arms and shook her head. "It's you that's the problem here. By not being completely honest with Kline, you've lost her trust. The only way to get her back is to *show* Kline she's the number-one priority in your life. Not with words. Actions. And I have an idea that might buy you some time until you figure it all out."

Actions? Wasn't it enough that he loved her? That he'd do anything for her? What more could he do? "What should I do in the meantime?"

"Have zero contact with her. She needs to see what it'll be like without you in her life again. Trust me. It'll throw her off because it's not something you'd usually do. Make her dig deep and figure out what she really wants. She'll eventually come to you for the explanation she needs."

That was just crazy. "I have to talk to her. She needs to hear the truth."

Casey laid her hands on her desk and leaned forward until her face was an inch from his. "She needs to come to terms with living here, and what it'll take to be with you again. You can't make her stay and you can't make her love you or Anderson Butte. It has to be her choice. The only thing you can do is figure out what would show her how much *you* love her. Women need to know they matter. What would you be giving up by asking her to marry you?"

"Nothing. But why—"

"What would Kline be giving up by saying yes to marrying *you*?"

Ben leaned back in his chair and pondered the question. "I don't like to think she'd be giving things up if she lived here. More like readjusting to a new situation."

"More like rearranging her whole life. What can you do to show her you'd be willing to rearrange yours for her? Figure that out, and you might have a chance to get her back."

He had no idea. Before he could come up with anything, Casey said, "I know this will kill your Mr. Fix-It heart, but what happens after that is out of your control."

It went against his nature to sit back and let things play out. But if it meant keeping Kline in his life, he'd get over it.

Kline threw her suitcases on top of the bed and started emptying all her dresser drawers into them. She was so angry that she didn't want to speak to her mother. Did her mom think pretending to be sick was some kind of game? That manipulation and lying were okay?

She'd just leave before her mom got back. That way she wouldn't say the things she wanted to. Things she'd never be able to take back.

Kline turned to get her toiletries from the bathroom and nearly ran into her mom. "Sorry." She moved around her to leave but her mother grabbed her arm.

"Why are you packing?"

Kline was so mad she couldn't even look at her mom. Instead, her gaze settled on the basketball trophies lined up on the opposite wall.

"Cut the act, Mom. I just read your e-mails. It was bad enough the whole town was in on your scheme, but how could you have lied to me like that? I was so *worried* about you."

Her mother cringed. "For the unnecessary worry, I'm sorry, Kline. But not the rest."

Kline's hands balled into fists. It took all of her control to keep her voice at a reasonable level. "So rallying the whole town into luring me into some false sense of welcome and security is acceptable behavior?"

"That's not what happened, Kline. True, I faked being ill. It was the only thing that I could think of to draw you home again. Don't you think I could hear how lonely you were at times when we'd speak on the phone? I hated that you moved from place to place, leaving before relationships got too complicated."

"I was *helping* people."

Her mom sighed and then sat on the bed. She patted the bedspread beside her.

Kline shook her head. She was too upset to sit and have a calm conversation.

"Nate told me how it really was, Kline. That when your relationship started to get serious, you bolted."

Kline closed her eyes and counted to ten. "You said you knew he wasn't right for me."

"That's only because I know Ben *is* right for you. I love you more than anything in the world. I only want what's best for you, sweetheart. You know that, right?"

She knew it in her heart, though she had some choice words dying to escape her mouth. But she didn't operate that way, so she just nodded.

"Then you need to understand that I know you better than you think. You don't get close to people because you're so afraid they'll hurt you. Doing the job you had was the perfect way to keep your heart intact, but it didn't make you happy. That's why I wanted you to come home. To see how things have changed around here. And how many people care for you, Kline. Especially Ben. His family told me he never married because he never got over you. We wanted you to have the chance to see that before it was too late."

Kline's wounded heart wasn't soothed in the least. "You could have just told me that."

"Really?" Her mom laughed as she stood to leave. "Think about that for a minute. And while you're thinking, remember you've made a commitment to your cousin. She needs to rest and can only do that if you keep your word and show up for school tomorrow."

Dammit! She'd forgotten about that. "Of course I'll keep my word. But then I'm going to leave as soon as classes are over."

"Not with my car, you're not. But before you run away again, please have the decency to talk to Ben." Her mother shook her head. "I was so looking forward to finally having a Grant run this town. You've disappointed me, Kline." Her mom softly closed the door behind her.

Disappointed her? How had this suddenly become all her fault! Kline grabbed her coat and walked toward the front door. She needed to see about getting her car charged so she could get the hell out of town.

She called out, "I'm going to see Uncle Zeke. If Ben is here when I get back, I'm going to the hotel. Stay out of this, Mom!"

She slammed the front door closed behind her and headed out into the dark, wet evening. How was doing what a person set out to do "running"? She'd put her life at risk a time or two for those needy kids. It was for them that she'd taken the job.

And damn Nate for his big mouth. She'd broken up with him because he wanted a commitment from her she couldn't give.

It didn't matter. They were better off as friends. It wasn't because she was afraid he'd hurt her like Ben had. It was because she hadn't been in love with him.

She pulled her hood farther down as she leaned into the wind and icy rain that pricked her cheeks. Her skin was so numb she barely felt her warm tears tracking down her cheeks.

Ben was the only man she'd ever loved and now he'd gone and lied to her again. He'd broken her heart for a second time. How could it hurt even worse than the first time?

Lights were still on in Zeke's workshop, so she wiped away her tears and slid the heavy door open. Warm air greeted her along with screaming country music. She had to tap on her uncle's shoulder to get his attention.

He jumped a foot in the air.

"Holy mother of . . . Kline, you about scared me to death."

She forced a smile. "Sorry. The music was so loud it was the only way to get your attention."

"I have to have it loud if I want to hear it. Getting old stinks, I tell you."

"You're not old." She stood on her tiptoes and kissed his wrinkled cheek. "You're just vintage. How is my charging station coming?"

He got a sheepish look on his face. "Seems I forgot to order those parts until just yesterday. See, proves I'm getting old."

Kline crossed her arms. "Or you're in cahoots with my mom and are trying to keep me here?"

Zeke chuckled. "You always were a smart one, Kline."

"How long before they arrive?" Kline had to restrain the frustrated scream that wanted to escape.

"Could be a week or so. I figured you'd be staying for Thanksgiving, so why pay the rush fee, you know?"

"Yeah. I don't suppose I could talk you into flying me to Denver tomorrow evening, could I?" She could rent a car, find a house to buy, and then ask Nate to drive her back for her car after she'd cooled down a bit.

"Nope. Not gonna lie to you, Kline. Your momma called just now and said she'd kick my butt if I flew you to Denver. But the truth is, I wouldn't have anyway. I think you have an honest chance to beat the mayor. We need you around here."

"Is telling me that part of the 'welcome Kline home' plan?"

Zeke pulled a red rag from his back pocket and slowly wiped his hands. He took so long she wasn't sure he'd answer the question. Finally he said, "Have you enjoyed your time back here? Until today, I mean?"

"Yes. But everyone was told to be nice to me."

"Since when do you think people are going to do anything they don't want to do? Especially those damned Andersons."

"I think everyone did it for Ben. Who doesn't like Ben, the town savior? If something is wrong, Ben'll fix it."

Zeke frowned. "They did it for you, Kline. Some maybe because they realized they owed you from before and others because they're glad to see you back. But speaking of Ben. The whole town knows I've always had a thing for his grandmother. I spent over forty years wishing for something I was too damned proud to ask for after we'd had a misunderstanding in high school. If you love Ben, you can work anything out. Because anything is better than being without the one you love."

She'd never heard the part about a misunderstanding in high school. "But don't I deserve to be told the truth? And to have an uninterrupted meal with the man? To be the most important person in his life, not third or fourth behind whichever family member Ben needs to please or rescue first?"

"A lifeguard rescues the drowning person in the most danger, then goes back for the others. Because Ben has obligations, it doesn't mean he loves them more than you. Ben's a good man. And I recognize that same hurt in his eyes when he looks at you that I used to see every morning in my bathroom mirror. Afraid he'll never have the love of his life again."

"Why, just once, can't someone in this town be on my side?"

"We're all on your side, Kline. You just need to put the past away and see what's right in front of you." He turned back to his engine, giving it his full attention rather than her. "Think about it."

Zeke giving her his back hurt. "Please just get the parts as soon as possible."

"I'll call first thing tomorrow and see if I can expedite the shipping."

"Thank you. See you later." Why would shipping the parts sooner make her feel like such a jerk? Had she disappointed Zeke now too?

Kline slowly walked home, grateful she'd forgotten her cell in her rush. Ben had probably called ten times looking for her by now. Maybe she'd just let that battery die too. He was the last person she wanted to talk to.

She walked into her mom's house and softly closed the door behind her, regretting her show of temper by slamming it the last time.

Her mom was sitting on the living room couch reading. She looked up from her book. "Want some dinner?"

What she wanted was a hug, but she was too upset with her mom to ask for one. As it was, she could barely resist the urge to cry. "No, thanks. I'm going to bed."

"At seven thirty?" Her mom stood and wrapped Kline up in a hug.

Maybe her mom did know her better than she'd thought. Kline let her tears fall as she hugged her mom back. "I'm so mad and hurt by what you did, Mom."

Her mother just nodded against Kline's shoulder. She was right. There was nothing more to say. Her mom had told her what her intentions were. Now the ball was in Kline's court.

She leaned away and wiped her tears with the back of her hand. "Did Ben come over?"

"No. And he hasn't called either."

Huh. That was odd. "Okay. Good night."

"Good night, honey."

Kline walked into her bedroom and checked her cell. No calls? She checked the battery to be sure the phone had juice. The green bar glowed at the halfway point. Was he giving her time to cool down? Yeah, that was it. He'd probably show up at her window later with something yummy to eat and be all full of remorse.

Well, she'd just let him stand outside and freeze his lying butt off.

CHAPTER TWENTY

 en finished up his lunch and then picked up his cell to text Kline. Just like the ten other times earlier, he laid the phone back down on his desk before his fingers betrayed him. He needed to listen to Casey's advice. He'd wait and let Kline come to him. Betty had texted that Kline had left for school earlier, so she was still in town. Kline's mom promised to let him know if it looked like Kline was leaving, so he needed to let things play out as they should.

Being patient was killing him.

Would asking her to marry him again be enough to show Kline how much he loved her?

He reached inside his white lab coat and pulled out the box that held her former engagement ring. Maybe he should upgrade it now that he could afford to do so. He'd happily buy her any ring she wanted.

No, that wasn't the answer. Kline couldn't care less about material things. She wore simple jewelry. It had to be something more meaningful.

Casey had asked if he'd be willing to rearrange his whole life for Kline. She wanted to live in Denver. Could he do that? He loved his patients here. He loved his family. His family and his patients needed him. Or was it the other way around? Did he need to be needed by them as others had suggested? God, it hurt to think of moving away. But not having Kline in his life just wasn't acceptable anymore.

So if it meant the difference between losing Kline again and having his life in Anderson Butte and the clinic, then yes. He'd rearrange his whole life to be with Kline. As much as he'd hated the idea, he *would* do anything to be with Kline again.

He picked up the phone and dialed Sam's number, hoping she'd be up for what he had in mind. As he waited for Sam to pick up, guilt brewed in his gut for icing out Kline. But like Casey said, Kline needed to realize on her own that they belonged together. Kline sometimes needed anger to make her face her real emotions.

It went against his nature to cut off all communication with Kline, but it might be the only way to make his point.

Now to show her in no uncertain terms that he'd do anything to be with her.

Kline checked the time and then called out to her first-period class, "Five more minutes. Hurry and finish up, everyone."

As the kids completed their tests, she opened her purse and surreptitiously checked her phone. Still no word from Ben. What the heck was going on? Ben wasn't one to let things hang. He loved resolution. Probably part of his control thing, but his behavior confused her.

She was still so hurt and angry by what Ben had done. Especially how he made a deal with his dad to talk her into pulling out of the race so he'd get his precious clinic. How could he have ever agreed to something like that? She understood the need for a better clinic, but why did he have to side with his father against her to get it? How could she ever trust him again?

It wouldn't be an issue anyway because she'd left a voicemail with Ben's grandmother to be pulled off the slate. Had her mom and Ruth told people in town to pretend to support her as part of the welcome home scheme? Well, she hoped everyone got their laughs at her behind her back for even thinking of running against Mayor Anderson.

The bell rang, and one by one the kids rose and laid their tests on her desk on their way out. She forced a smile as she gathered up the pages. "Have a good day, everyone."

Ally was the last to hand in her test. Kline asked, "How do you think you did?"

"Crushed it," she said with a smile and without a stammer.

Kline held out her fist for a bump. "Good job. Now go crush the rest of your day too."

"'Kay. Bye." Ally returned the bump then quickly disappeared out the door as the next class of kids filed in.

Kline passed out the tests and then started grading the ones from first period so Barb wouldn't have to do it when she got back the next day. Assuming Barb got back the next day—she hadn't heard anything from her cousin. She'd have to call later when Barb got back from Denver.

Kline couldn't help but grin as she graded the tests. The kids had been paying attention for the most part. She was thrilled with all the As and Bs. A few poor grades, but that was to be expected. And Ally was right; she'd crushed a perfect score. Kline would've liked to see Ally's face the next day when she got her test back. It just added to her sadness that she'd miss that.

By Kline's last period, Ben still hadn't even texted. She'd gone from hurt and sad to full-out mad again. Part of her wanted to hunt him down and let him have it. Yell like she'd never yelled before so he'd get it through his thick skull how much he'd hurt her again.

The bell rang and the last of her students handed in their papers. After they were all gone, she used the planning period to finish up her grading. She tried to focus, but her mind kept wandering back to Ben. He and her mom had accused her of running away from and not facing her problems. Would she just prove their point if she left town without having it out with Ben once and for all? Maybe she'd go find him after school and get that over with.

The door opened and Lisa walked in with a deep frown creasing her forehead. "Kline? Do you have a second to talk?"

Seeing Lisa still made Kline's stomach clench with bad memories. "Sure. What's up?" She laid down her red pen.

Lisa sat in one of the front row desks. "I just got a call from the mayor."

"Let me guess. He told you not to give me a job, right?" She'd heard him threaten it while yelling at Ben. Looked like whatever plan the mayor and Ben had cooked up was coming to fruition.

"Yes. But I don't care if he's the mayor or my father's cousin, I won't be told whom I can hire or fire. I wanted to be sure you knew that you still have a job here if you want it."

That Lisa, who had teased Kline relentlessly as kids, would stand up to the mayor on her behalf made a lump form in Kline's throat. "I appreciate it, but—"

"And Ally would like it too. You made a big impression on her yesterday. Maybe she recognized a kindred spirit in you." Lisa stood and headed for the door. "Please stay, Kline."

After the door closed behind Lisa, Kline dropped her head into her hands. Something Uncle Zeke had said the night before kept echoing in her head. She *had* been happy while she'd been back. But Ben was right. The town wasn't big enough for the both of them. He obviously had no intentions of patching things up this time, or he would've called her. She needed to confront him to know for sure. She didn't want to break up a second time without getting all the facts straight like the last time. So that meant she had no choice. She'd man up and go talk to Ben.

But there was no way she could bear the thought of seeing him all the time if what she'd heard was true and she stayed. If her suspicions proved correct about Ben, then she had no choice but to move forward with her original plan and move to Denver. Her mother could just come see her there from now on. And when Mom really did get too old to live alone, she could live in Denver with Kline.

She had Nate and a few other friends in Denver. Surely she'd make more friends if she stayed in one place long enough to meet people. It'd be a little lonely at first, but she'd adjust. She always had before.

Kline quit pondering her dreary future and got back to grading the papers. She finished a few minutes before school let out for the day, so she headed down the quiet hallway for home. The air was brisk on her walk, but Kline embraced it. Used it to fortify her for the confrontation she'd have with Ben. He'd see a side of her he'd never seen before. She'd show him how wrong he was about her. He was going to regret suggesting that she didn't face her problems. Because she was going to let him have it. Maybe then she'd feel like she could move on with her life and shake off the doom and gloom that filled her.

Her phone buzzed in her pocket and her stomach dropped. It was probably Ben. Finally. She pulled the phone out but was disappointed that it was her cousin Barb. "Hey there. How are you feeling?"

"Okay. My doctor suggested I take another day or two to rest up, though. Could you take my class for the rest of the week?"

The charging parts for her car wouldn't arrive for a few more days anyway. "Of course. But hey, how come you didn't mention Lisa was the principal now?"

Barb chuckled. "Because I knew you'd avoid her like the plague and never agree to sub. But she's changed."

Avoid her? That hit a little too close to home. "Yeah, she has changed. And Ally seems nothing like her mother was."

"Ally is a great kid. So I'll e-mail you the lesson plans. Then I'll buy you dinner after you win the election, day after tomorrow, Mayor Grant! We're all so proud of you, Kline."

Proud of her? "Barb, I asked to be removed—"

"Sorry, it's Lisa beeping in on the other line. I'll talk to you later, okay?"

"Okay. Bye." Kline hung up and put her phone away. Proud of her? That made her want to cry again. But she needed to stay tough. Just until after she had it out with Ben. Then she could fall apart.

Every step closer to the clinic chipped away at her confidence. And made her consider putting off her confrontation with Ben. She was going to be in town until the end of the week. It'd probably be less awkward if she yelled at him right before she left.

Nope. She could do it. She reached out and yanked on the front door to the clinic. The waiting room was empty except for Joyce, who was busy filing.

Kline sucked in a deep breath for courage. "Hi, Joyce. Is Ben busy?"

Joyce turned around and smiled. "Ben's gone until Thursday."

He hadn't mentioned any plans to be out of town. "Some sort of emergency?"

"Nope. Personal time off. He hasn't had any since I can remember. He said he needed to take care of something important in Denver."

"Oh. I guess I'll talk to him later then." Kline turned to go, embarrassed that she felt a huge wave of relief knowing she wouldn't have to confront him until the day after tomorrow. After the election was over and nothing mattered between them anymore.

Joyce yelled out, "You can always call him, Kline. I know he'd be happy to hear from you. He moped around here all morning over whatever is going on between you two."

He was mopey? Good!

Kline stopped and turned around. "What I have to say needs to be said in person."

Joyce tilted her head. "That doesn't sound good. We all had such high hopes for you guys."

"Why?" Kline suspected she knew what the answer would be. Because they wanted Ben to be happy. He was the town's favorite son.

"Because of the way you both light up around each other. Neither of you seems complete without the other."

"Oh." Kline's eyes suddenly burned with tears. "Gotta go."

"Bye." After a moment Joyce added, "I'd call him if I were you."

Kline let the door swing closed behind her. What could Ben have had to do that was so important? Probably some recruiting for his new clinic. Clearly he was willing to throw her under the bus to get it. Although he'd never asked her to drop out of the race. Maybe he just hadn't gotten around to it yet?

She couldn't stand it any longer and fished her phone from her purse and dialed Ben's number. It went straight to voicemail as if he was out of service range or his phone was turned off. She debated for half a second about leaving a message, but then it occurred to her that maybe he'd shut off his phone to avoid *her*, so she quickly hung up.

As she passed by the diner, deep in thought, Gloria came barreling out the door. "Kline. Come inside and see this!"

Before she could open her mouth to protest, Kline was being dragged by the arm into the diner. Gloria sat her down at the counter and said, "Be right back."

When she reappeared a few seconds later she had a slice of chocolate mousse pie and a list in her hand. "After-school snack. And . . . the latest poll results."

Kline hated to look. "Things have changed, Gloria. I withdrew my name."

Gloria's face fell. "But you can't, Kline. Look at the numbers. You're ahead! By two votes."

Kline blinked at the page in her hand. Sure enough she had a small lead. But it was just Gloria's poll. Nothing official. And two votes wasn't much. "This is great, but I just don't think I can live here long term. Ben's father is probably the better choice. He's proven he's good at the money aspect, if not the social, anyway."

"I heard you and Ben had a falling-out." Gloria slammed her hands on her hips. "I never thought I'd see the day that Kline Grant would become a quitter."

A quitter? God, if only it were that simple. She dug into her pie, hoping to offset the deep sadness that had settled around her heart. She'd definitely miss Gloria's pie after she left. Heck, she'd miss Gloria. She'd forgotten how much she liked her. "Maybe things worked out for the best. As much as I wanted to make some needed changes, I really don't have any experience running a town. What if I had done more harm than good?"

"We wouldn't let you. We're all here to support you, Kline. Promise me you'll put yourself back on the slate and finish out the race, at least. Let fate decide?"

"How about I promise to think about it?" Kline finished up her pie and then dug out her wallet.

Gloria lifted a hand. "Nope. On the house."

"No, I insist. I saw the 'be nice to Kline' e-mail on my mother's computer. So I'm on to you all now."

"Oh, that." Gloria waved a hand. "Meggie sent that shortly after you arrived. She just wanted to help you and Ben get back together. It was as innocent as that, Kline. No big conspiracy. Folks were already happy to see you again."

Meg and Casey had proved their desire for her and Ben to get back together by trying to make her jealous at the bar. Maybe she'd go back and read those e-mails again tomorrow, when she wasn't so angry. "Well, I'd still feel better if you'd let me pay."

Gloria shook her beehive hairdo. "You didn't order it, so I can't ask you to pay for it. But can I give you something else for free?"

Kline tilted her head. Gloria was up to something. "What?"

"Advice. You know that Brewster and I fought like cats and dogs for so long we thought it'd be best if we went our separate ways. But after looking back a few years later, I realized something. I wished I'd understood that the only person I can change is me. Hoping for Brewster to change was futile. Now I have to live with that decision every day. Alone."

"So you still love Brewster?"

She nodded. "I do. But I hurt him so badly by wanting him to be something he isn't that he'd never have me back. Believe me, I've tried. If Ben has flaws you can't live with, then fine. But you're not perfect either, young lady. Sometimes we have to weigh living without the one we love or learning to love them, faults and all. Can you fix this thing with Ben?"

Kline shrugged. "Ben's not talking to me at the moment."

"Well, hurry up and decide if it's worth fixing. Now give me my poll back and go think about all the good things you can do as our new mayor."

Kline smiled. Gloria was still mothering everyone in town no matter how old they were. "Yes, ma'am. Thanks for the pie."

As Kline walked toward the door, Gloria called out, "Do yourself a favor and patch things up with Ben!"

Kline's smile faded as she walked out the door. Assuming Ben had some reasonable explanation for his actions, fixing things wasn't looking like an option when the man wouldn't even take her calls. Had she somehow hurt him as badly as Gloria had hurt Brewster?

If it had all been a misunderstanding, would she want to live her life without Ben?

CHAPTER TWENTY-ONE

*W*ednesday after school, Kline was walking past Town Square when her feet changed direction on their own and led her to the mayor's office. She'd replayed the snippets of conversation she'd overheard between Ben and the mayor two days ago around in her head so many times she was sick of them.

She wanted some answers about this so-called agreement they'd made regarding her and Ben's clinic. Since Ben wasn't talking to her, she'd go straight to the source.

She knocked on the mayor's closed office door and waited. She wasn't afraid of the mayor, but that didn't mean she liked talking to a man who had told her in no uncertain terms that she wasn't good enough for his son. When he said, "Come in," her stomach clenched, but she turned the knob anyway.

He looked up from the papers on his desk and sighed. "What do you want, Kline? I can't think of a thing we need to say to one another."

"Fine." She turned and pretended to leave. "But I know about your heart attack. I overheard you and Ben arguing the other day."

She was almost all the way out the door when he called out, "Wait."

When she returned and sat in one of the chairs in front of his desk, he said, "Why haven't you told everyone? It'd guarantee you a win in the election."

"I withdrew from the election. But I, unlike you, would never use such a personal issue against an opponent. I'm here because I want to know what deal you made with Ben about me and his clinic."

The mayor leaned back in his chair. "You're still on the slate. We'd have to have a board meeting to remove you, but my mother convinced the whole board to be busy until Friday."

"So I'm still in the running?" That'd make Gloria happy. Kline was batting a thousand at disappointing people lately. And after Gloria's pep talk, and reassurance that people would help Kline learn the ropes, she was glad to still be on the slate.

"Yes. But you never belonged here, Kline. It'd be best for us all if you just snuck away in the night."

That got her blood boiling. "I belong here just as much as you do, Mayor. And you never answered my question. What was the deal you and Ben struck regarding me and the clinic?"

"I told Ben he couldn't have his clinic unless he made sure you withdrew from the race. Obviously, he chose not to do that."

So he hadn't thrown her under the bus? That was a huge relief, but dammit, then why wasn't he talking to her?

She stood to leave. "Well, may the best person win tomorrow."

The mayor frowned. "You'd really stay if you won?"

"You'll just have to wait and see, I guess. Get ready for a fight, Mayor. Last I heard, I had the lead."

Kline stood and walked out the door, relieved. Ben had finally stood up to his father and hadn't chosen him over her. Why had she been so hasty to think that Ben hadn't changed? Standing up to his father was something he'd never been able to do before, and that he'd chosen to stick up for her filled her with hope for their relationship. That is, if Ben was ever going to speak to her again.

Later that evening, Kline still hadn't heard from Ben and it was making her downright cranky. He was due back in the morning for work, according to Joyce, so he was probably in Anderson Butte by now. So what was taking him so long to come find her and explain things?

She walked into her mother's study and pulled up the town e-mails. She'd given herself a day to cool off a bit before she read them again.

She reread the one about Ben knowing about her mother's fake illnesses. No wonder he'd never given her the name of a doctor in Denver and had asked to let him worry about her mom so they could have a nice visit. Ben was a staunch rule follower, so of course he followed HIPAA guidelines regarding her mom and his father.

Next, she read the e-mail Meg had sent. Taking into account Gloria's perspective, it *could* be just a matchmaking attempt. There wasn't any specific mention to give gifts. And after reading all the other e-mails that had been passed around in the last two days, it became clear that no one was laughing about her running for mayor. There was positive support for her. That must be chapping the mayor's butt pretty hard.

So maybe she'd jumped to a wrong conclusion about the e-mail loop too. The townspeople had actually been supporting her. But that didn't change the fact that Ben still hadn't been honest with her when she'd specifically asked him for that.

She shook her head and turned off the computer. Would she stay if she lost the election? Or if Ben had decided they were through? The parts for her car were supposed to come in on Friday, and Uncle Zeke said he'd have her all ready and charged up by Saturday, so she'd be able to leave soon if she chose to.

She'd actually regret not being able to take over Barb's classes. She had come to feel comfortable teaching in her old middle school the past few days. Most of the teachers had stopped by to greet her and wish her well. It was a tight-knit, cohesive group. Lisa probably had a lot to do with that, and it was clear she had really changed.

Kline went to the kitchen to grab some warm tea to take with her to bed. She hadn't been sleeping well the last few nights and was exhausted, so crawling into bed early sounded like a good plan. Maybe she'd read a bit and hope to make her brain tired enough to shut off.

But she kept coming back to Ben, and how he'd always felt the need to shield her from things like she was a child. It'd probably never change. He should have just told her that the mayor wanted her to withdraw and let her decide what to do. The real question was, could she live with Ben's faults rather than be apart from him again?

And Gloria was right. Kline wasn't perfect either. She hated talking about feelings and shied away from emotional and complicated friendship issues rather than face them head-on. Could that be part of the reason Ben had treated her like he did? If she'd been able to get past the initial hurt when Ben had broken up with her and had tried to find a solution instead of taking off as fast as she could, things might have turned out differently.

She loved Ben but was so confused by his behavior. He'd never just flat-out ignored her before.

As she pondered the mess she'd made of things, she got ready for bed and settled in with her new tablet. Who was she fooling? She wasn't going to fall asleep. She was waiting for Ben. He'd probably come tapping on her window any minute.

When three hours had passed, she couldn't stand it any longer. She was going to go to his house and find out what the hell was going on. Would it have killed him to send a simple text? He could be dead on the side of the road somewhere for all she knew. How freakin' inconsiderate could the man be? She'd told him that she loved him! Shouldn't that imply that she'd worry about him if she hadn't heard from him in three days?

Kline quickly dressed and then grabbed the package she'd ordered for Ben earlier. She slipped into her jacket on the way out the door, not caring that it was after eleven. If he'd gone to bed, she'd drag Ben out of it and make him talk to her. She was tired of whatever game he was playing.

It was cold, so Kline set out at a jog to stay warm. What if he *was* lying hurt and bleeding on the side of the road? Or, what if something had gone wrong with the chopper? She grabbed her cell and picked up the pace as she dialed his number. The call went straight to voicemail again, and she went into full panic mode.

When she got to his house it was dark.

Her stomach sank.

Maybe he was just in bed already. She opened the door and stuck her head inside. "Ben?"

No answer.

She flipped on some lights and walked toward his bedroom. The door stood open and the bed was made. Perfectly, of course. She could drop a quarter on the bedspread and it'd probably bounce right back.

Maybe he was flying back early in the morning?

She turned around to leave and noticed a duffle bag on a barstool in the kitchen and Ben's cell phone, watch, and wallet on the counter. She picked up his cell and pressed a button. Fully juiced. So he'd ignored her calls on purpose then.

Next to all of his things lay her engagement ring box. Like he'd just dumped everything and left in a hurry. But the ring was still there, so was he dumping her?

Where was he so late at night? She was going to strangle him when she found him for making her worry. She laid the gift she'd bought for him on the counter and turned to leave.

The front door opened and Ben walked through it all out of breath, like he'd been running. When he saw her he said, "There you are. Your mom thought you'd left when you weren't in your bed."

Thank God he was okay.

He must've taken the back route to her house and they'd passed each other. "I'm still here because my mother and uncle conspired to be sure I didn't have any car battery power to leave on my own. Which you would have known had you bothered to call me. I was worried about you, Ben!"

"Really?" His eyebrows shot up and he crossed his arms. "I would've never known by the way you drove off like a bat out of hell and left me standing in the rain."

She blinked at him. "I was upset. I'd just overheard your father saying you'd made a deal with him."

"There was no deal. But you tearing off like that made me decide it was time for one of us to compromise so we can move forward with our relationship." Ben shook his head and switched off the hallway light. "I was going to tell you everything after I got done telling my dad to go to hell. But then after thinking about this for three days, I'm *pissed* you didn't trust me enough to at least give me a chance to explain! So now it's done, and I hope you'll be happy!" He threw his arms up in frustration.

Kline was totally thrown off balance. Ben *never* yelled at her. "Fine. Here's your chance to explain! So what's your *big* plan?" She shouldn't have yelled back at him but she was so frustrated by his cavalier behavior—cutting her off for three days while he formulated some plan. She'd at least tried to call *him*.

"We can talk about it all in the morning." Ben walked toward his bedroom. "It's late and I'm going to bed. You're welcome to join me. But text your mom, she's worried about you."

Kline stood in the hallway with her mouth gaping and both palms in the air like an idiot. What the heck was going on? And he was *not* going to bed until they settled things! She pulled out her phone and texted her mom and then went to make Ben talk to her.

Ben forced himself to walk calmly to his bathroom and brush his teeth. His sister had been right to tell him not to talk to Kline. She was as flustered as he'd ever seen her. And she'd been worried about him. That made him smile.

That she'd finally yelled at him was a good thing. Kline not holding back for once hopefully meant she was digging deep and figuring out what she really wanted. Hopefully what she wanted was *him*.

He'd bet any minute she'd march in and let him have it.

Sure enough, Kline's frowning reflection showed up in the mirror beside his. "We aren't finished, Ben. What did you do?"

"I arranged for a job in Denver so we can be together. Sam is coming here to take my job and I'm taking a job at her hospital. They offered me a one-year contract."

Her jaw dropped. "So you're giving up your town, and being near your family, and your new clinic, everything you love, to be with me in Denver? Don't you think we should have talked about something that drastic first?"

He washed his face and then wiped it with a towel. "What is there to talk about? You don't want to live here, so I'm moving to Denver. Because I love you, dammit!"

"That's not even the point! You just did it again. You went behind my back and made a decision for the both of us. You should've asked me what I thought about this before you went and did something so permanent!"

"But I did it for you!"

Kline shook her head. "What if I win the election tomorrow? And I'm stuck here for two years while you're in Denver?"

"I never thought you'd actually stay!" Dammit. By reacting and not thinking this through, he'd really messed things up. Now what choice did they have? "I guess we can see each other on the weekends?"

"What if I don't want to only see you on the weekends? What if I want to see you every day?"

He slowly turned around and leaned against the counter. "Do you still want to see me every day?"

She closed her eyes and clenched her teeth. "Of course I do. I love you too! When we were younger, I thought you wanted to leave as much as I did. I'd never ask you to leave Anderson Butte or your family for me. I was coming to tell you that I'd decided to give Anderson Butte another chance that day when you were arguing with your father."

So she really *was* willing to stay? "But I'd never ask you to live here just for me. So by signing a one-year contract in Denver, I just made it easier for both of us."

"Oh. My. God. You still don't get it! When you're in a relationship you make decisions *together*!" She poked her finger into his shoulder. "We'll talk about this after the election tomorrow. Maybe if I lose it won't matter. But I don't know how we can *ever* be married if you don't figure this out!" She turned and walked away.

A few seconds later his bedroom door slammed shut.

He'd text her in a few minutes to be sure she got home okay.

Kline had actually talked about marriage. And slammed a door. Things she'd never done before. So Casey's plan must've worked.

But he'd figured if he moved, she'd move with him in a heartbeat, regardless of the election. And be thrilled with his decision. What if she actually won and decided to stay in Anderson Butte? He'd done it again and hadn't even realized it. Why hadn't he talked to her first?

Crap!

He needed to find a way to fix things. To show Kline he could change. He started to go after her but found her sitting on a barstool in the kitchen with her head on top of her folded arms.

She hadn't run for once.

"Kline? What are you doing?" He laid a hand on her back.

She drew in a deep breath. "Gloria said that I needed to decide if it was better to accept you as you are than to live without you. Like when you go and do things for me but forget to talk to me about them first. And do nice things like giving up your whole life for me to show that you love me."

"I do love you. And I'd do anything to be with you. I'm sorry I was so focused on a solution that I didn't stop to think beyond it. I should have talked to you first, instead of trying to solve the problem on my own." He sat on the empty stool beside her.

She nodded. "And I should have trusted you enough to hear your side of the story instead of just reacting when I was hurt. We both have stuff we need to work on, I guess."

"Yeah." He ran his hand up and down her back to soothe her. "I'm willing to try, if you are. So what's the verdict on Gloria's question?"

"I hated not being able to talk to you these past three days. And I was scared when I thought something might have happened to you. It made me realize that sharing you with your family and this town is a small price to pay for being with you the rest of the time." She slid the box she'd brought toward him.

"Sorry. I didn't mean to worry you. And for the record, I missed you too. What's in the box?"

"Something I owe you."

What could she possibly owe him? Short of a smack upside the head for his stupidity.

He quickly opened the package. When he spotted a pair of the latest Ferragamo loafers, he smiled. "Thank you. These are perfect. Just the ones I wanted."

"Figured. But I still feel compelled to point out you could buy enough school supplies for fifteen African villages for the price of those."

Typical Kline. "Then how about you return them for me and donate the money? Would that make you smile again? I miss seeing it."

"Yes! Thank you." She grinned widely and sat up. Then she took his hand. "When I got out of jail, I vowed to stop wasting time. To appreciate all the good things in my life because I deserve to be happy. You make me happy you're mine about ninety-five percent of the time, Ben."

He chuckled. "Ninety-five percent's still pretty good, right? Like getting an A from my favorite teacher?"

After she wiped the tears from her cheeks, she nodded. "Yeah. I'd still give you an A for effort because I know your heart is always in the right place. Is there any way out of the job?"

"I'll call first thing in the morning and see. Maybe I'd better take you to bed now and see if I can improve on my grade point average."

"Good idea. And maybe I can think of some extra credit work to help keep that GPA up." Her lips slowly bloomed into a mischievous grin. "It might involve that huge tub of yours again."

"My kind of homework." He leaned down and kissed her. "Thanks for sticking around to settle things."

"I'm going to work on doing that from now on." Fresh tears sprung into her eyes. "And no matter where we end up living, it'll be okay because we'll be together. I love you, Ben."

"I love you too." He scooped her up off the barstool and carried her toward his bedroom. "Let's get started on that extra credit."

Getting through the next school day was torture for Kline. Her stomach had been in knots about the election all day. She was excited at the prospect of being the mayor, but Ben's last text said he still wasn't sure if he could get out of the contract. She hated to think of seeing Ben only on weekends, but they'd have to work it out if that's what happened.

Only five more minutes and then she could go to the library to vote. She'd always gotten the absentee ballots every few years if her mail could find her, because with online bill paying, she'd never officially had another permanent address other than her parents' house. That might not change anytime soon depending on the election results.

The bell finally rang, so she smiled and waved to the kids and then cleaned up before calling it a day.

The door opened and Ben appeared. "Hey. You want to go vote and then grab something at the diner while we wait for the results?"

"Depends." She grabbed her laptop case and stuffed her notes inside. "*Whom* are you voting for?"

"The next mayor of Anderson Butte. So far, I've never been wrong."

She rolled her eyes. "Very funny."

He reached out for her laptop bag so she handed it over and they started out toward the main exit. "Thank you."

"Welcome." Their footsteps echoed off the shiny hallway floors as he finally got around to answering her question. "In a recent act of self-preservation, I've decided I'm apolitical." Ben slung her bag's strap onto his shoulder. "So rather than flipping a coin or something unscientific like that, because that'd surely drive you nuts, I'm simply voting for the strongest candidate." He held the front door open for her.

She loved that he knew she was nervous so he was teasing to distract her. "That's actually not a bad plan based on nature. Usually the best of the species tend to survive longest."

It was cold outside, so Ben wrapped an arm around her shoulder and pulled her close as they walked toward the library. She smiled at the familiar warmth that filled her when she touched him that had nothing to do with his body heat.

He said, "But I have a feeling *my* survival might depend on this vote." Ben opened the library door for her and when they stepped inside, everyone cheered.

Kline had never voted in person before, so she wasn't sure what the setup would be. But there among the kiosks of paperback books stood two electronic voting machines. Kline asked, "So how long before we know the results?"

Mrs. Anderson replied, "Depends. We have to count the paper ballots too, but your mom and I worked our fannies off to get these fancy electronic machines for quicker results. It helped that we got permission to hold a special election today rather than on Tuesday. So hurry up, you two. Most everyone else has already voted."

Ben winked at Kline before he stepped up to his machine and started punching buttons. It'd probably make more sense if they both voted for his father. It would solve the living-in-Denver-with-Ben problem. But then she wouldn't be able to do what she set out to do. Make Anderson Butte a better place to live.

Kline took to her own machine and quickly voted for herself. Would she actually get her chance to finally change the way Anderson Butte was run?

Ben sat across from Kline at the diner as they ate their supper and waited for the election results. Many in town had squeezed inside, including his father. When his dad glanced their way with a hard stare, guilt arrowed through Ben's gut.

He'd voted for Kline because she was the strongest candidate. And because his father needed to take things easy. He'd done the right thing on both counts, so he pushed the guilty feelings aside.

He glanced at Kline, who was playing with the food on her plate. "Sam is coming in a few minutes. She's spending the night at my house, if that's okay with you?"

Kline laid her fork down and smiled. "I don't mind if she spends the night. Thanks for asking."

"What are we going to do if you win tonight?"

Kline arched a brow. "Ah, so it's finally *we*, huh?" She leaned across the table and kissed him.

He whispered, "See? I'm trainable."

"So no more busting out your Superman suit to save me?"

"Nope. But I hope you'll tell me when I *can* help you. You don't have to be so tough, Kline. No more lone-wolfing it, okay?"

Her eyes misted. "I don't want to be alone anymore, Ben. We'll figure this communication stuff out yet."

"Yeah." He reached out and took her hand. "I know the job thing is my fault, but I really don't want to only see you on weekends for an entire year. I need to put that out there before we see the results."

"Me either." She lifted their entwined hands and laid a kiss on the back of his. "But I'm not a quitter. I doubt those owls will survive if I don't win. And I can't disappoint all the Grants."

"Then we'll just have to make this work no matter what."

Just as she was about to say something, his grandmother opened the door and announced, "The results are in!"

CHAPTER Twenty-Two

Kline held up a finger to indicate to Ben's grandmother that she needed a second. Kline stood at a crossroads about the election results. Which path should she take? No matter what she chose, this was it. No going back.

One option would be to ask Mrs. Anderson not to announce the results and forfeit to Ben's father. Then she and Ben could move to Denver and be together. Or, another option was to stay in Anderson Butte, do what she set out to do if she won, and see Ben only on the weekends for a very long year if he couldn't get out of the contract.

She whispered to Ben. "I want to come home. For good. No matter if I win or not. I want to teach here and be near my family. Are you okay with that? Even if it means things will suck for the first year if you can't get out of the contract?"

He nodded. "Yep. We'll work it out."

Sam squeezed through the crowd. "Sorry I'm late! Here, Ben."

Ben held out his hand for the piece of paper Sam waved and said, "I asked the hospital personnel director to intercept my contract before the president got a chance to sign it. I owe the guy a weeklong stay here for him and his family." He held up the pages and tore them in two.

"I'm fired before I'm hired. We can stay now. But I need to ask Kline a question."

The whole diner went library quiet.

Kline's heart skipped a beat when she realized what booth they were sitting in. The same one as when he'd asked her to marry him before. When the jukebox played the exact same song that had been playing while he proposed the last time, she couldn't stop the mile-wide smile that stretched her lips. "But do you think we should wait to find out if I won?" she teased.

"I think you'll want to hear this first." Ben slid out of the booth and onto one knee. Then he pulled out her engagement ring box and tilted the lid. It took all she had not to reach out, snatch the ring, and slide it back on her finger where it had belonged for over ten years.

"But I take being the mayor pretty seriously, Ben."

He shrugged and snapped the box closed. "Okay. I guess this can wait."

As the crowd groaned, Ben's grandmother said, "You're gonna give me a heart attack here with all the anticipation. Ask her already!"

"That's up to Kline." Ben grinned at her. "Which is it?"

"In the interest of everyone's health, I think you'd better ask your question." Her hands shook with excitement as she laid them in his outstretched palms. That his were slightly moist with nerves melted her heart. It was shaping up to be the best day of her life. Win or lose the election.

Ben cleared his throat. "Kline, I've loved you all my life. I know I come with lots of meddling family, and patients who sometimes call me away during dinner, but I'd like nothing better than to know you'll be there for me when I come home. Because as much as I've tried to make my house a home, it never felt like one until the other day when you were standing beside me in it. So will you marry me, Kline? Flaws and all?"

All eyes in the room shifted to her.

She'd come back to the US to lay down some roots, to make a home, and couldn't think of a better life than one with Ben in it.

Nodding, because it was hard to speak, she finally croaked out, "Yes!"

When Ben slid her ring on, the dam burst. She wrapped her arms around him and whispered in his ear, "I *will* always be there for you, Ben. And I can't wait to get started with the rest of our lives. Together."

"Me too." He kissed her so tenderly it made her start crying all over again. When he leaned away, he said, "Now we should probably find out if I'll be living with the mayor of Anderson Butte."

"'Kay." Kline blinked away her tears as everyone slowly settled down. "Okay, Mrs. Anderson, so what's the news? Good or bad?"

"The news is looking good for me. I won Gloria's pot. I knew you two were so stubborn that it'd take a few weeks for you to work things out. And now it looks like I've got myself a new relative and Anderson Butte has got a new mayor! Congratulations, Kline. You won!"

Kline found herself pitched high into the air and on many shoulders as Ben's father stomped out the door. She almost felt sorry for the guy. But not enough to withdraw. She was going to make some big changes in town.

Ben's uncle called out, "Let's go back to my place. Drinks are on the house!"

Kline was carried by her new constituents the block or so to Brewsters. She looked over her shoulder and found Ben as he walked close behind and smiled sweetly at her.

She smiled too, and drew in a deep breath of cold, fresh air, grateful her mother had tricked her into coming back. Because for the first time in her life, she finally felt like she was home. With Ben. Right where she belonged.

INAUGURATION DAY

*O*n a cold Saturday in January, Kline stood before the mirror in Ben's oversize bathroom wearing her big terry cloth robe and feeling a bit sick to her stomach as she was about to take on the job of mayor. The distillery was going to be moved, Ben's clinic was going to be built, and the birds would be saved, so she was pleased with that. But now to learn how to run a whole town when Ben's dad wasn't speaking to either of them.

She lifted a hand to brush back her hair and smiled at the way the bright light made the diamond on her left hand sparkle.

She'd worn the same ring when she'd been in college, anticipating her big fairy-tale wedding day, but now she just wanted to get married and get busy having kids. They'd waited long enough. She'd rather just do something quick and get it over with. But Ben said he was only getting married once and wanted the whole deal, a big celebration, with everyone in town, dancing and partying long into the night.

Then they'd fly somewhere warm that had private huts and sandy beaches where they could make love whenever they wanted for an entire week. Nobody to interrupt their meals with family drama, no medical emergencies, just the two of them. The time alone together trumped the wedding part to her by far.

Their wedding was the one big thing she and Ben disagreed on—every other day—and why they couldn't settle on a date. When he'd asked if she'd trust him to take care of all the details, she'd agreed, but now there was a new complication and she needed to talk him into moving a tad quicker.

Ben appeared behind her in his brand-new suit that fit like it was made just for him and wrapped his hands around her waist. "Ready for the big day, Mayor Grant?"

She nodded. "I hope your dad changes his mind and comes. I could really use his advice on a few things. This not talking to us can't be good for the town. Or his heart." She hated how Ben's father had cut Ben off too. It obviously hurt Ben and she hated to see him sad.

"About that." Ben's jaw clenched. "You remember that I went to see him a few weeks ago and we talked? I had to promise him something to get him there. I'm not sure you're going to like it at first, but please give it a chance. And know, it's you I was thinking of when I promised it. If you absolutely don't want to do it, the deal is off. No harm, no foul."

Her eyes narrowed in the reflection of the mirror before them. "What deal?"

He nibbled on her neck and made her shiver. "It's a surprise." His lips moved to her jaw and made their way to her earlobe. He whispered, "One that I think will make many of your new constituents happy. It's all about the greater good, right?" His mouth found hers and he slowly turned her body so she was pressed against his hard, sexy-in-a-suit one. He kissed her sweetly, and wasn't fooling her for a second.

She ended his attempt to distract her with a nip to his bottom lip. "Your theme song in life should be all about the greater good, Ben. Now go away and let me finish dressing."

He stood right where he was and let his hands wander all over her curves. "I love what a good sport you are, Kline. Have I told you that lately?"

She wrapped her arms around his neck and whispered, "No. And for your sake, I hope whatever you've cooked up doesn't end you up on the couch tonight."

Ben chuckled. "It's still *my* house. You can't make me sleep on the couch until you marry me."

"I can make wedding plans this afternoon. We can be co-owners of this lovely home by the end of next week. Just say the word."

"No thanks. I'm on top of it." He patted her rear end. Then his phone buzzed in his pocket.

Of course. Just when she was ready to try to get the whole wedding thing settled.

"Saved by the cell." She smacked *his* sexy butt in return. "Give me ten minutes and we're out of here."

"'Kay." He laid a quick kiss on her lips, then took his call.

By the time Kline was ready, Ben's phone had buzzed with five more texts and he'd excused himself to take two more calls. It was a Saturday, for goodness' sake. Couldn't everyone leave the man alone for one day? Shaking her head, she grabbed her coat and was about to put it on when Ben appeared by her side and took it from her.

He held it out to help her into it. "Sorry about that. This is your big day. I promise I'll do my best not to run off and spoil it."

"Thank you." She wrapped her scarf around her neck. "But if it's a medical emergency, I'll understand."

Sam appeared in the hallway from the guest room. She'd said she wouldn't miss the chance to see a Grant take office in Anderson Butte. "I'm on call for Ben today if anything comes up."

Ben crooked his arm for Kline to take. "See? I'm all yours now."

"Perfect." Kline would bet a buck that wouldn't last long, but she appreciated the thought.

When they pulled up in front of the high school the parking lot was packed. Kline grabbed her cell from her purse to be sure they weren't late. They were thirty minutes early, just as Ben's grandmother had instructed. "Wow. It looks like almost everyone in town has come out for this."

After Ben helped her out of the car, they climbed the front steps and headed for the auditorium. Before they got there, Ben's grandmother, her mom, and his sisters all rounded the corner. Casey said, "About time. Let's go. We have to hurry and get you changed!"

Changed? Kline turned to Ben. "What's going on?"

Ben smiled sheepishly as the women surrounded them. "You told me to handle this and I know the auditorium isn't the most romantic location, but if you agree, I have these." Ben pulled two boarding passes from his inside pocket. "Tahiti. For ten whole days, starting tomorrow."

Tahiti? "Wait a minute. I can't be sworn in as mayor and then leave town the next day."

"Not even for your honeymoon?"

"Honeymoon? Are we getting married today? That's the deal you struck with your father?"

Ben nodded. "Right before the swearing-in."

Ben's grandmother held up a piece of paper. "I got myself all ordained online just so we could pull this off. Casey took care of the rest. You don't have to do a thing, Kline, but say I do."

"This makes no sense. Your dad can't stand me, Ben. Why would us getting married get him to come today?" She crossed her arms. "What's really going on here?"

Ben's grandmother said, "This was my idea, Kline. I hate Ben and Mitch not talking and we've always had an Anderson run this town——"

"Oh, now I get it." Kline cut her off. "You marry us and then I become an Anderson, *before* I take office? That way Ben's dad can calm down because an Anderson will still be running the town?"

All the women nodded.

"And Sam, you're here to take over for Ben while we're on our honeymoon, right?"

"Yep. A working vacation." Sam chuckled. "Kline, you look a little dubious. But let them show you the dress first, and I think you'll start to see this is the perfect solution."

Kline turned to Ben. "You could've just taken me up on my offer to go to the courthouse in Denver last month and had the same result."

He wrapped his arms around her and pulled her close. "I know. But this way, my dad can come too. You know his pride would've never allowed him to show up to our wedding otherwise, and it means a lot to me to have my only parent here today."

When Ben's voice cracked with emotion, it made her eyes mist. The mayor was a jackass, but Ben still loved him. It was probably one of the many reasons she loved Ben. "How did you pull all of this off behind my back?"

He smiled. "Everyone in town wanted to be a part of this day so badly that they've all kept this a secret from you for weeks, Kline. They love you. And I do too. So what do you say?"

Kline glanced at her mother, who was nodding her head along with Ben's sisters and Sam. Finally Ruth thumped her cane and said, "Make up your mind, Kline. I'm getting older by the second here. And I'm hungry for some damned cake!"

"Thank you for doing all of this for us, Ben." She leaned up on her tiptoes and kissed him. "It sounds perfect. See you out there."

Kline let the Anderson girls and her mother drag her to an empty classroom, where all sorts of makeup was scattered about and tons of shoes were lined up to choose from. Tara was fluffing the most beautiful lace wedding dress Kline had ever laid eyes on. "Wow," was all Kline could squeak out, she was so impressed.

Tara carefully pulled the dress off the hanger and laid it across Kline's arms. "This is Ryan's and my wedding gift to you, Kline."

Kline shook her head as she studied the intricate beading and gold thread details. "This is too much, Tara. I can't—"

Meg appeared with a matching veil. "Yes, you can. Now stop crying or your eyes will be all red and puffy. Here." She stuck out the gossamer material with the same beading.

Casey swatted her sister's arm. "Be careful, Meg. It's delicate, not a pair of jeans, for goodness' sake."

Meg rolled her eyes. "Whatever. Let's just get the show on the road, please. The natives are getting restless."

Kline smiled at the playful bickering that continued the whole time they dressed her and did her makeup.

This is what having sisters must be like.

She turned to see her mom blinking back happy tears and it made Kline want to cry all over again.

Kline asked Tara, who had her hands in Kline's hair, putting it up, "Is Ryan standing up with Ben?"

She nodded. "He asked Josh and Zane too."

That meant Kline needed three. "Since we're all going to be sisters now, will you guys do me the honor of being my bridesmaids?"

Meg said, "About time you caught on and asked us, Kline. Geez."

It was almost time, and Ben still hadn't seen his father. He hadn't promised he'd come, just that he'd think about it. Ben paced in the hallway as he waited.

Ryan joined him all decked out in his new suit and leaned against a locker. "He'll be here."

Ben shook his head. "It doesn't matter. What's important is that Kline is happy about all of this."

"It does matter. That's why I stopped by his house this morning and threatened to quit if he didn't show. As I was walking out his front door, Casey showed up to tell Dad the same thing. Meg called him last night. He'll be here."

His father couldn't run his businesses without all of their help and he knew it. That they'd do that for him made Ben's throat clog up a little. "Thanks."

Zane and Josh showed up with big grins on their faces. Josh said, "All ready, buddy?"

Ben glanced out the front doors one last time and then nodded. He'd done all he could do. If his father didn't show, it'd be his loss. "Let's do this!"

Ben opened the double doors leading to the auditorium and stood in the back until his grandmother gave the signal. Then he walked up the white runner someone had laid that covered the length of the center aisle.

When he got to the raised platform up front, he gave his grandmother a peck on the cheek and then turned around to face the crowd. Seats on both sides of the aisle were filled to capacity with Grants, Andersons, and all the rest happily mixed in with each other.

The music changed as the rear doors opened again and his niece and nephew started toward him. Haley held a basket of flower petals and threw them with wild abandon. Ty, looking sharp in his new suit, walked beside her carting the rings and looking like he'd rather be just about anywhere else. It made Ben smile. Screw his dad. He'd not let him ruin the wedding.

It was getting hard to breathe as the music got louder and Meg and Josh started up the aisle. Meg, the town's tomboy mischief-maker, had given Ben many sleepless nights in her youth, but now she was married to a great guy and had two fantastic kids. There were times he thought she'd never get her act together, but to see her now, with her hair actually up, makeup on, and that same sly grin on her face warmed his heart. Casey was right—he needed to stop babying Meg.

Meg went to the other side of the dais and Josh joined Ben, as Ryan and Tara started up the aisle. Ryan, so shy Ben worried he'd never get over the girl who'd broken his heart in high school and be happy again, walked beside his beautiful fiancée, Tara, the one woman able to make Ryan want to speak in complete sentences. Ryan and Tara looked happy, and that made Ben glad.

Next came Casey and Zane. Ben would've never guessed that Casey, the one who'd stayed home from college to help him raise Ryan and Meg, the Goody Two-shoes of the family, would be the one who was engaged to a bad-boy rock star. It was finally Casey's turn to put herself first and allow herself the joy written all over her and Zane's faces.

Yeah, Kline was right. His job was done. They were all just fine. Who needed his father? He wasn't the one responsible for Ben's sibs turning out so well. That was Ben and Casey's achievement, so his father could go straight to—

His father and Sue Ann slipped in a side door and quickly sat in front beside Kline's mother. After they were settled, his father glanced Ben's way and hitched his chin. The closest thing he'd get to his father's approval. It'd have to be enough.

The music changed again and Ben's heart raced in anticipation. As everyone stood, Kline appeared in the rear with her uncle Zeke. Kline's eyes locked with his, and when she smiled, he nearly lost it. She was such a beautiful woman, but in that dress, and with that smile, she was radiant. He was the luckiest guy in the world.

When Kline finally joined them, he took her hands and couldn't take his eyes off of her. She was glowing in her gown, and her eyes turned misty as his grandmother said words Ben couldn't hear. All he could think about was how close he'd come to never having this moment and it choked him up again.

His grandmother's foot landed on his shin. "Snap out of it, boy. Gonna need you for this part."

Ben rushed through his vows, eager to get to the kissing part to make her his forever.

Kline wiped away a tear and then said her part next. They slipped rings on each other's fingers and then Ben looked at his grandmother for the declaration he'd waited forever to hear.

She said, "By the power vested in me by the Internet, I now pronounce you husband and wife. You may kiss your bride, Benjamin."

He pulled Kline close and laid his hungry mouth on hers. Loud clapping faded away as she kissed him back, and he got lost in Kline. She was all his for the rest of their lives. And he couldn't wait to get her to Tahiti and all to himself for ten solid days.

When his grandmother's shoe found Ben's shin again, he took that as his cue to slowly break the kiss.

Grandma declared, "Settle down now, everyone. We're not done here. We still have us a mayor to inaugurate. If you two would, please?" Grandma held her hand out to a table filled with papers to sign. Ben signed the marriage license above the witnesses' signatures first and then stood back to let Kline sign the license and what looked like the inauguration papers.

While Kline scratched her name by all the little colored tabs, Grandma whispered, "Anyone else want to get married while we're all here gussied up and I'm still breathing? Tara?"

She shook her head. "My mother would kill me. She's been planning our wedding for months."

Grams turned to Zane. "How about you two?"

He glanced at Casey and a guilty look passed between them. Casey whispered, "We didn't want to wait until September anymore to get pregnant. We were married last weekend in Lake Tahoe. But this is Kline's big day, so not a word, Grandma."

"Dagnabbit!" Grandma threw her hands up. "You eloped again on me, Casey?"

She nodded. "How about you and Zeke? We gained an Anderson today, so we could stand to lose one to become a Grant."

Zeke suddenly appeared with a ring in his hand. "How about it, Ruthie? Will you marry me?"

Grandma picked up the ring and examined it. "Not bad. I guess I could live with this weighing my hand down for the few years we got left. But I don't want all this fuss. I always secretly wanted one of them Elvis impersonators to marry me in Vegas. That way we could party all night after and play the slots. It'd be fun to win a jackpot or two while we're at it."

Kline burst out in laughter as she wrapped her arm around Ben's waist and gave a squeeze. "See? I wasn't the only one who wanted a quick wedding."

Ben shook his head and then kissed his grandmother's cheek. "Then a Vegas wedding you'll have. Congratulations." He shook Zeke's hand. "Welcome to Club Crazy."

Grandma chuckled and then slipped her glasses onto her nose. She shuffled through the pages. "These look like they're all in order."

After swearing Kline in as the new mayor, Grandma grabbed Kline's arm and raised it above her head. "I present to you the new mayor of Anderson Butte. Kline Anderson! Now let's go get us some fancy champagne and cake. I'm starving!"

The wedding party crowded around to hug Kline as Ben's chest filled with pride. Kline would be a fantastic mayor. He turned to gauge his father's reaction. Dad's jaw clenched, but he clapped along with the rest of the people. Maybe he'd help Kline after all.

After all the obligatory pictures, the cake cutting, and the shoving pieces into each other's faces, Ben finally dragged Kline out to the dance floor in the school's gym for a moment alone with her. She snuggled close to him and sighed. "I'll bet I go down in history as the only mayor to ever be inaugurated in a wedding gown."

"That, and the best-looking mayor this town has ever seen. I haven't had a chance to tell you how pretty you look today, Kline."

She leaned back and smiled. "You didn't have to. I saw it in your eyes. Something I'll never forget." She laid a soft kiss on his lips. "This was perfect, Ben. As easy as a courthouse wedding."

"Yeah, for you. I did all the heavy lifting."

"But at least we discussed the wedding plans together. Mostly. We're getting the hang of this." She gave him another quick kiss. "And we're very proud of you for doing all of this and pulling off the perfect wedding."

"Wait. Did you say we? As in plural?" His heart nearly soared out of his chest. "Are you pregnant already?" They'd decided she'd go off birth control, figuring it'd take a few months to get pregnant.

She nodded. "I was going to tell you this afternoon. That's why I wanted to move the wedding up so badly. But looks like all three of us are going on the honeymoon. Not that we'll mention that part to little baby Grant-Anderson."

He stopped dancing. "You hyphenated your name when you signed everything earlier?"

"What? Do you think I should've talked that over with you before I did it?"

Well, yeah! What was she think—"Nope." He'd better not go there. Not after the stunts he'd pulled in the past. "Did I mention how pretty you look, Kline?"

"Gotcha." She laughed. "I was just kidding about the hyphen."

"Thank you, Mayor Anderson. But speaking of that, there is this one other little thing I did that maybe I should've told you about . . ."

"Stop." Kline laid a soft finger on his lips. "I vowed I'd take you as you are, but maybe you'd better tell me after the honeymoon so I don't have to kill you and go alone."

"Deal." He smiled and pulled her closer. Yeah. He was the luckiest guy in the world, all right. Well, until after the honeymoon, anyway. Then he'd just have to take his chances.

The End

$\mathcal{A}$CKNOWLEDGMENTS

I owe a heartfelt thanks to my critique group, Sherri, Robin, and Louise, and to my family for always being there to support me. And to my editors, Maria Gomez, Charlotte Herscher, and the whole Montlake team for just being such awesome people to work with. And to my many writer buddies who continue to inspire and encourage me, particularly Gina Robinson and Lauren Christopher.

But mostly, I'd like to thank my readers. Thanks for believing as much as I do that everyone deserves their own happily ever after.

ABOUT THE AUTHOR

Photo © 2012 Robyn Adams

Tamra Baumann got hooked on writing the day she picked up her first Nora Roberts novel from her favorite bookstore. Since then, she's dazzled readers of contemporary romance with her own lighthearted love stories. She was the 2012 Golden Heart winner for Contemporary Series Romance and has also received the Golden Pen Award for Single Title Romance. Born in Monterey, California, Tamra led the nomadic life of a navy brat before finally putting down permanent roots during college. When she's not attending annual Romance Writers of America meetings, this voracious reader can be found playing tennis, traveling, or scouting reality shows for potential character material. Tamra resides with her real-life characters—her husband, two kids, and their allergy-ridden dog—in the sunny Southwest.